perfect
ruin

also

by

Lauren
DeStefano

◆·····································◆

The Internment Chronicles
burning kingdoms
no intention of dying

The Chemical Garden Trilogy
wither
fever
sever

Lauren
DeStefano

perfect
ruin

The Internment Chronicles
Book One

SIMON & SCHUSTER BFYR

New York | London | Toronto | Sydney | New Delhi

An imprint of Simon & Schuster Children's Publishing Division
1230 Avenue of the Americas, New York, New York 10020
This book is a work of fiction. Any references to historical events, real people,
or real places are used fictitiously. Other names, characters, places, and events
are products of the author's imagination, and any resemblance to actual events
or places or persons, living or dead, is entirely coincidental.
Text copyright © 2013 by Lauren DeStefano
Cover photograph copyright © 2015 by Kevin Twomey
All rights reserved, including the right of
reproduction in whole or in part in any form.
SIMON & SCHUSTER BFYR is a trademark of Simon & Schuster, Inc.
For information about special discounts for bulk purchases,
please contact Simon & Schuster Special Sales at 1-866-506-1949
or business@simonandschuster.com.
The Simon & Schuster Speakers Bureau can bring authors to your live event. For
more information or to book an event, contact the Simon & Schuster Speakers
Bureau at 1-866-248-3049 or visit our website at www.simonspeakers.com.
Also available in a SIMON & SCHUSTER BFYR hardcover edition
Book design by Lizzy Bromley
The text for this book is set in Stempel Garamond.
Manufactured in the United States of America
First SIMON & SCHUSTER BFYR paperback edition March 2015
4 6 8 10 9 7 5
The Library of Congress has cataloged the hardcover edition as follows:
DeStefano, Lauren.
Perfect ruin / Lauren DeStefano. — First edition.
pages cm — (The Internment chronicles ; [1])
Summary: "Sixteen-year-old Morgan Stockhour lives in Internment, a floating
city utopia. But when a murder occurs, everything she knows starts to
unravel"— Provided by publisher.
ISBN 978-1-4424-8061-2 (hardcover : alk. paper) —
ISBN 978-1-4424-8063-6 (pbk) — ISBN 978-1-4424-8062-9 (eBook)
[1. Science fiction. 2. Utopias—Fiction.] I. Title.
PZ7.D47Pe 2013
[Fic]—dc23
2013014392

For

my family,

who knows

the importance

of dreaming

beyond the edge

of our world

Out beyond
ideas of
wrongdoing
and
rightdoing,
there is
a field.
I'll meet
you there.

Jalāl ad-Din ar-Rūmī

The first humans were especially ungrateful. After the birth of the sun and the moon, they asked for stars. After the crops rose from the ground, they asked for beasts to fill the fields. After some time, the god of the ground, weary of their demands, thought it best to destroy them and begin again with humbler beings. So it goes that the god of the sky thought the first humans too clever to waste, and he agreed to keep them in the sky with the promise that they would never again interfere with the ground.

— *The History of Internment,* Chapter 1

1

You have all heard the warnings about the edge. We have been told its winds are a song that will hypnotize us, and by the time we awaken from that trance, it will be too late.

—"Intangible Gods," Daphne Leander, Year Ten

We live encapsulated by the trains. They go around in a perfect oval at all hours, stopping for thirty-five seconds in each section so the commuters are able to board and depart. Beyond the tracks, after the fence, there's sky. Engineers crafted a scope so that we can see the ground below us. We can see tall buildings and other sorts of trains—some of which disappear underground or rise onto bridges. We can see patches of cities and towns that appear stitched like one of Lex's blankets.

We've never been able to craft a scope advanced enough to see the people—it isn't allowed. We've been banished to the sky. I'm told they can see Internment, though. I wonder, what must we look like to them? A giant oval of the earth with rocks and roots clinging to the bottom, I suppose. I've seen sketches of what Internment looks like as a whole, and it's as though a giant hand came down and took a piece right out of the ground, and here we are floating in the sky.

When I was a child, I used to think about the day Internment was ripped from the ground and placed in the sky. I used to wonder if the people were frightened, or if they felt fortunate to be saved. I used to imagine that I was a part of Internment's first generation. I'd close my eyes and feel the ground under my feet going up and up and up.

"Ms. Stockhour," Instructor Newlan says, "you're dreaming with your eyes open again. Page forty-six."

I look at the textbook open before me and realize I haven't been keeping up with the lesson since page thirty-two.

"I don't suppose you would care to add to our discussion." He always paces between the rows of desks as he lectures, and now he's stopped before me.

"The festival of stars?" I say, but I'm only guessing. I have an incurably wandering mind, a fact that has given Instructor Newlan much cheerful cause to torture me. The chorus of chuckles from my classmates confirms I'm wrong.

"We've moved on to geography," Pen says from beside me. She glances from me to the instructor, curls bouncing around her cheeks and creating a perfect ambiance for the look of contrition on her face; if Instructor Newlan thinks she's sorry for speaking out of turn, he won't give her a demerit. He likes her; she's the only one left fully conscious after his geography lectures—she'd like to work on the maps when she's older. He gives her a wry glance over his glasses, flips my book to the correct page, and goes on.

"I do realize that it's December first," Instructor Newlan says. "I know we're all excited for the festival of stars to begin, but let us remember that there is plenty of class work to be done in the meantime."

The festival of stars is a monthlong celebration, and in the excitement and preparations, it's common for students and adults alike to daydream. But while the rest of Internment daydreams of normal things—gifts and requests to the god of the sky—I dream of things that are dangerous and could have me arrested or killed. I stare at the edge of my desk and imagine it's the end of my little world.

After the class is over, I wait for Basil before I move for the door. He always insists on catching the same shuttle to the train so he can escort me home. He worries. "Where does your mind go?" he asks me.

"She was thinking about the ground again," Pen teases, linking her elbow around mine and squeezing against me. "I swear, with all your daydreams about the ground, you could be a novelist."

I will never be disciplined enough to write a novel, not like my brother, Lex, who says I'm too much of an optimist to have any artistic prowess.

We walk quickly. Pen is trying to avoid Thomas, her betrothed, and the way she keeps glancing behind us, she isn't even being inconspicuous.

We make it into a shuttle with hardly a second to spare.

The shuttles are electric vehicles that are much smaller than train cars and therefore are usually crowded. We stand huddled by the door. Pen deflates with a quiet sigh of relief. Thomas is just leaving the academy as we depart.

Basil grips the overhead handle, and I grab his arm as a jolt knocks me into him. The reason for our betrothals is never explained to us, but I like to think the decision makers knew Basil was going to be taller than me. It can only be an act of good planning, the way my head fits into the hollow between his neck and shoulder.

I keep hold of Pen's wrist so she doesn't stumble, but she has no problem keeping her balance. She's staring out at the clouds full of evening sunlight. They meander alongside Internment, but just when I think they'll hit us, they evade, slipping under or over our little world like we're a stone in their waters. Internment is encased by a sphere of wind that prevents the clouds from entering our city, though they seem close enough to touch.

The shuttle stops, pushing strangers into us. We're lucky to be so close to the door, because everyone rushes to get out at once, hoping to catch the train so they won't have to wait for the next one.

The train is not very crowded when we board, aside from the seats at the head of the car that are occupied by a group of pregnant women, chattering with one another about the details of their birthing class. Judging by their stomachs, I'd guess they're carrying a round of January births.

The higher grades let out an hour after most work shifts

end, and the younger children have another hour yet of classes. We find an empty row of seats wide enough to fit the three of us, and I deliberately usher Basil in first so that Pen won't be the one to sit by the window. She has spent enough time staring at the clouds.

"They've already started decorating for the festival of stars," I say, nodding to the silver-colored branches that frame the ceiling of our train car. From the branches hang little metal toys and trinkets that are meant to symbolize human desire—toy trains and books and miniature couples holding hands, the brass silhouette of true love.

The festival of stars overtakes the city in the month of December. It's a time for giving gifts to our loved ones to show our gratitude for having them in our lives. And on the very last day, we're allowed to make one big request of the god in the sky. Each request is written on a special piece of parchment that we aren't meant to share with anyone else. The entire city gathers together, and our pieces of parchment are set on fire and cast into the sky, like hundreds of burning stars. We cling to one another and watch as our greatest desires are carried off and eventually extinguished, to be answered or denied.

"They've asked me to help with the murals this year," Pen says, raising her chin in a modest show of pride. "Apparently one of the instructors recommended me to the festival committee."

"It's about time," I say. "You couldn't keep your talent a secret forever."

She smiles. "I'm a bit nervous, if I'm going to be honest

about it. All those people telling me what to draw. I've never been good at taking orders."

She takes my shoulders and faces me away from her so that she can weave my straight dark hair into a braid. She says I waste my beauty, letting my hair fall over my shoulders like a mop.

Basil doesn't comment on my appearance at all, although sometimes he says he hopes our children have my blue eyes; he says they make him think of what the water on the ground must look like. We've never seen it from up close, but we have the lakes here, which are sort of green.

"If they boss you around, just call it artistic license," Basil says. "You can convince them to see it your way. You're a good debater."

"That is true," Pen says cheerily. "Thanks, Basil."

The train stops, and everyone getting off at the nearest section rises to their feet, but their haste is replaced by confusion. This isn't the platform. Basil cranes his neck and tries to see ahead, but Pen is the one to notice the lights first. She abandons my braid, and my hair falls, undone. She jabs my ribs and says, "Look."

Red-and-white medic lights are flashing off in the distance.

People around us are murmuring. There are medical emergencies sometimes, and despite the organization of the shuttles, accidents happen when people get too close to the moving vehicles. Once, there was an hour's delay after one of the cattle animals broke through a fence and was struck by a train.

Pen and I start to get to our feet for a better look, but a jolt forces us back into our seats. We start moving again. But something is wrong. The scenery moves in the wrong direction.

We're going backward.

Pen is alight with excitement. "I didn't even know the train could *go* backward," she says. "I wonder if it puts any strain on the gears." At times her curiosity makes her brave.

I bite my lip, look out the window because no matter which direction we go, the sky looks the same. And the sky is familiar. The sky is safe.

There's a half mile of land on the other side of the fence that lines the train track; I've never set foot on the other side of the tracks—we aren't supposed to—but Lex has.

On Internment, you can be anything you dream—a novelist or a singer, a florist or a factory worker. You can spend entire afternoons watching clouds so close that it's as though you're riding them. Your life is yours to embrace or to squander. There's only one rule: You don't approach the edge. If you do, it's already over. My brother is proof of that. He has successfully quieted any delusions I held about seeing the ground for myself.

My stomach is doing flip-flops, and I can't decide if it's excitement or fear.

I force myself to look away from the window, and my eyes find Basil's.

Some of the other passengers seem excited, others confused.

A man several seats down, in a black suit, has begun talking to Pen about how trains have emergency systems, and shuttles too. He says that the train has moved backward before, several years before she was born, when repair work needed to be done on the track.

"So it could be that something just needs to be fixed," he says.

One of the pregnant women is staring past Basil and me, out our window at the sky. Her lips are moving. It takes me a few seconds to realize that she's talking to the god in the sky, something the people of Internment do only when they're desperate.

"All this backward motion is starting to make me dizzy," I say.

"It's only because you're worried," Basil says. "You have great equilibrium. What was that spinning game you used to play when we were in first year?"

I let out a small laugh. "It wasn't a game, really. I just liked to count how many times in a row I could spin without falling down."

"Yes, but you would do it everywhere you went," he says. "Up and down stairs, and in the aisles of the train, and all along the cobbles. You never seemed to get dizzy."

"What an odd thing to remember," I say, but it makes me smile. I would spin around the apartment from the time I awoke in the morning, jumping around my older brother and spinning after each step as we shared the mirror in the cramped water room. It drove him mad.

One morning as he was fixing his tie, he warned me that

if I kept spinning, I'd be stolen by the wind and carried off into the sky. "We'll never get you back then," he said. The words were meant to frighten me, but instead they filled me with romantic notions that became a part of my game. I began to imagine being carried on the wind and landing on the ground, seeing for myself what was happening below our city. I could imagine such great and impossible things there. Things I didn't have words for.

The madness of youth made me unafraid.

2

Our genders are determined for us before our parents have reached their turn in the queue. How much are we leaving to the god in the sky?

—"Intangible Gods," Daphne Leander, Year Ten

You didn't have to walk me all the way to the door," I say as Basil and I stop in front of my apartment. His building is within reasonable walking distance, but I'd hate to be the reason he isn't home when his little brother arrives from classes.

"Are you feeling better?" he says. "Your knees have stopped shaking."

I nod, stare down at my hand when he drags his fingertip over my knuckles, our clear rings catching the light. We had to wear them on chains around our necks until last year, when they finally fit us. When we're married, the jeweler will open them and they'll be filled with our blood—mine in his ring, his in mine. I don't think about what it will be like to marry him; according to my mother, I don't think about the things I should be thinking about now that I'm two months past my sixteenth birthday. But I do look at my ring and wonder if the blood drawing will hurt. Alice says it doesn't.

"I can be here in the morning if you'd like," he says. "To walk you to the shuttle for the academy."

I feel my cheeks swell with a smile and I can't meet his eyes. "No," I say. "It's out of your way, and anyway Pen will be with me. I'll meet you there."

He touches the sharp crease of my uniform sleeve, runs his hand down the length of my arm. Something within me stirs. "All right," he says. "See you tomorrow."

"See you."

I watch him enter the stairwell, and as he goes, I notice the flushed skin at the back of his neck.

The apartment door opens, and my mother, wearing an apron stained with flour, ushers me inside. She was listening at the door.

"You should have invited him to dinner. There's plenty," she says. And, "You're late. Did you miss the train?"

"There was a problem with it," I say, shrugging my satchel over the back of a kitchen chair.

"A problem?" She sounds only mildly concerned as she opens the oven and considers the state of the casserole.

"It stopped, and then it had to go backward."

She closes the oven door and looks at me, eyes narrowed in concern.

"It started going the right way again eventually," I say, unknotting my red necktie. With the anxiety I feel today, the tie is starting to have the effect of a noose.

"But you're all right?" she says. "Nobody was hurt?"

"There were medic lights up ahead, but I didn't get a good look." I don't want to worry her; she's been doing so well lately. It has been a while since she's gone through an entire prescription. "I'm sure it's fine," I say.

She stares at me a moment longer, face unreadable, then blinks to free herself from whatever it is she's thinking. "Here," she says, fitting me with oven mitts and thrusting a covered dish into my hands. "Take this upstairs to your brother and Alice."

"Mom, if you keep feeding them, Alice is going to think you have something against her cooking."

"Nonsense," she says. "I just worry. She knows that." She's already opening the door for me; she can't have me out of her kitchen fast enough. Usually she loves my company after class; she lets me nibble on mini fruitcakes and she asks about my lessons. She used to ask about Basil, but not so much since he and I started wearing our rings; she says it's important for betrotheds to share secrets with each other.

"And tell your brother I expect that dish to come back empty," she calls as I'm entering the stairwell.

She has unrealistic expectations. My brother can live on ideas and water for days. His apartment is directly above ours, and his office is over my bedroom. I hear him at all hours, but especially late at night, wearing down the floorboards, and I know he's whispering his novels into the transcription machine. If I listen closely, I might hear his indistinguishable murmurs, Alice asking him to come to bed.

My brother is frequently irritated by my visits, especially

if I'm under our mother's orders to bring him food. He says he's too old now to be treated like a child. But when he and Alice married, they applied for an apartment in this building, so he must not mind being near our parents too much.

I knock on the apartment door, and from the other side I hear Alice cursing. When she opens the door, her hair is falling out of a cloth tie, and water and flower petals are spreading out on the kitchen floor. She's holding shards of the unfortunate vase in a dustpan. There are always flowers in her apartment, and Lex is always knocking them over.

Meekly, I hold up the covered dish. "From my mother," I say.

"Lex!" she calls to the closed door at the end of the hallway. She steps aside to let me in. There's no answer and she paces to the door and knocks angrily.

The windup metal vacuum discus is repeatedly knocking into the corner, trying to find its way out. The copper is scuffed, the gears whining for their efforts.

Alice goes back to picking up the shards. "You try getting him out of there," she says. "Maybe he'll come out for you. He's holed up in there so often that I'm starting to forget I have a husband."

As she gathers the shards, I watch the red blood in her band.

I set the dish on the stove before heading down the hallway—my mother's instincts were right; the stove hasn't been turned on.

I stand outside the door to my brother's office, ear

pressed to the door. I never know what he's writing. He tells me that when I was a baby, he would read his earliest manuscripts to me—he would whisper them through the bars of my crib until I stopped crying in the bedroom we shared, and he could finally go to sleep. He won't tell me what the stories were about. "They were gruesome, brutal," he'll say. "But you didn't understand. You'd smile and go to sleep."

Now I can't hear what he's saying to his transcriber. I knock. "Lex?"

His murmurings stop. I hear him shuffling around, but I don't ask if he needs help. Words like "help" have been banned from his apartment like Internment has been banned from the ground.

The door opens, and I'm hit with the smell of burnt paper. Through the darkness I can just see, on a table in a far corner, a long strip of paper trailing from the transcription machine to the floor, curling into and around itself like hills and valleys. Wisps of smoke are rising from the exposed gears.

"You're supposed to use that thing for only an hour at a time," I say, frowning. There are bags under his eyes and he's staring through me with eyes that used to be blue like mine. But they've faded since his incident. They're gray, bloodshot, and they tell a different story from the rest of his youthful face. He could be my twenty-four-year-old brother or he could be a hundred.

"What happened?" he asks me.

"Mom sent me up here with dinner. She's going to send

me right back up here if I don't convince you to eat. You just have to take a bite; you know she can tell if I lie."

"What happened?" he asks again. He always knows when I'm uneasy.

"Nothing," I say. "There was a problem with the train. Come out and eat something."

"I was in the middle of a thought. Just leave it on the table."

"You're going to break that machine," Alice yells from the kitchen. I've never understood how two people who are so clearly in love can act as though they hate each other at the same time.

Lex relents, though, closing the door behind us and feeling his way along the wall toward the kitchen. Alice has mopped up the water and flower petals. The apartment is kept sparsely furnished, which is Alice's doing. This is her way of helping Lex in secret; she's always a step ahead of him, quietly making sure he's safe.

In a rare feat of accomplishment, I've convinced Lex to eat some of the casserole. He has just taken his first forkful, and he's just about to complain, when the door bursts open.

My father is standing in the doorway, red and out of breath. Sweat stains the collar of his blue patrolman's uniform.

"Dad?" Lex and I say at the same time. Lex is gripping Alice's arm. He's always worrying she'll disappear.

My father needs a moment to catch his breath, but then he seems relieved. "Morgan—" he wheezes. "Your mother told me she sent you up here alone—she didn't know about the king's order."

"What order?" Alice asks, pouring him a glass of water from the tap. He shakes his head, doesn't accept.

"What is it, Dad?" Lex says. "You're making everyone panic."

"Morgan needs to come back downstairs," he says. "The king is ordering everyone to be in their own apartments tonight. There was a body on the train tracks."

Some distant part of me understands, just barely, but another part of me has to ask, "Was there an accident?"

"No, heart," he says. "The other patrolmen and I have been investigating. A girl was murdered."

3

Up until someone I loved approached the edge, I had no reason to question the hand of any god, much less my own god's hand. But to see that no amount of love or will on my part could make that little girl open her eyes as she lay unconscious in a sterile room— How could I not question this god that watches over us? Maybe what frightens us about the edge isn't the fear of our mortality, but the thoughts it leads us to have.

—"Intangible Gods," Daphne Leander, Year Ten

We eat dinner in silence, my mother and I. My father is out investigating the incident and going door-to-door making sure everyone is home and accounted for.

The word keeps replaying in my head: "murder." It's a dusty, cobwebbed word; there hasn't been cause to use it on Internment in my lifetime. It's something I've only read about in novels. It's something that happens on the ground, where there are so many people and most of them are strangers to one another, where there are many places to stray and conspire, where people so often go bad. At least that's what I imagine it's like; nobody knows for sure what the ground is like. Not even King Furlow.

We have engineers who study the ground from afar and educate themselves on ways to further our own technology. Internment has evolved drastically in the last several hundred years; we've learned to set underground wires and indoor plumbing for our sinks and water rooms. The city's electricity is generated by the glasslands, which is a series of panels and globes that gather the sun's energy and store it so that it can be converted into electricity. But there are ground technologies we don't use because the king believes they would complicate our world, make it too dangerous. The king says that the ground makes people greedy and wasteful, while the people of Internment are resourceful and humble.

I think about the murdered girl. I wonder about her final moments. I'm horrible and selfish—I must be—because all my thoughts lead to the idea that she could have been me instead.

My mother's dinner sits untouched on her plate. She's weaving the fork between her fingers and staring out the window across the apartment. The sun has gone away and the train speeds past, rattling our walls for the second time since we've heard the news. The girl's body has been cleaned from the track and the train is back in service. Things must go on. There would be more cause to worry if they didn't.

"It's good that Basil walked you all the way home," she says. "Maybe he should from now on."

"Will there be academy tomorrow?" I ask.

"I'm sure there will," she says, not moving her eyes from the window. The view is exactly the same as it has always been—other apartments and windows full of light. But something has changed; there's something dangerous out there, and to look now, we'd never be able to find it.

There was a murder when my parents were young. Two men had been fighting, and somehow they'd reached the swallows, and one pushed the other in. The fence surrounding the swallows has since been rebuilt to ensure such a thing can never happen again.

Hundreds of years ago, the swallows were a farmland, but something changed. There have been theories about atmospheric pressure, or else the god in the sky becoming angry. The dirt began shifting, and over the decades, it began to churn into itself, swallowing the animals and the crops and anything else that touched it. I've seen slide images of it—a whirling darkness always in motion.

The murderer had been driven mad by a tainted elixir that should have been discarded by the pharmacists. He was feverish and deranged when they found him, and the king had no choice but to have him dispatched.

I clear the dishes, scraping the uneaten food into the compost tube, where it's immediately sucked away to the processing chamber in the basement. I try to keep my mind busy with homework, and my mother doesn't offer to double-check my answers. She's curled in the armchair, touching the fringe of Lex's blanket that's wrapped around her thin shoulders. I hate when she gets this way, so uncertain.

I go to bed two hours early, and I listen to Lex pacing upstairs. When I stand on the bed and knock on the ceiling three times, there's a pause and then he knocks three times with his foot. I think his muffled voice is saying, "Go to sleep."

When we were children, we shared a two-tiered bed, and he slept on the top tier. His lantern would burn late into the night, and sometimes I would lie awake watching his shadows move across the ceiling as he wrote. I would knock on the underside of the bed, and the only reply I ever got was, "Go to sleep."

But I'm too restless, and I wander to my bedroom window and thrust it open. If I stick my head out far enough, I can see a bit of the glasslands to the left. It's viewable from most everywhere because it sits at the heart of the city. Only the sun engineers are permitted to enter the buzzing fence that surrounds it. From afar, though, it looks like a miniature city made of glass. When I was little, I used to imagine that people lived there. Sometimes I still do. A city within a city. What could be safer than that?

I tell myself that I'm safe. The murdered girl didn't have a betrothed who protected her like Basil protects me. She didn't have a brother upstairs and a mother in the next room and a father on the patrol force. She didn't keep to her routine. She wasn't like me. She couldn't have been.

I dream of an angry god in the sky, filling the atmosphere with lightning and inky swirls of wind. He has come alive from my textbook; he doesn't show his face, but he's the maestro in an orchestra of elements. His winds cause the city to shake, the edges to crumble away. We've already been banished from the ground, and now the sky has turned on us. There's nowhere left to go.

My father's voice is what wakes me. He has turned on my bedside lamp, and its glow casts hard shadows on his face. "Morgan?" he whispers. He's still in uniform; he must have just gotten in.

I push myself upright. "What's wrong?" I say, trying to rub the sleep from my eyes. The nightmare is already dissolving as I remember the dark circumstances of the day.

"Morgan," he says, sitting on the edge of my bed. "I worry sometimes that you've been too sheltered."

"Sheltered?" I say. "From what? Things like this don't usually happen."

"You're getting old enough now to see life for exactly what it is."

"What is it?" I say.

"Unpredictable. Mostly good, but awful sometimes. The screens are going to turn on in a few minutes, and King Furlow is going to talk about the incident on the train tracks. It's going to be an honest account. I know you've read about other incidents in your textbooks, but this will be more upsetting. I think you should come watch, but I'm leaving it up to you."

I don't even have to deliberate. "I want to go," I say,

throwing back the covers, reaching for my robe hanging over the bedpost.

My father ruffles my hair as he stands. I worry for him; he rarely talks about his work as a patrolman, but I imagine it's very taxing keeping order, making sure we're all safe, all the while knowing these are things that cannot truly be controlled. He must take the murdered girl as a personal failure; somewhere on Internment tonight, there are parents without their daughter. How long did the murdered girl's parents wait in the queue to have her? Whose birth will be granted now that she's dead? When a person dies alone before his or her dispatch date, the decision makers usually allow two children to be born so they can be betrothed.

"Careful not to wake your mother," my father says as we move through the common room and kitchen.

"Won't she want to see?" I ask. The screens are turned on so rarely.

"No," he says, opening the door for me. "She won't."

Downstairs, the broadcast room is filling with weary-eyed tenants, many in slippers and robes, some in patrolmen uniforms. Aside from a sleeping toddler in a woman's arms, there are no children. Everyone talks in hushed tones, finding friends and relatives in the thin crowd. It's nearly midnight, and most of the city would be asleep by now, except for the patrolmen, and the ones like my brother who never sleep at all.

The lobby has already been decorated to signify the

start of the festival of stars. Paper lanterns hang from the ceiling on strings, lit by small electric bulbs and covered in slantscript to symbolize the requests we'll ask of the god in the sky.

I wonder what the murdered girl's request would have been.

I force the thought away and look for Lex and Alice, but instead Pen and I find each other. She breaks away from her parents to run to me and grab my hands. "Can you believe it?" she says, her green eyes wide with excitement and fright. "Does your father know who it was?"

"I probably know as much about it as you," I say, comforted by the way she coils her arm around mine. I have the horrible thought that the murdered girl could have been her, that by next week she would be nothing more than a handful of ashes cast to the wind. And then I feel selfishly relieved that the murdered girl wasn't anyone in my life. It wasn't Pen or Alice or my mother.

Across the room, my father has found Alice. Lex isn't with her. I understand; he has known enough awful things for a lifetime. I still think of how he used to be, attentive and intense, his face magnified by the beaker he'd hold up to the light. He used to be one of the top pharmacy students, honored with tasks most others can't take on until graduation. But after his incident, he burned all of his notes and abandoned the trade entirely. He earns money by sewing quilts now—his work is erratic but deft, and the quilts always fetch a higher price than the others, his skill and precision cause for envy among the other makers.

Pen presses close to me and says, "Look."

A patrolman is jostling the screen, twisting its knobs and trying to make the static subside. The screen is more than a hundred years old, its bronze facing chipped down to oblivion; the wires are frayed, and a little burst of sparks makes someone in the crowd gasp.

But the image comes through, distorted at first, King Furlow trembling, warped, and green, before the patrolman hits the screen, knocking the image into reasonable clarity in time for us to see the king remove his red bowler hat and hold it to his pudgy stomach.

King Furlow's lineage traces back to the dawn of Internment itself. His oldest ancestor is in the history book as the only man chosen to hear from the god in the sky. No one knows for certain how the god in the sky speaks with the king, but it's Internment's longest standing tradition, passed down from generation to royal generation. I've never envied him; it's surely a terrible burden to be the voice of an entire city.

The rest of us speak to the god in the sky when we're frightened or grateful, and we don't expect to be answered.

Standing at either side of the king are his children: Princess Celeste, and her older brother, Prince Azure, both of whom may be trying to appear somber but instead seem bored. Though the screen is sepia and the image a bit out of focus, they both look like their mother, and their mother's mother, and so on as far as records trace. Blond hair and clear sparkling eyes, a bit of plumpness to the face. They're sixteen and seventeen, making them closer in age than any other siblings on Internment. The king's children are traditionally born outside the queue. When the queen announces her pregnancies, she and the king go through the list of hopeful parents in the queue, and they hand-select the applicants they see fit to bear their children's betrotheds. Of course the hopeful parents can refuse, but no one in Internment's history has ever passed up the chance to have a child without the long wait.

"At four-oh-five this evening," the king begins, "the coroner made his official statement that the death of a sixteen-year-old young lady was the result of murder. I warn those of you watching at home that many of the details about to be shared are graphic, and young children should not be present."

The other tenants are huddling together. Pen and I have our arms around each other; my view of the screen is partially obstructed by the people ahead of me, but I don't crane my neck for a better look.

Across the room, Alice chews her thumbnail and nods at something that my father has just said to her.

There's an assortment of gasps and "Oh no" and mutterings as the murdered girl's class image is shown. She's got a coy smile and her eyelids are dusted with glitter. My first thought is that she's radiant. Through the sepia, I can imagine her face alive with color.

"Oh," Pen whispers into my ear. "I know her. We were in a romantic-literature course together."

"Daphne Leander," the king goes on, "a tenth-year student and aspiring medic, is estimated to have died this morning. Her parents informed our patrolmen that they last saw her boarding the shuttle for the academy."

The details turn dark after that. She received absences from all of her instructors. No report from other morning passengers that she ever boarded the train. She was found early in the evening. Throat and wrists slashed. Everything indicates that she bled to death. As to how her body came to be on the train tracks during daylight hours—that's still under investigation.

"Patrolmen will be stationed in every train car, at every platform, and outside the doors of every building of Internment until the criminal responsible for this vicious act is found."

Pen's mother stands a few paces away with her arm out, waving her daughter to come over and allow herself to be embraced, but Pen resists.

"It's important for you to all go about your lives normally," the king says. Daphne's image is replaced with the sketched map of Internment. "The theater and the businesses in the shopping sections will keep their usual hours. There *will* be patrolmen in sight at all times; report any suspicious activity, no matter how minor it may seem at the time."

The panic reaches through me like vines curling up from my toes to my stomach, twisting and knotting and tightening around my organs. Internment looks so small on the screen. It would take a train less than two hours to circle it entirely. Within that circuit is everyone I've ever loved and every place I will ever go. But it has been sullied, ugliness spreading out like the color from a steeping tea bag, until everything is covered by it. There's someone out there capable of slashing open a young girl's skin and leaving her to be found.

"I feel sick," I say.

"Me too," Pen says.

When the broadcast is over, the screen goes to static.

"Margaret," Pen's father calls impatiently. She grunts. He's the only one who uses her real name; even her instructors call her Pen, despite what her forms and her student identification card say.

Numbly I watch her return to her parents, but she squeezed my hand before she went. The crowd is dwindling, but I don't go to my father and Alice; I go to the stairwell, and once the door is closed behind me and I'm alone, I run up the four flights of stairs to my brother's apartment. The door is locked; it's never locked. I fight the doorknob and then I pound frantically on the door. I can hear shuffling inside and I know he's coming to let me in, but there are footfalls in the stairwell and there could be anything around the corner, where a bulb has gone out and shadows spread into the light.

The door opens and I spill inside, pushing it shut behind me.

"Morgan?" he says. Even without his sight, Lex always knows my presence. His dark hair is bunched on one side; he pulls at it when he's writing.

I try to speak, but my lip is quivering and my heart is in my throat and I'm out of breath from the climb.

"You watched the broadcast, didn't you?" he says. "It's

all right. Breathe. Sit down." He pulls out a kitchen chair for each of us.

"Pen knew her," I blurt. "She wanted to be a medic. She was my age. And she was pretty." I don't even know what I'm saying. Words are blurring like the city through the train window. My lungs are aching.

"Morgan." My brother reaches across the table and puts his hand over mine. "Every generation has its horror stories. It was only a matter of time before something awful happened in front of you. It's an awful thing to be alive sometimes."

"Don't say that. It isn't awful at all."

There's so much beauty out there that Daphne Leander will never see again.

Lex has such a piteous look on his face, as though I'm the one to feel sorry for.

"Why do you say things like that?" I ask.

"Because I saved lives when I was a pharmacy student," he says. "And you can't be the reason someone is alive without giving thought to what being alive means."

I pull my hand away from his. "Remind me to never implore your aid if I'm dying."

"Don't be angry," he says. "I'm sorry. Morgan, I'm sorry. I wish it hadn't happened. I wish you never had to know such things."

"But you write about it," I say. "Don't you? People dying and getting sucked up into the swallows and things."

"Sometimes," he admits. "You've read dark stories, haven't you? People die in them?"

"But I know they aren't real," I say. "I put the book down and I go on with my life."

He frowns. "Things are changing, Little Sister, and not for the better. I have a feeling about that. But I would dock Internment to the ground and take you someplace brilliant if I could."

"Internment is brilliant," I say. "It's more than enough."

More than enough. I repeat the words over and over in my head, forcing them to be true.

4

Virtuousness—how is it defined? We are taught not to approach the edge, and certainly not to jump. But is bravery not a virtue?

— "Intangible Gods," Daphne Leander, Year Ten

The train ride to the academy is so quiet that I can hear the wheels squeaking on the tracks, and the hum of the electricity. The students, like the families in my building during the broadcast, huddle together, talking softly if at all.

Even Basil and Thomas aren't speaking.

Pen watches the clouds blurring past us, and in the window's reflection I think she's watching the patrolman standing at the head of our car. As promised, there was no lack of them this morning, holding open doors for us, nodding, saying, "Good morning" as though to reassure us that our little world is safe. They cast suspicious glances at the men in particular. I don't know that I like this. The vigilance of the patrolmen is supposed to make me feel safe, but all it does is further the knowledge that something has changed.

There are patrolmen watching us step off the train; Pen stays close to me, huffing indignantly as she tugs her skirt pleats down past her knees. "Are all these eyes really necessary?" she says.

"They're only looking out for our safety," Basil says. "Try to ignore them."

She looks over her shoulder after the patrolman who opened the academy door for us; she crinkles her nose but says nothing more.

Normally we'd have at least ten minutes of free time in the lobby, but today we're supposed to report to our first classes immediately. "I'll see you at lunch," I say to Basil.

He reaches for my hand, hesitates, and drops his arm back at his side. "See you at lunch." I watch him disappear into a group of his morning classmates.

"What was that about?" Pen says after we've rounded the corner.

"I think he's going to kiss me soon," I say, suddenly feeling very awkward about what to do with my own hands. "It seemed like he wanted to yesterday when he walked me home."

"At last, my little girl is growing up," she says.

"I'm three days older than you," I say.

She bumps me with her shoulder. "But I know all the things you're too sweet to know."

Her laugh gives me more reassurance than all the patrolmen on Internment combined.

The cafeteria at lunchtime, in contrast to the rest of the academy, is alive with chatter.

"I've found a few things out about Daphne Leander," Pen says, setting her tray on the table across from Basil and me. She rifles through her satchel and pulls out a folded piece of paper. "These were tacked up in the ladies' locker room. They're all handwritten but they say the same thing. Look at the date—it's from last month. It was her essay on the history of the gods. But we had to read our essays aloud, and this isn't the one she read. If I had to guess, it was a draft she didn't intend to have anyone find."

As I'm unfolding the page, Basil says, "Should we be invading her privacy like this?"

"They're all over the academy," Pen says. "Someone wanted them seen, to be sure."

I smooth the page flat against the table and begin to read. *Intangible Gods, Daphne Leander, Year Ten.*

"You look lovely today," Thomas says, seating himself beside Pen.

She glares at her lunch tray and mumbles a dispirited, "Thank you."

I fold the paper before Thomas notices it, and tuck it into my skirt pocket.

"How are you handling the news?" Thomas asks, glancing between Pen and me. "It must be pretty frightening for you girls."

"Everyone's frightened," Pen says. "Not just the girls."

"Of course," Thomas says. "I only meant that you must feel more vulnerable. The fairer sex and all that."

"How do you know it had anything to do with being a girl?" Pen says. "The patrolmen aren't watching *just* the girls. They're watching all of us. We don't know why this murderer victimized a girl or if that even mattered, and we don't know who could be next."

"I didn't mean to offend," he says, looking between Pen and me. "Forgive me."

I concentrate on my tray. It isn't hard to understand why Pen is always avoiding her betrothed, even if to an outsider they'd seem like the perfect pair; he's every bit as attractive as she is, in that pristine, bright-eyed way. And he has her same spiritedness, but they are far from compatible most days. She has confided in me that she'd cheerfully marry a dead trout in his place.

Thankfully, Basil is an excellent conversationalist, and he and Thomas begin talking about last week's squares tournament and some apparent controversy about a referee's call on a blunder.

Pen pushes her vegetables around with her fork.

"You should try to eat," I say.

"I will if you will."

We make a silent game of synchronizing our bites.

After lunch, we drop our utensils, trays, and uneaten food into the respective recycling and compost tubes and we move in four different directions to our next classes. The paper in my pocket feels heavy.

The evening train is less somber than the morning's was. Basil is trying to cheer me with plans for the weekend.

He thinks we should go to the theater; one of his favorite books has just been adapted into a play.

I rest my head on his shoulder. His collarbone presses into my cheek, and I breathe in the sharp linen of his uniform and something faintly spicy-sweet. Up until last year, he smelled only of soap, if anything at all.

"You don't have to walk me to the door," I say. His train stop is right after mine, and if he walks me inside, he'll have to walk a section over to his apartment.

"I don't mind," he says as the train begins to slow.

"You'll be safer on the train," I say. "It'd make me feel a lot better. Please."

"Don't worry. I'll protect her," Pen says, tugging me to my feet after the train's final jolt.

"Come by tomorrow afternoon," I tell him. "We'll see the play if you want."

We step off the train and Pen checks her reflection in her wristwatch. "You're lucky, you know," she says. "You aren't doomed to marry a complete ass."

The patrolmen open the double doors for us, nod as we pass through.

"Maybe Thomas isn't as bad as all that," I say. Her being envious of Basil would defeat the purpose of arranged betrothals. "Plenty of couples argue."

"I'll never fancy him," she says. "He has a face like composted broccoli."

I laugh. "No he doesn't."

"He does. Which is why I intend to never enter the queue. I couldn't inflict such awful cheekbones on future generations, even if there's a chance our children could look like me."

Though it's a long way off, I've given some thought to the queue. I might like having children, but more than that, I think my parents would want a grandchild. Lex and Alice will never be eligible now that he's disabled, but they applied for it six years ago when they were newlyweds.

Because of Internment's land limitations, there can't be a round of pregnancies until there has been a sufficient amount of deaths. It's a long wait—years—which is why so many couples enter the queue while they're still university students. My parents reentered the day my brother was born, and it was more than seven years before they were allowed to have me.

Alice got pregnant out of turn. It wasn't intentional; she'd been neglectful with her pill. She pleaded with the decision makers, even writing a personal appeal to the king himself, but she was years from the front of the queue. She offered to give her child to the next eligible couple, as a last-ditch effort to let her child be born, but of course that isn't allowed—giving away a child could lead to resentment and jealousy, which could prove dangerous. There's a story in *The History of Internment* to prove that, something about a woman who decided she'd rather smother her child than allow it to belong to someone else. Pen knows it better than I do. She has the history book memorized.

After weeks of fighting for her cause, Alice was forced to have a termination procedure. She came home from the hospital with darkness under her eyes, and she retreated immediately to bed, where she stayed for days. Her skin and even her hair seemed to have lost their color.

It took her a very long time to act like Alice again. I would follow her around the apartment and on her weekend errands, coaxing her to take me shopping for new jewelry and to tea shops, throwing my arms around her without warning on shuttles and while she was cooking dinner.

Lex won't have anything to do with pharmaceuticals now. In studying medicine, he used to help manufacture the elixirs that precede the termination procedures, among other things.

Pen is still musing about the queue. "You do have nice eyes," she tells me. "Blue isn't very dominant against brown, though, is it? Well, still, Basil isn't *un*attractive."

We're standing in front of her apartment door now.

"You should come to the play with us tomorrow," I say. "Bring Thomas."

"Maybe," she sighs. "If my mother is having one of her headaches, she'll want me out of the apartment anyway. See you later."

In my apartment, I find my mother sleeping on the couch, curled in Lex's blanket. There's a hot plate waiting in the stove for me, but I'm not hungry. I work on my homework for a while, but the silence feels crushing and it doesn't take long for me to get restless enough to go upstairs.

As always, there are signs of life in Lex and Alice's apartment. Alice is standing on the kitchen table in impractical black heels, trying to change a lightbulb.

"Morgan's here now," Lex says before I've even stepped into the apartment. "Let her help you. You're going to fall and break your face."

"I am not going to break my face," she says, cursing when she burns her fingertips on the bulb.

I grab a new bulb from the package at her feet and hold it up. "You're a peach," she says, stooping to take it.

"We're going out in a few minutes, you know," Lex says. "It's Friday. Jumper group."

"I was hoping you'd let me tag along."

Alice climbs down from the table and dusts her hands on her shirtfront. "I don't see why not," she says. "It'll give me someone to talk to, at least. I'm always left waiting in the hallway. They don't even offer me any of their snacks."

"Tell Mom so she doesn't worry," Lex says.

"She's sleeping. Already left a note."

Alice runs the tap and smoothes water over some defiant strands of hair. She's done it up in elaborate curls held in place by bronze clips that compliment her curls' many shades of red. She's wearing a blue dress that curls and billows around her knees and elbows as she moves through the mundane tasks of putting away the bulbs and straightening an image on the wall. Sometimes she's unreal. Something that floated down from the sky.

Before the incident, she and Lex were seldom home. She had a dress for every color the sun illuminates and there was always cause to wear one. Even when I was a child, I admired the love they had, the way every outing, every dinner party or hike through the woods was an adventure.

Now Alice dresses up only for weekend errands, and Lex's jumper group every Friday, even though the only people to see her are the shuttle and train passengers. Her job in the gardens requires a drab uniform that I've always thought looked like it was trying to smother her.

I feel underdressed in my academy uniform, yet I know that I won't have time to change. Alice, reading my mind, disappears to the bedroom and returns, pressing silver earrings into my palm; they're shaped like stars cascading down little chains.

"Better get moving," she says, jostling the back of Lex's chair. "If we miss the train, we'll have to walk."

Outside, the sky has become a deeper blue, filling fast with stars. As we step onto the train platform, Lex crushes a daisy that's growing between the cobbles. I wonder if he remembers what flowers are, not only what they look like, but that they exist at all. He's knocked over plenty of Alice's vases, and he has no idea what the shattering glass was before he ruined it. He's told me that he can't remember how eyelashes are shaped. He can't conjure an image of our mother's window boxes full of tomato plants, though he had looked at them every day of his life.

The seven thirty train isn't crowded. There's a group of men in suits at the far end of the car; one of them tips his hat flirtatiously to Alice, and she tugs on her earring, smirking for a moment before turning her attention to ushering Lex into his seat. There's a mother listening patiently as her young child recites the multiplication tables. There's a girl traveling alone, which I wouldn't have found strange before the murder. She's wearing the blue necktie worn by sixth- through eighth-year students. She's young but her face is pointed up, and something about the ferocity in her eyes is vaguely familiar.

Beside me, Alice rests her head on Lex's shoulder, and he rubs her arm, says something in her ear that makes her smile.

A patrolman paces the aisle after the train has begun to move, and the girl in the blue tie plays with the ring hanging from her neck as she watches him. I'm sure I'm imagining the snarl she gives once he has passed by. Her eyes meet mine and I look away. I watch the sky slowly turning darker blue. In the long season, the sun burns until late evening, but the short season is approaching now and the days are getting shorter.

"We'll have two hours to burn," Alice says. "There's a tea shop at the end of the block we could try."

I smile. "Okay."

"Are you feeling okay?" she says. "You seem a little distant."

I feel the eyes of the girl in the blue tie watching me, though I don't look in her direction to confirm. And I feel the patrolman watching me, not just here but everywhere I go. For the first time in my life, I feel unsafe and I don't know how to help it. The king has insisted that we go about our lives as normal, that the patrolmen will keep us safe, but who was there to keep Daphne Leander safe?

"I'm okay," I say.

"Dad shouldn't have let you watch the broadcast," Lex says. "All it's done is cause you to worry about everything."

"I needed to see it," I say. "I don't need to be sheltered."

"Says the girl who still sleeps with the light on after I tell her a harmless ghost story."

"That was years ago," I say. "I'm not a baby, you know."

"I am certain it was only last season," Lex says, and his voice deepens when he adds, "The tale of the ghost birds that flew into the city and pecked everyone to death."

"I don't recall leaving any lights on," I say, and am impressed by my cool tone.

"Don't listen to him," Alice says.

"Do they sell sweets at the tea shop?" I say. "I skipped dinner and now I'm hungry."

"I'm sure they do."

Lex says something about my teeth rotting out of my head and how the only way to stop me from crying as a baby was to give me sugar water, and the conversation moves into the comfort of trivial things. But in the window, among the clouds, I see the reflection of the girl in the blue tie. I can't shake the idea that she looks familiar, even though I can't remember ever seeing her in the city.

The train stops and Alice and I guide Lex onto the platform, keeping him out of the way of passengers entering and exiting. I feel a tug at the back of my shirt, and when I turn around, the girl in the blue tie is holding a silver star earring in her palm. "You dropped this," she says. Her eyelids are smeared with pink glitter, and it isn't until after she has walked away that I realize why she looks so familiar. She's a younger version of the murdered girl. They could be sisters. And they probably are.

The jumper group is held behind a closed door in a recreational room of the courthouse that used to be a holding cell for criminals decades ago. Even spouses, siblings, and parents aren't allowed inside.

Alice straightens the collar of Lex's shirt and kisses him. "Handsome," she accuses. "I'll be right outside when it's time to go home."

"I'll be waiting, gorgeous," he says.

"Gorgeous," she says, exhaling a little laugh. "For all you know, I've colored my face green."

"Then you'd be gorgeous and green," he says.

She does her best not to show it, but it's hard for her to relinquish her husband into the care of a fellow jumper, who ushers him to the circle of chairs. They've always shared everything, and this is something he never talks about. There's a camaraderie among these group members that never leaves the room.

The girl in the blue tie slips past us into the room and finds a seat. She looks so small and out of place there among the others. Most of the jumpers are old enough to have grown cynical about our little world, discontent. I've never heard of a child jumping. The others are disfigured and disabled from their attempts, but she looks polished and thin in her pressed uniform. Her hair, the same sweetgold blond as the murdered girl's, is held back by a white band with a bow on one side. Someone hands her a paper cup and she manages a polite if despondent smile.

"Okay," Alice says, putting her hand on my back and guiding me toward the door. "Let's get out of here." We pass others who linger in the hall, waiting for their loved ones while reading or talking amongst one another. This is where Alice would have waited in her pretty dress, and when she went home she would have simply hung it in the closet again. I don't know that I can ever forgive Lex for squandering her. And yet she has never complained about having to care for him. She could go out more if she wanted to; if he's in the throes of a novel, he probably won't even notice. But she mostly just leaves for work in the greenhouses.

A patrolmen opens the door for us. "Ladies." He nods as we pass by. "Be safe out there tonight."

The orange glow of street lanterns outlines the cobblestones with shadows. Yet in the distance, the glasslands shimmer in the moonlight.

"That little girl is part of the jumper group?" I ask, once we're beyond the earshot of the patrolmen.

"I've seen her the last few times," Alice says.

"So she's jumped?"

"She must have . . ." Alice's voice is trailing off. She takes a deep breath and says, "Look at that moon, Morgan. It's so close. As if we could just walk right up to the edge and reach out and take it." She closes one eye and holds up her hand, balancing the moon on her palm.

I hook my elbow around hers. I don't like what she has

said. I don't like the thought of her crossing the tracks and chasing the moon to Internment's edge. People go mad there. They see all of that sky and nothingness and they lose themselves.

"Is this the tea shop?" I say.

"Oh! Yes, it is. Look, the sign is shaped like an actual teacup. Isn't that quaint?"

It would be, if not for the patrolman standing at the entrance.

5

Every moment is a gift, from the frivolous to the dire.
The taste of sweetgold, and the rough paper of our
favorite books. I find a god in these things—which
god, I cannot say, but I'm grateful to it.

—"Intangible Gods," Daphne Leander, Year Ten

Pen fixes the hem of my red velvet glove that's
starting to unroll from my elbow. "You look classic," she
says, and then holds up her own blue gloves with a look
of disdain. "Aren't these archaic? They're my mother's.
She used to wear them on dates with my father. You know,
back when Internment was still part of the ground."

"I think you're a vision," Thomas says, coming up
behind her, gripping the overhead handle as the shuttle
begins to move.

She looks over her shoulder at him, and the sunlight
catches the shadows of her neck and collarbone in a way
that makes her seem more woman than girl. "I thought for
sure you'd missed the shuttle."

"I caught it just as the doors were closing," he says, and looks at me. "I take it your other will be joining us shortly?"

"We're taking the train to his section and walking from there," I say, feeling strange about the word he has used: "other." He likes to talk like a period actor; he's always reading romantic classics—a woman on the cover with an elaborately floral hat, looking faint as a man in a tuxedo steadies her. Things of that nature.

When the shuttle jolts and pushes Thomas toward her, Pen swats at him, complaining that he'll make her hat go crooked. She's wearing a candlebox hat that has been dyed the same color as her gloves. Candles come in small, cylindrical stiff paper boxes that can be taken to a clothes maker to be recycled into a hat. They're dyed desired colors, given a brim, and affixed to a band so that the hat will sit firmly on one side of the head.

They look ridiculous on me. Few girls are bold enough to pull them off, but Pen is the sort of girl who can wear anything.

Thomas smiles at her averted face. "I'll have your heart yet, Margaret Atmus."

"You already have it." She holds up her hand, betrothal band gleaming in the light. "Not that I had any say in the matter. And you know I hate when you call me that."

When we make it to the train, I notice that it isn't very crowded, which is strange for the weekend. "Looks like a lot of people decided to walk today," Thomas says.

Pen flattens her dress against her knees, indifferent to his arm around her shoulders.

"I've been reading a peculiar little story," Thomas says, looking at me because he knows Pen won't humor him with interest.

"What about?" I say.

"It's about the people of the ground trying to reach us. They craft a sort of machine and harness it to birds."

"Birds couldn't lift something that heavy," Pen says. We don't know very much about birds—they've never flown so high as Internment, but we've seen images of them taken with the scope. Skinny white blurs traveling alone or as beads in a necklace of *V*s.

"Well then, you've figured out the conflict," he says. "Anyway, they don't make it. The story was really more about their trying to reach us. Some think they are, and others say we're nothing more to them than a giant rock in the sky. Perhaps they think we're a dusty moon."

"I wonder about that all the time," I say.

"Don't get Morgan started on the ground," Pen says, rising as the train rolls to a stop. "She'll be lost in thought for the rest of the day, and I need someone to whisper with if this play is no good."

Basil spots us as we're stepping out onto the platform. The gold trim of his jacket matches the flecks of light in his brown eyes. Pen calls it a shame that my eyes aren't dominant, but I think it would be nice if my children look like Basil. He holds his arm to me, and I look at my velvet glove against his gray suit, imagining we're figures in a very old image. Though I know I shouldn't, I imagine that the steps leading down off the platform will go all the way down the sky until we reach the ground.

"How are you?" he asks, so close that his breath reaches the nape of my neck.

"I'll feel better once they've caught the person responsible," I admit. "My father came home last night with an extra bolt for our door. Every time I look at it, I see that girl's face."

"A lot of people in my building are installing locks, too." He frowns. "They'll find whoever's behind this. Internment is only so big. There aren't many places to hide."

That's what has me so afraid. I've always liked the smallness of Internment, always liked lying in bed at night and hearing the trains rush by, always on time. But now it's starting to feel smaller, as though every day since Daphne Leander's murder has crumbled the edges a bit more, and the city is closing in on me.

Even the seats in the theater feel smaller and closer together, the dim lights getting dimmer.

"Are you okay?" Pen says. "Your cheeks are bright red."

Basil touches my forehead. "Do you feel sick?" His touch is supposed to comfort me, but all I want is to get away from him, to get away from this air that everyone else is breathing.

"I need to use the water room," I say.

"I'll go with you," Pen says.

"No," I say, too quickly. "No, you might miss the opening. I'll be fast, I promise."

I can see that she's wary, but she doesn't try to stop me as I shuffle down the aisle.

With all of the shows about to start, the lobby is empty aside from the ticket vendors, who pay no mind as I stumble toward the water rooms. But when I push the door open, I find that I'm not alone.

Though she's not in uniform, I recognize the little girl from last night. She's kneeling on the edge of the sink, tacking a piece of paper over the mirror. But she stops when she sees me, stumbles to her feet, and backs against the wall.

"I didn't mean to scare you," I say.

There's a piece of paper over each of the mirrors. A quick glance and I can see that they're select passages from Daphne Leander's essay. All of them are handwritten. Typewriters are a rare luxury afforded to those who write for a living; a past king once considered making them a household item, but decided against it. He said that if words could be easily printed and erased, we would lose our appreciation for what we wrote.

I'd like to ask her about the pages, but she runs past me and pushes her way through the door.

"Wait!" I run after her.

She's quick, but so am I, and I catch up to her on the sidewalk outside the theater, where she has come to a stop. She doesn't seem out of breath, and I'm trying to figure out why she stopped, but then I follow her gaze to the building at the end of the block, engulfed in flames.

She looks at me, and her eyes are full of so much pain that it astounds me. They're the same as the murdered girl's eyes, and yet different somehow.

"It's only going to get worse," she says.

That's the jumper's code, if Lex's similar outlook is any indication.

A patrolman is running from the theater, shouting for us to get back inside. She doesn't move, though, and I grab her arm and pull her along. She doesn't resist, but she watches the flames over her shoulder. It was one of Internment's oldest buildings, back when they were still made of wood as opposed to stone. Over the centuries it has been everything from a prison, back when those still existed, to a recycling plant. In my lifetime it has been only a flower shop. Alice has taken me there dozens of times.

It's only a few paces back to the theater, but before we've reached the doors, the sky has changed. Ash is heavy on the air and it's as though something has covered the sun. Even the patrolman has stopped to watch. Sirens begin as distant warnings, but soon they're screaming as the emergency vehicles rush toward the flames.

The girl's arm is still in my grip and she lets me bring her inside, but then she twists away, presses her hands to the glass doors and watches.

The lobby is crowded now, everyone rushing to windows, calling out the names of their friends. "Are you here with anyone?" I ask.

She shakes her head. "I'm not supposed to be here. I'm supposed to be practicing my music."

"Come on, then," I say. "You can come with me. I'm going to find my friends and make sure they're okay."

"I don't know you," she says.

"Morgan Stockhour," I say. "There, now you do."

The room has gotten very loud around us. A woman screams.

The girl looks up at me, hesitating. Some pink glitter has clumped in her eyelashes.

"I'm Amy," she says.

"Morgan!" Somewhere in the melee, Pen raises her gloved arm. She twists away from Thomas, fighting him and shouldering her way to me. She crashes into me, squeezing me so hard that my feet almost come away from the floor. "What's happening? They stopped the play, and . . ."

She sees the smoke through the glass doors for the first time. Her mouth is open and breathless. She pales.

"The flower shop caught fire," I say, though the words don't do justice to what I just saw. I should be panicking like everyone around me. I should be frightened. But I feel the same as I did after watching the broadcast, like none of it is real.

"Your parents will be worried," I tell Amy.

"They won't notice I'm gone." She seems like the type who can slip in and out of a place unnoticed, which is likely how she snuck into this theater without formal attire.

Basil wraps his arm around my waist from behind. Thomas does the same to Pen, and for once she seems grateful that he's there to hold her. Amy stands between us, and we all watch the clouds and the sun get swallowed whole.

It feels like hours before the flames are extinguished. Patrolmen fill the lobby, escorting us from the building to the shuttle in droves. Pen lets Thomas hold on to her, and Basil hasn't taken his arm from me since we were reunited. Amy walks a pace ahead of me, tugging at the ring on the chain around her neck.

"Where do you live?" Basil asks her as the five of us cram onto a shuttle bench meant to hold four.

"Section three," she says.

"I'm in two," he says. "But it's a short walk back for me. I'll see you home."

"You don't have to," she says. "I'm old enough to take care of myself."

"Yes, right, okay, we're all old enough," Pen snaps. "But in case you haven't noticed, Internment has kind of gone into a complete state of lunacy."

"I know that," Amy says, and looks sharply out the window, where the smoke has turned the city into an old image.

"Are you frightened?" Thomas asks Pen.

She's looking at her lap, but he tilts her chin and she meets his eyes.

"I won't ever let anything happen to you, you know."

She nods, leans her forehead against his.

For all their arguing, they have kissed. It first happened several months ago. He kept dropping hints and she decided to just be done with it. It wasn't terrible, she told me. It wasn't great but it wasn't terrible. I had a hard time believing it—she's always evading him—but I'm starting to see that there's a reason they were betrothed. There's always a reason.

Basil grips my hand as the shuttle comes to a stop. "It's going to be chaotic. Don't let go of me even if people rush between us," he says. With my free hand, I grab on to Pen and we rise to our feet.

An instant too late, I remember that Amy is behind me. In that instant, she dodges under Pen's and my interlocked hands and disappears into the crowd.

"Amy!"

"Let her go," Pen says. "Where did you find such a strange child, anyway?" She's trying to act nonchalant but the fear is still in her eyes.

I'm scanning the crowd for Amy; with the patrolmen steering us all right onto the waiting train, there's nowhere for her to go, and I still want to ask her about the essay.

But it's taking all my efforts to hold on to Basil and Pen; I've never seen Internment in such a panic, and other worries start to invade my mind. My father is patrolling today; that means he must be out in this mess. And Alice will be out running errands; she frequents the flower shop, has a side job designing event bouquets.

And what started the fire to begin with?

Amy said it was only going to get worse. I see this panic all around me, while news of Daphne Leander's murder is still fresh, and I cannot fathom what worse should look like.

By the time we make it to our seats on the train, Pen isn't the only one with tears in her eyes. Other passengers have the same frightened expression.

Even Basil is looking worriedly at the city through the

window. A patrolman is standing at the head of the car, instructing us not to check in on family and friends, to step off the train at our appropriate sections and go straight home. The train will stop for an extra two minutes on each platform to ensure everyone has a chance to exit the over-crowded cars in time.

"Something is happening," Basil says, "isn't it?"

"I'm sure it was only an accident," Thomas says. "That building was so old that it has never been properly outfit-ted with electricity. Most of the rooms were lit by flame lanterns. One of them probably tipped over."

"Do you think so?" Pen says.

"I'm almost certain."

None of us believes it, but we don't have the nerve to say so.

"Your mascara is running," Pen says. "Here." She rubs her gloved thumb under my eyelid.

"Thanks," I say, though from the black smear on her glove I suspect she's made it worse.

When the train stops in our section, Basil squeezes my hand. "I'm sorry I can't walk you in," he says.

"I'll be fine; my building is right there," I tell him, wish-ing desperately that I wasn't about to leave him behind. "Stay safe."

I don't know what it is—the noise or the distant smell of the ashes or the fear—but I get the thought that I'd like to kiss him. I lean forward and press my lips against his fore-head, pleasantly surprised by the softness and the warmth of his skin.

I don't get a chance to see his reaction; Thomas is pulling Pen, and Pen is pulling me.

We can still smell the fire, though it happened several sections away and has since been extinguished. The blue of the sky is still up there, if a bit obscured, and I might have started to feel relief if only there weren't a patrolman forcing me down the steps.

Thomas lives in the same section that Pen and I do, but his building is a block over, and at the fork in the pathway, he leans in for a kiss and Pen backs away. "Let's not capitalize on a tragedy," she says. "I'll see you on Monday, provided the academy is still standing."

He smirks, nods to us, and turns into the crowd.

She shakes her head. "Strange thing, him."

"He's just a little old-fashioned," I say.

"And you!" she says. "Don't think I didn't see what you did as we were getting off the train. We'll be talking about that some other time when we're not being manhandled by patrolmen."

"Move along, please," the patrolman says from somewhere behind us. "Move along, toward your own buildings."

It is wildly inappropriate that Internment is crumbling around me, but all I can think about is the warmth of Basil's skin lingering on my lips.

Alice is frantic. When I open the door to my apartment, she's got her arms around me before I know what's happening. "She's home," she calls to Lex, who's got an unfinished quilt draped across his lap and a spool of thread in one hand and a needle in the other. He does his best work when he's anxious. But he drops all of these things and starts making his way to me.

Alice is holding me by the shoulders now. "Are those bruises?"

"She's hurt?" Lex says. He rarely seems to regard me at all, much less show concern. Normally I'd appreciate it, but right now it only adds to this feeling that Internment has gone mad.

"It's cosmetics," I say, reaching my arm out to Lex so he can find me. "I'm perfectly fine. Where are Mom and Dad?"

"Dad has been patrolling all day," Lex says. "Mom was at the market. We came down so someone would be here when you got back."

"They're making everyone go home," I say. "The trains are running slowly. The cars are all overcrowded, so they want to make sure everyone has time to get off at their stops." I thought I was doing better, but there's a stone in my stomach at the thought of my mother and father out in all that chaos. And I can still smell the burnt air, though maybe it's just clinging to my dress.

Alice sets me in a kitchen chair, moves to the sink, and returns seconds later to wipe the cosmetics and sweat from my face with a wet cloth. My tears are only from the abrasiveness of the ashes, but they still earn her sympathetic touch.

Lex, sitting across the table, still has his hand over mine.

He keeps pressing his palm into my knuckles like I might vaporize into nothing if he doesn't hold tight. Sometimes he hides in the darkness of his blindness, and other times he fears it will swallow everyone up and leave him alone.

Alice dabs the cold cloth to my forehead and then drapes it across the back of my neck, still fretting that I'm too red.

"Thomas thinks it may not be cause to panic," I say, trying to reassure her. "He said the flower shop still uses flame lanterns and it was probably an accident."

"There will be a broadcast tonight for sure," she says. "Thank goodness you're safe. We heard the fire was near the theater and we've just been all over the place about it."

Lex is squeezing my hand. I close my eyes, trying to pretend that I'm blind, trying to understand what it means to be in this world without seeing any of it, not knowing where anyone is, if they're safe.

I can see the red of my eyelids, but it's still horrifying. It isn't simply that I was missing in that chaos—without the sound of my voice, to him I'd disappeared into that darkness entirely. I could have fallen over the edge of Internment.

"I'm sorry I made you worry," I say. I lean over the table so that I'm closer. "I'll never disappear. I promise that every time I leave, I'll always come back."

"Not coming back wouldn't be the worst thing," he says. "For any of us."

"None of that talk," Alice says. "You're going to scare her."

"She should be scared," Lex says.

"I'm not," I say, but I am.

"Everything is going to be fine," Alice says. "We'll know more when the broadcast goes up. And if there is no broadcast, then it can't be too serious, now, can it?" She's handing me a cup of tea, ushering Lex and me to the couch.

Soon, I feel myself falling asleep under the unfinished blanket, as Lex works skillfully at its edges. Some distant part of me understands that there's cause to worry and that I'm frightened, but it's safe and warm inside, and Alice is moving about the kitchen, cooking up the smell of something sugary sweet. She asks me a question, something about my hair, and though I don't hear her I nod assent, and in the next moment she's peeling off my velvet gloves and gently unclasping the wooden barrettes in my hair.

When I was small, my brother would let me follow him on the train for entire afternoons without a destination. We would ride until we were hungry or had to find a water room. The train would always be crowded and I'd stay so close to him that I could hear his murmurs as he wrote on scraps of paper. He never spoke to me, always writing or looking at the city passing by. But it didn't matter. I knew the honor of having been invited. We were two parts of the same set then, our skin as pale as the sunlight that washed over us through the glass, both of us silent and blue-eyed in the bustling crowd. On these trips I began to feel we were the same. I would catch our reflection in the window and fancy myself a perfect miniature version of him.

The train that circles Internment couldn't carry him far enough, though. My brother, the peripatetic, the sage, was too restless to stay in one place, but one place is all we're given. The only one who could quell this restlessness was Alice, always Alice, who swears she was born already in love with him. When she wasn't allowed to have their child, something fell apart and they lost themselves for a while.

The train speeds past the apartment, rattling the walls, and I dream that I'm riding it in my theater dress. I'm on my way to meet my betrothed waiting for me on the platform. I dream about the other passengers, and I wonder who's waiting for them. I wonder what keeps the conductor conscious as he navigates through the night. I dream about the murderer, out there somewhere, and wonder where he is when the train passes him by.

6

Break the sky. Look up. Look down. Beyond what
is familiar. If you've never been afraid, you haven't
had your moment of bravery just yet.

— "Intangible Gods," Daphne Leander, Year Ten

In the morning, I awaken with stiff muscles and the notion that something is wrong. But it isn't until I realize I'm still on the couch, Lex's unfinished quilt replaced with the heavy blanket from my own bed, that I remember.

"Good morning, love," my mother says, setting down her sampler when she sees that my eyes are open. "Would you like breakfast? I brought home some fresh strawberries."

That's right. She was at the market when the fire happened. "Are you okay?" I sit upright. "When did you get home?"

"There was a broadcast," she says by way of an answer. "Your father wanted me to wake you for it, but you seemed so exhausted." She's sitting on the edge of the couch now, smoothing back my hair. When Lex grew too old for her affections, she lavished me with double, and to make up for his absence I've always welcomed them.

"What did the broadcast say?" I ask.

"The king's investigators are looking into the cause of the fire. He just wanted to reassure us that everything will be fine." While my father is trying to introduce me to a more honest view of the city, my mother is still trying to coddle me.

"Investigators?" I say. "I didn't know the king had investigators."

"He does. For incidents like this."

I don't like that word, "incident." Three years ago I was pulled from my classroom and told my brother had had an incident, and I was brought to see him at the hospital, where he lay unconscious and within a sliver of his life.

I think of what Basil said yesterday on the train, and the worry clouds into panic. "Something is happening, isn't it?"

My father has never been one to lie to me, but the same can't be said of my mother. Now, though, perhaps because I'm old enough to wear my betrothal band, she says, "It's possible, love. We're all waiting to find out what's happened. They've stopped the train for today; nobody is supposed to leave home. The shops will stay open late tomorrow so people can do the rest of their weekend shopping after work and class."

I've always wanted for her to be honest with me. When I was little, I'd try on her dresses and fantasize about the day when they would no longer pool around me. The highest honor was when she'd sit me on her overstuffed red stool and brush colors onto my eyelids and lips and cheeks. I wanted very much for us to be equals.

Now, suddenly all I want is to put my head in her lap, for her to tell me it's going to be okay and this feeling that I'm trapped in my own city will pass. I want the mother I had before Lex became a jumper. I want to stop pretending that I don't need her, that I'm not a child.

Instead, I ask for strawberries. We eat breakfast and make meaningless talk about nothing important—homework and what should be for dinner.

"Your father won't be eating at home tonight," she says. "I do hope he doesn't work himself too hard. He was barely able to take a nap before he was called in this morning." She's staring past me, through the window that overlooks the city.

She has been a bit distant these days, my mother. There has always been a little worry in her eyes. I follow her gaze to the city and I can still taste the smoke on my tongue no matter how many strawberries I've eaten. A girl with glittery eyes was found on the train tracks with a slashed throat. Saying nothing, I stand, go to my mother's chair, and put my arms around her.

"What was with that strange little girl in the theater?" Pen asks. As she walks, she holds her hand over her head, watching the way her betrothal band fills with light where there will one day be blood.

"I think she's Daphne Leander's sister," I say. "I caught her putting up passages of Daphne's essay."

"Really?" She stops walking and swirls to face me, eyes wild with excitement.

Basil looks sharply at me.

"Keep it moving, ladies, please," the patrolman behind us says.

"Being herded into the academy like animals to slaughter," Thomas complains, appearing from nowhere, as is his skill. "I feel like we're in section seven with all the beasts."

Pen makes some comment about his smell resembling that of a cow, and he artfully retorts with a compliment about her redolence-dabbed wrists. Basil leans close to me and says, "You didn't tell me about Amy being the murdered girl's sister."

"There was no time," I say. "And I'm not certain. Not yet."

"Maybe it's best not to get involved," Basil says. "Copies of Daphne's essay were in the men's water room, too. I read it, and it's pretty sacrilegious. With all that's going on, that's bound to draw unwanted attention. People are already nervous."

He's right, of course. But I can't stop thinking about it.

In the lobby, Basil takes my hand and squeezes it before we're to part ways. I think there's something more he'd like to say, but a patrolman interrupts us. He's standing on one of the benches and yelling for all of us to stop chattering and turn our focus to him. His voice echoes off the marble walls.

"Your classes will resume as planned in a moment," he says. "I was asked to inform all of you that throughout the day, students will be taken individually from their courses and interviewed by a specialist employed by the king. It's nothing to be alarmed about."

I wonder if there are others who see my father the way I see this patrolman—intimidating and cold. I wonder if there's anyone who sees this patrolman the way I see my father. Whenever there's something I don't like about a stranger, I try to imagine that someone out there loves them, and it puts them in a different light. Most of the time, anyway. Not now. All I can feel right now is anxiety.

The patrolman stops talking, but he has successfully extinguished our chatter. There's not so much as a murmur as we shuffle to our classrooms. All the lessons pick up where they left off in the textbooks, but the instructors seem distracted by the absence of each student who's called. Even our morning instructor lacks his verve as he discusses the history of section fifteen's abundance of minerals and how they are to thank for our towering apartments.

A student returns and there's a synchronized shuffle as we all turn in our chairs to face him. The instructor, after a pause, says, "Well?"

"They want Margaret Atmus in the headmaster's office, sir," he says.

Pen gives me a look that is part reassurance, part worry. She takes her time stacking her notes, tucking them into the cover of her textbook, and filing the book away in her satchel before she stands.

She's gone for the rest of the period.

At lunch, the cafeteria is subdued. Basil rubs my arm and tells me I should try to eat.

"Pen's still gone," I say, twisting my fork. "Could they still be speaking to her?"

"They spoke to me this morning," Thomas says. "It's nothing horribly elaborate. They just want to make sure we haven't gone mad. You haven't gone mad, have you?"

The sharpness in his eyes frightens me. He realizes this and he softens. "It's not anything to be concerned about," he says.

Somehow, this doesn't feel true. The king is looking for something by sending his specialists out here.

I don't see Pen again until our last class of the day, which is more of Instructor Newlan's passion for our little world. It's torturous not being able to ask her about where she's been, but she seems intact. She's taking notes, at least.

Instructor Newlan is talking about section nine's cow pastures. Or maybe it's section seven. I can't concentrate, though I try. I've never noticed how wedged together we are, each section like a thin slice of a pie in the window of the bakery. Below us, is the ground just a larger version of what we have up here? Is there a bigger train that goes in a bigger circle? Do the people on the ground also fear stepping over their edge? What if there's a bigger ground below them? What if everything is floating in the sky?

Maybe I am going mad. Maybe I'm turning into my brother, so hypnotized by the edge that I can't stop myself from scaling the fence, so frenzied by the idea of the ground that I forget where I belong.

Another student returns from the headmaster's office, and this time nobody else raises their head to listen for their name. Everyone in this room but me has already been called.

"Hello, Morgan," the specialist says. She's tall and wiry and dressed all in gray. "My name is Ms. Harlan. May I call you Morgan?"

Ms., not Mrs. For a woman to be unmarried at her age, it can mean only that her betrothed is no longer living.

"Yes," I say, mindful of sitting very straight. I fold my hands in my lap, which is something my mother taught me when I was a fidgety child. I've always fidgeted too much. I've always thought too much. I'm very like my brother that way.

"As you know, we've had a couple of tragedies. Did you know Miss Leander?"

"No," I say. "But I was sorry to hear about what happened."

I've never been in this room. I've seen the door in the headmaster's office and always assumed it was a closet. It's not much bigger than one; there are only two chairs to fill the space, and the persistent clicking of the specialist's pen, which ceases only long enough for her to scrawl the odd note.

"It was an especially violent crime," the specialist says. "It must have scared you to know something like this could happen in your lifetime."

"Yes," I say, grossly understating it.

"It must make you feel that Internment is unsafe," she says.

"Internment is my home," I say. "I've always felt safe here."

She smiles, but there's something unsettling about it. She leans forward, resting her arms on her crossed knees. "Morgan, I'd much like to be honest with you. You seem like a bright young lady. May I be honest?"

Uncertainly, I nod.

"I've read your academy file, and it shows that three years ago you suffered a pretty traumatic incident."

My blood goes cold. I don't like where this is heading. "I didn't," I say. "It was my older brother."

"But surely that was traumatic for you also," the specialist says. "To have someone close to you fall victim to the edge's allure."

"He couldn't help it," I say, repeating what I've been taught, what every student is taught in their first year of academy and reminded of every year after that. "We have the free will to stay on this side of the train tracks. If we cross over to the other side, we get too close to the edge, and it mystifies us. We see how infinite the sky is and we lose our senses. Even the people we love most disappear from our thoughts in that moment." I am quoting a textbook exactly.

The specialist takes notes. I clench my interlocked fingers in an effort to keep still.

"What about your parents?" she asks.

"My parents?"

"Your father is a patrolman—please congratulate him for me, that's quite an honor—and your mother works in a recycling plant in section fourteen. Has either of them ever discussed the edge with you?"

I think of my father waking me for the broadcast, the darkness of my room doing little to conceal the sadness in his eyes when he told me that life could be awful sometimes. "Only to warn me to stay away," I say.

"Would you say they're protective of you?"

"Yes," I say.

"And your brother, Alexander, does he talk about his experience with the edge of Internment?"

I'm starting to feel ill. This conversation has moved far from Daphne Leander. Were the others questioned so personally?

And then I make the connection. Most of the others don't know someone who tried to jump over the edge. Daphne Leander knew someone, though. And now she's dead.

"He doesn't talk to me about it," I say. "He goes to his support group every week. What happens behind the closed door is confidential."

More notes.

"Morgan, I know that these personal questions are probably uncomfortable for you to answer," the specialist says. "Right now, the king has asked me to speak with you and your classmates only to ensure your safety. Several years ago, we had a murder. Your parents probably told you about that. It spurred a lot of talk about Internment being unsafe, and many people became, as you put it, mystified by the edge. We had a few very close calls. I found myself standing on the platform contemplating the other side."

I can see the platform under my feet, the black rails and the gray pebbles that fill the space between the wooden planks. The fence far on the other side, bold and stoic against the meandering clouds.

I look at the king's specialist and I do not believe her when she says she's contemplated the other side. I believe that she is testing me.

"If you feel tempted, please come and speak to me at any time," she says. She's handing me a small card, gray like her uniform, with the address for a section three apartment complex.

"Thank you," I say, tucking the card into my skirt pocket.

"You're free to return to your class now," she tells me. "You were my last student of the day."

I take great care not to stand in a hurry. Just as I'm turning the doorknob, she says, "Morgan?"

I turn.

"Have you had thoughts of going over the edge yourself? Even for a fleeting moment?"

"No," I say. My palms are starting to sweat, which happens when I lie.

On the train home, Pen stares into the loose-leaf pages of her notes. Thomas tries to talk to her and she shushes him repeatedly, swatting him when he tries to read over her shoulder.

"How'd it go with the specialist?" Basil asks me.

"I don't know," I say. "What sorts of questions did she ask you?"

"She asked about my parents, mostly. Their trades, and if they told me about the murder several years ago." He tucks a stray lock of hair behind my ear. "Then she asked about my studies."

"That's it?"

"That's it."

"Me too," I say, but I think he catches my hesitation. "My father said that everyone doesn't have to come right home after class and work anymore," I say. "You can come over for dinner if you want. My mother always cooks too much food during the festival month." There are things I'd like to tell him, if not for the patrolman pacing the aisle, making sure we're safe and that our feet and our minds lie firmly on Internment's floating floor.

"I'd love to," he says. "I don't have to be home to watch Leland. My mother is taking him to get fitted for a new uniform."

"Don't tell me he managed to lose an entire uniform," I say. Basil's brother is famous for losing things. It's a wonder he still has his betrothal band on a chain around his neck.

"He didn't lose it, exactly. He's pretty sure it's at the bottom of the lake. Part of it, anyway."

Even Pen looks up from her notes at that.

"He was trying to use the pant legs as a net to catch fish." Basil sighs. "These are the sorts of things that happen when I take my eyes off him for five minutes."

I laugh. "Poor Basil," I say. "The great fun in being a younger sibling is getting to torture the older."

"You were an uncorrupted compared to Leland," Basil says.

"What about the time we were seven and we tried to bake a cake?" I say.

"I don't recall any baking," Basil says. "I recall cracked eggs on the floor and a sack of flour that was too heavy for you to carry."

"That mess happened on Lex's watch," I remind him. "He's the one who had to clean it up."

Now Basil is chuckling with his lips pressed together. He's looking at me.

"What?" I say.

"I'm just remembering all the flour in your hair."

"It got up my nose. I couldn't stop sneezing."

We're both trying to quiet our laughter so as not to disrupt the solemn mood of the train.

"Is this what passes for romance between you two?" Pen says.

"Yes," I say. "And we like it this way, don't we, Basil?"

"Quite," he says.

The evening sun catches every bolt and scrap of metal on the train, and for an instant we are suspended in an atmosphere of stars.

perfect ruin

My mother is of course thrilled that my betrothed is joining us for dinner. Not only does she find him charming, but
she is also eager for a sense of normalcy. Though the ash
from the fire at the flower shop has long since disappeared,
a grayness still blankets the city. I've never known anything
like it, but something about my mother's despondency of
late tells me she knows it well.

My father's absence at the table doesn't help.

I force myself to eat everything on the plate, despite the
lingering dread in my stomach after my interview with the
specialist, which I leave out of the dinner conversation.

After we've cleared our plates, I say I'm feeling tired
and I'm going to lie down, and I pull Basil toward my
bedroom.

"Did you take your pill this morning, love?" my mother
asks.

I feel my cheeks burning. "Yes," I say, and I can't meet
Basil's eyes. I've been taking my sterility pill since about
the time my betrothal band started to fit on my finger. I
know my mother doesn't want for me to repeat Alice's
mistake, and I've heard it isn't uncommon for girls my
age to be intimate with their betrotheds, but the idea still
embarrasses me.

When I close my bedroom door, I sag against it with a
deflating sigh.

Basil sits on the edge of my bed and holds his arms out
to me. "Come here," he says, and when I take his hands, he
pulls me down to sit beside him.

"Today was awful," I confess, making a little game of

rolling and unrolling his red necktie. "In just a few days, I feel as though everything has changed."

"I keep thinking it'll all go back to normal," he says. "Each morning I wake up and tell myself there won't be a patrolman at the door when I leave. They'll have found the murderer. The fire will turn out to have been an accident."

We sit without speaking for a while, me staring at my lap, as the sunset makes everything orange.

"You can tell me anything, you know," Basil says.

He knows something is wrong, then. He's an excellent reader of people, and I am terrible at hiding things. Another reason we're probably a good match—he keeps me from getting lost in myself. And I always relent, telling him the little things, like my fear of giving verbal presentations before the class, or that I don't like his mother's walnut cookies—which she gives me every year for my festival of stars gift—as much as I let on. But how can I tell him that I fear I'm becoming like my brother, or that I have perhaps always been like him? That for all of last night I dreamed of Internment's edge, Amy scattering pages into the clouds, and a fire raging behind her so that she had no choice but to jump?

I think of the specialist's card in my pocket.

"Basil?" I say. "You want me to be safe, don't you?"

He puts his hand over mine, and his tie unrolls from my fingers. "Of course," he says.

I can't tell him, then. If he knew that I was this curious about the edge, he would drag me to the king's home atop the clock tower himself. He would ask to have me declared irrational, and I'd be fitted with an anklet made of blinking lights and never be allowed to step outside again. Just like the woman who used to live downstairs. I used to pass by her door and see her sometimes, standing just inside her threshold after her husband left for work. I'd hear the whimpers of pain when she tried to follow after him.

"What is it?" he asks.

I'm trying to think of a way to answer without lying, but then I'm saved by a knock on my door. "A patrolman was just here." My mother's voice. "There's going to be a broadcast. They've found that poor girl's murderer."

Even gods must have their secrets.

—"Intangible Gods," Daphne Leander, Year Ten

The building is shaking, for all the footsteps fighting to get down the stairwells at once. Our fascination is as great as our horror, as though knowing the name of the person responsible will explain what has been done. As though it will bring us peace.

I hold Basil's hand, and when we make it downstairs, the broadcast room contains what I'm certain is everyone in the apartment complex.

Even my brother, who never comes down for these. I spot him standing along the wall with Alice. He's most comfortable when he can be near a wall or sitting on the floor; he's told me it's the only way he can keep from feeling like he's falling through the sky. In the first months, when he was still adjusting to the permanent darkness, he used to crawl.

Alice waves us over.

"They found the murderer?" Basil asks.

"That's what we've heard, too," Alice says.

Lex mumbles something I don't catch. I touch his arm, to let him know where I am and to console him before he starts to get angry. He has never had a kind thing to say about the king, or his announcements. Especially since Alice's ordeal. He could get us all arrested for treason.

I stand on tiptoes to reach his ear. "It'll be okay," I say.

"It's already plenty not-okay, Little Sister," he says.

Alice shushes him. A patrolman is shaking the screen, trying to get it to work. There are a few seconds of static, and then the king appears, wobbly and distorted on the screen.

Everyone in the room has gone quiet. When the roar of the static reduces itself to a faint crackling, we can finally hear what the king is saying. "—are appalled by our findings early this evening that after a thorough investigation, based on extensive evidence, there is reason to believe that Judas Hensley is responsible for the murder of Daphne Leander, his betrothed."

My blood runs cold. Basil squeezes my hand.

"No," Lex murmurs beside me.

Rather than an academy image, there's live footage of the accused, his arms shackled behind him, his head down, and his face half-covered by blond hair as he's lead up the steps of the courthouse by several patrolmen. I'm uncertain what awaits him on the other side of those heavy wooden doors. Many generations before I was born, crimes were a routine part of Internment. Jealousy and greed bred most of them, and it was determined that arranged betrothals and assigned housing would diminish many such crimes. Things will never be perfect, of course. With free will comes inevitable error and misjudgment. There are still disputes and accidents that are resolved in the courthouse. If it's an involved case, people are selected to serve as part of a jury.

But a murderer? What sort of trial would have to take place? Where would they keep him in the meantime?

Alice has her finger to Lex's lips now, because he just said something I didn't hear. What could this possibly mean to him? In the last moment before the image switches back to the king, I see Judas Hensley in the courthouse lights. I've seen him at the academy; we've had classes together, but I don't think we've ever spoken.

"Do you know him?" I ask Basil.

"I've seen him," he says.

The king is still speaking, telling us there will be more updates to follow, but I'm distracted by Alice, who is pulling Lex out of the room and trying not to make a scene. I don't understand why he's so upset by this. What does he have to do with a murdered girl's betrothed from the academy?

The broadcast ends, and the room reaches a crescendo of chatter. Lots of speculation, but no answers among the lot of us.

All night, my dreams are pervaded by my brother's furious pacing overhead. I fear the floorboards will splinter and break.

The cafeteria is filled with morbid, fascinated gossip. Judas is the name of a hero in the history book. The right-hand man to the king, he penned the first page of *The History of Internment*. The sky god favored him, and when Judas died, Internment experienced its one and only water storm. To think a boy named after Judas could commit such a crime.

Pen pulls excitedly on my sleeve. "It's all like a tawdry romantic horror," she says. "Can you even believe it?"

It's all anyone in the cafeteria is talking about. I know because I overhear pieces of conversation—"Did anyone know them?"—"always a little strange"—"pretty girl"—"stuck up, if you ask me." But I don't find myself among them. I'm not interested in the gossip. I'm more worried about the aftermath.

"Wonder when the trial will begin," Basil says.

"They'll have a difficult time finding a jury, I imagine," Thomas says. "It's supposed to be unbiased. Who can be unbiased about murder? It's clearly wrong."

"Unless he didn't do it," I blurt, surprising myself. Everyone's eyes are on me. "I mean—that's what the trial is for, isn't it? To determine innocence?"

Pen shrugs. "Guess we'll see. Is there a math exam this week?"

And the topic of Daphne Leander and Judas Hensley dies away.

"Lex?"

"What is it?" he says after a pause. I knocked, but he won't open his office door to me. Lost in his brilliance, I suppose. He was always like that—going off by himself. But his blindness has intensified it.

"I wanted to talk to you," I say.

"Talk about what?"

"Things," I say. "That's what sisters do. You know, because you're my brother and I care about you?"

"You bug me," he says. "That's what sisters do. How do you know I'm not trying to nap?"

"You aren't," I press. "The ceiling is practically crumbling over my bedroom."

He ignores me. Alice, standing at the end of the hall, frowns in apology. Lex has even begun to elude her. I worry for him, alone in all that blackness.

I sit on the floor and lean against the door.

"Who was that little girl at your jumper group?" I ask. "She had a bow in her hair." Too late, I realize a physical description won't do my brother any good. "She can't be more than eleven or twelve."

No answer.

"The day of the fire, I caught her putting up papers in the ladies' room at the theater. I think she put them up at the academy, too. They were copies of a paper Daphne Leander wrote about the gods being a myth."

The door opens, and I tense to keep from falling backward. Lex reaches out for me.

"Where are you?" he says.

"Down here." I hold up my hand and he takes it, feeling his way until he's on his knees across from me.

"That girl is none of your concern," he says.

"Is she really a jumper?" I say.

"Yes. And you have no business talking to her."

"She's Daphne Leander's sister," I say. "Isn't she?"

"I'm not kidding, Morgan. You stay away from her."

He's in a miserable mood, and there's no sense pressing him for more, but all he's done is pique my interest.

"Since you're out, come on and eat something," Alice says. "I made berry cobbler."

Later, when Lex has retreated to his office once again, Alice is washing the dishes and I'm drying them.

"He is right," she says. "It's best if you stay away from that girl."

"Who is she?" I say. Alice takes her husband's side about most things, but she's always had a soft spot for me.

"You were right," she says, handing me a dripping plate. "She's Daphne's sister. She may be a little girl, but she's got a lot of demons. It's best if you let her alone."

I've heard that saying used to describe my brother. "A lot of demons." That's what my father said while we all kept vigil at Lex's bedside in the hospital. I didn't know what he meant. But now I'm thinking of Amy Leander, and what it must have been like to learn her sister wouldn't be coming home. It was the most awful thing I could imagine, watching my brother fight to breathe in that sterile room. But at least he *was* breathing.

Alice starts talking about frivolous things—greenhouse vegetation and silver earrings in jewelry shop windows that she thinks will make my eyes sparkle—and I play along, but she isn't fooling me. There's something happening to Internment. That's as certain as Daphne Leander is dead.

8

*Every star has been set in the sky. We mistakenly
think they were put there for us.*

—"Intangible Gods," Daphne Leander, Year Ten

Basil throws a stone into the lake, trying to
make it skip.

"Like this," I say, pitching the stone into the water at an
angle. It hits the surface and promptly sinks. Basil tries not
to laugh.

"Well, I was good at it when I was little, anyway." I fall
back into the grass and watch a cloud that's sloping over
the atmosphere.

"Our engineers spend so much time studying the
ground," Basil says, settling beside me. "Ever think about
what's above us?"

"The tributary," I say. "The god of the sky."

"But those are intangible," Basil says. "Spiritual. What
I mean is, what if there's more land up there? What if there
are people living on the stars?"

"I've never thought about that," I say, and suddenly I feel overwhelmed by how much there is to know, and how much I will never live to figure out.

In the distance, there are patrolmen sitting in the gazebo, trying not to seem as though they are watching. I can no longer tell if they're trying to protect us, or if they're suspicious of us.

Basil tilts his head against mine. From a distance, we're just another young couple lazing about in the park after class.

"You aren't crazy," he says.

"What?"

"I've known you all your life, and you've always tried to hide the parts of yourself that you think are wrong. But nothing is wrong with you."

Those may be the best words he's ever said to me. I mutter "Thank you" but it doesn't feel adequate.

I don't tell him about the card Ms. Harlan gave me, and I don't tell him that I'm beginning to think I need her help.

Don't focus on the edge, I tell myself. Stay inside the tracks. Stay in this little place where awful things happen, but where beauty hides in beams of sunlight, in the green grass and the gentle lapping of the lake forming and destroying watery shapes. Ignore the men in uniforms that stand at length, sullying the image. They'll be gone soon. Everything will go back to normal.

On Friday, Lex doesn't go to his jumper group. Instead, there's a cavalcade of footsteps above our common room, rattling the hanging light.

It sounds as though they're having a party upstairs, but that can't be right. Lex would never allow something like that. I'd like to ask my mother about it, but she's asleep, which is something that happens more and more lately with the prescription she's taking. I don't tell Lex; he's opposed to all the pharmaceuticals, even the mildest ones. But she'll often be asleep when I get home, and then late into the night, I'll hear my bedroom door creaking open as she checks in to be sure I'm safe. I pretend to be asleep when this happens. I have to seem unburdened. After all that has happened with Lex, I can't give my parents cause to worry about me.

When I can take the stomping no more, I head upstairs and knock on the door. Alice opens it just as far as the chain latch will allow. She never uses the chain latch.

"Morgan." She blinks. "Is everything okay?"

I try to see behind her, but whatever's happening is in another room. I can smell something baking—apple pie, I think. "Are you having a party?" I ask.

"We can't get into the courthouse until the trial's been had," Alice says. "So Lex is having his group here this week. I'm sorry, love. I can't let you in. I've been stuck in the kitchen myself. Come back later and we'll have some desserts, if they haven't eaten everything in the cold box."

She closes the door before I can get in so much as a word.

The door opens again just as I reach the stairs. "Morgan," Alice calls, and I spin around, hopeful. She hands me an envelope. "Would you mind dropping this in the message bin for me?"

I don't have to read the envelope to know what it says:

Clock Tower
Medicinal Affairs

Every week she fills out a mandated report of the pharmaceuticals she and Lex pretend to be taking, and orders more to keep from arousing suspicions.

I drop the envelope in the tall metal bin outside the apartment. In the morning a messenger on a bicycle will retrieve the envelopes and take them where they need to go. A messenger comes in the afternoon and evening too, but never this late.

I'm too restless to go home; the thought of listening to clocks ticking until I fall asleep is unbearable. Pen won't be able to leave; her parents don't let her out after dark since the fire happened, even if it's just upstairs to my apartment. She's their only child and her mother is particularly protective. Though, as Pen says, her mother's protectiveness is subject to her whims and sobriety.

It isn't late, and Basil will go for a walk with me. He might be a little unhappy to know I traveled to his section by myself, but the murderer, also suspected to be the arsonist, has been caught and there are still patrolmen at every turn.

A patrolman opens the front door for me. "Be safe out there tonight," he says. It's a phrase that's starting to lose meaning now.

But somewhere out there, my father is saying the same

thing, over and over. I wonder if he believes any of us are safe now.

Outside, warm lantern light greets me. The sky is smeared with stars like the glitter over Daphne's eyes in her class image. I don't know why this makes me feel at peace. Like everything is connected in some way, that humans are just that, whether they're on the ground or in the sky, and that we all belong to the same greater something.

I gave a lot of thought to the gods when I thought my brother was dying. Pen says people get the most spiritual when things are at their worst. She was right about that. I wondered about the atmosphere that keeps us contained on Internment, and when my brother reached the edge, I wondered if the sky god felt betrayed. I wondered if the god of the earth had called out a temptation and set it on the wind. In the texts, we're taught that it's a hypnotic melody.

If Lex were to die, I wondered what would become of our family then.

I try not to dwell on it anymore. He lived. I don't have the answers and it would be ungrateful of me to ask for them.

It's a beautiful night; a bit colder, as the short seasons tend to be, but I don't mind. It's a short walk to Basil's section, and I'll pass the lake on the way. There will be patrolmen, inevitably, but if I'm lucky, they won't send me back home. Now that the murderer has been caught, things are starting to relax. Or so the king would like us to believe.

There are fewer patrolmen than I expected. They stand guard outside apartment buildings and on certain corners, but then I see none for several blocks.

The lake is serene.

It casts a flawless reflection of the stars, as though it isn't a lake at all, but a hole in the city itself. Lex and Alice used to take me here when I was small. They taught me how to swim in the shallows, and how to stand very still so that the trout would flutter up against me. I have a memory for every part of this city. With the exception of the sections accessible only to workers, I've been everywhere.

The stillness is broken by something rustling in the shrubs that outline the park. In the darkness just beyond the street lanterns, I see what looks like a figure hurtling toward me. Whatever it is, it brings the sound of more footsteps approaching, voices shouting, "This way!" and "You cover that area!"

If I can hardly make out the figure, it definitely can't see me in the darkness, because in the next instant, it crashes into me and we grab each other to steady ourselves. There's heavy breathing and the smell of sweat and possibly tears.

In the starlight, I can just barely make out the person holding my wrists.

I'm staring right into the face of Judas Hensley.

The voices are getting closer, and I hear bodies breaking apart the shrubs. Of course they're coming for him. He murdered his betrothed. Supposedly. Maybe not.

"Help," he says softly.

I think he's surprised by the way my fingers tighten around his forearms. "Quiet," I say, and push him under the lake water.

He disappears under the surface immediately and without struggle.

I stoop down and gather a handful of pebbles, toss one into the rippling water just as a patrolman approaches.

"Are you alone here, miss?" he asks me, doubling over to catch his breath. It's been a long time since the uniforms have had cause to run.

"Yes," I say. "I saw someone run through here a while ago." I point toward the cobbles. I toss another pebble into the lake to mask the ripples being caused by the body under the surface. "He seemed to be in an awful hurry. Has he done something wrong?"

"He was caught stealing, miss," the patrolman says. "You shouldn't be out this late alone."

I'm not quick enough to come up with an excuse, but it's no matter. He's run off to chase the phantom thief, who is really no thief at all.

It isn't a moment too soon, because Judas bursts from the surface of the water, spluttering. I offer a hand out to help him, but he stomps past me, his bare feet making squishing sounds in the mud. He moves into just the right beam of moonlight and I see that his eyes are swollen from tears. I have seen enough crying eyes to be certain.

This is the boy that's got Internment so scared. He's tall

and lean, and his face is all sharp angles. He holds his chin up high. But I can't bring myself to fear him. It's the bleary eyes, I think.

He drops to the grass and huddles forward, and his shape protrudes through his wet shirt, the muscles moving as he takes in oxygen. Like some sort of machine. Like there are gears under his skin. He seems too exquisitely crafted to be all human.

Cautiously, I kneel beside him. "I've seen you," I say.

"On the king's broadcast?" he says bitterly.

"At the academy." There are four academies and universities on Internment. "We're in the same year."

"We *were*," he amends. "There's not much of an education on my horizon now." His jaw is trembling, and I wish that I had something to offer him for warmth.

I don't see something deranged, like how the killer who went mad from tainted pharmaceuticals when my parents were children must have looked. I don't see Daphne Leander's murderer. Just a ragged shirt and water dripping from all the angles of his collarbone, moonlight darkening the notches of his throat. Just a boy.

"Your father is a patrolman," he says. "Stockhour? Am I right?"

"Maybe, maybe not," I say, feeling oddly brave. It's strange that he would know this about my father; if anything, most of my classmates know me for having a brother who's a jumper. "Your hands are bleeding."

He stares at his open palms, marred with bloody lines, and then he rubs them in the dirt. I wince.

"Why did you help me?" he says. "Don't you know who I am? I could have killed you."

"How? By wringing your wet hair out on me?" I say. "You need to get someplace warm before you catch a chill."

"Don't have that luxury," he says, pushing himself to his feet. He has already begun to walk away when I start after him.

"Where are you going?" I say. He can't be thinking of hiding. "There are patrolmen on almost every corner. At the doors of every building, for certain."

He doesn't answer, pushing through the shrubs and crossing into the small woods that encompass the park. The trees are mostly insubstantial, skinny things only as thick as arms.

Basil would never go for this—me chasing after an accused murderer in the darkness. He says there's nothing wrong with me, but it's entirely possible he hasn't been paying enough attention.

"You aren't thinking of jumping over the edge, are you?" I say, ducking a low branch as I keep several paces behind him. "That isn't the answer, you know. It's worse than suicide. My brother tried."

For a while there's only the sound of twigs cracking under our feet, and then Judas asks, "Does he regret it?"

"He went blind," I say.

"But does he regret it? Has he said he wishes he could undo it?"

I stop walking. He moves a few steps ahead before he

notices and turns to face me. I can see only his hair and one side of his face.

"No," I say. "He wouldn't tell me something like that. He doesn't talk to me like he used to. It's implied, though." I'm not oblivious to the uncertainty in my voice, and Judas isn't either. I can just make out his sad grin before he turns away and stomps onward. It's amazing how little noise he makes for one with such angry footfalls.

I follow. I know where we are. When we were kids, Pen and I found a shallow cavern here made up of rocks and we turned it into our secret house. I ruined the game when I told Basil and he brought Thomas into it. It was a full day before she forgave me. The boys have forgotten about it, but Pen and I still go there sometimes.

"If you keep following me, I really will have to kill you," Judas says.

"My father is a patrolman," I say. "You were right about that. But if you kill me, it'll be a week before he notices." It's been about that long since I've seen him.

The frail moonlight blurs and in the next instant a tree trunk is pressing into my spine and I can taste the blood and the dirt from Judas's hand against my mouth.

He begins with the word, "Listen."

I do. Listen to a heartbeat throbbing in my ears. The slight wind moving leaves gone silver all around. His heavy, grieving, shaking breaths that go toward and then around me like clouds to our atmosphere.

"Go back," he says. "Go back home to your safe apartment high above the city, and forget that you saw me here."

When he moves his hand away from my mouth, I'm not breathing. My arms are wrapped around the tree behind me and that's the only reason I don't fall forward when he moves away. There's a sense that I am weightless, that if I let go, I'll be carried on the wind of his strides and I'll go wherever he goes. Something keeps me here, my eyes straining to see what I can of him as he leaves. But the image isn't perfect. My memory of Judas Hensley will always be dark. It will always be moving away from me.

9

Novelists weave tales of ghosts and villains and what the ground must be like. This is accepted so long as these things are presented as fiction.

—"Intangible Gods," Daphne Leander, Year Ten

My father is sitting at the kitchen table when I return home. He's wearing his uniform and staring into a cup of tea.

"A bit late to be out, heart," he says without looking up.

"Is it?" The kettle water has gone cold and I set it back on the burner. "I'm sorry. I was visiting Basil." I don't know why I'm lying; he would have assumed that's where I was.

"Your mother," he says, "has she been sleeping long?"

I don't like this monotone voice he's using. And when I sit across from him, I don't like the circles under his eyes.

"Since I came home from class," I say.

"You should try to keep her company," he says. "Your brother's no good for that anymore. He's gone selfish. Not you, though. You've always cared about others."

Why are we talking about this when Judas Hensley has broken free? My father must have heard.

"She takes a lot of headache elixirs lately," I say.

He nods, twisting the cup around in his fingers.

"Dad?"

"Yes, heart?"

"I know there are many things on your mind, with the murder and the fire and keeping all of us safe. I know that it's a great burden. I just want you to know that you don't have to worry about me."

I won't end up like my brother, is what I don't add. At least my parents have one child they don't need to worry about.

He gives something like a smile for a moment, but then it's gone. The kettle whistles and I reach for his cup to refill it, but he stands.

"I've got to get back out," he says. "Get some sleep. Lock the door."

He rustles my hair before he leaves.

The train speeds by, shaking the walls. There's a portrait that my mother colored hanging over the kitchen table. In it, a little girl is crouched in the tall grass, cupping something in her hands. Whatever she's holding casts light through her fingers. A boy is beside her, staring up at little pieces of light that swim in the inky blackness. The children are luminescent, invincible, and lost. My mother says it's a dream she used to have when she was waiting in the queue to get pregnant with me. She says she knew that I'd be a girl, even though that's up to the decision makers. I've asked her what the little girl is holding, and what the lights are. She told me that they're part of another dream, one she hasn't had yet.

The portrait rattles and goes still. I wonder if that dream would do my mother any good. I wonder if all that blackness has ever frightened her. I always assumed the children were on Internment, but do dreams have to be confined to the same place as the dreamer?

"Mom?" I whisper.

She barely stirs as I climb onto the bed. There's a minty smell to the darkness, from the lotion she uses to keep her hands young. She's particular about her hands. The space under the bed and the spare closets are stuffed with things she's made—sewing samplers and colorings and statuettes made with scraps of metal she's salvaged from the recycling plant. She's a craftswoman and my brother is the ever-aspiring novelist-slash-playwright. And me? Every day I rearrange my thoughts and my words so that I can be ordinary. Maybe there's a craft to that.

"Do you have another headache?" I ask her.

"No. I'm dreaming," she says, sighing and turning onto her back. "The ceiling is made of roots. We're under a great tree."

She frightens me when she's like this. There's no line between make-believe and what's real.

"I saw something tonight," I tell her, only because I know she won't believe me. "A boy with eyes like knives.

He told me to go home where it was safe."

She reaches out her arm and gathers me to her side. "He was lying to you, then," she says. "It isn't safe here."

"Yes it is," I say. "There are patrolmen outside and I locked the door."

The ceiling is creaking and I wonder if Lex and Alice still have people over. There's no sense trying to listen in; footfalls carry through the ceiling, but voices don't.

My mother rests her chin on my head and mumbles something about the roots moving. "It's only Lex and Alice walking around," I say.

I don't think she heard me. Judging by her breathing, she's asleep again, if she was ever awake to begin with.

She dreams in her bed, above boxes of art she's abandoned. When she was my age, her work was a part of the mural for the festival of stars. And then she had Lex, and her colorings were of sweet things—children and flowers. After his incident, one by one, most of those colorings disappeared from the apartment. She began to focus on samplers with a set pattern, as if she were afraid to leave the charted path and enter her own thoughts.

She's like Pen in that way. Sometimes Pen destroys her art, and when I see the crumpled pages enter the recycling tube, I feel that a piece of her is gone forever.

I wait for there to be a broadcast telling us that Judas Hensley has broken free, or that he's been detained again. I wait to hear anything at all. But on Monday classes go on as usual. The trains go in the right direction. Patrolmen open doors and keep us moving in organized lines.

And all day I think of Judas Hensley disappearing into the trees. I think of his parchment that will not be burning along with the others at the festival of stars. If he asked for Daphne to return to him, his request would certainly be rejected. There are some things even a god can't do.

In the evening, as we're all filing into shuttles that will take us to the train, Pen grabs my arm, tearing me away from Basil. "I have to show you something," she says. "It'll only take a second."

I don't have time to apologize to my betrothed before I'm dragged back into the academy. Pen says something to a patrolman about having left her assignment at her desk. When we're alone, she leads me into a janitor's closet and shuts the door. She shuffles through the darkness and eventually finds the hanging cord that turns on the overhead light.

"Pen, what—"

"Finally." She claps her hands on my shoulders. "We're alone. I've been feeling that the boys have been hovering around us all day, haven't you?"

"Well, yes, they're betrothed to us. That's what they're supposed to do."

She shushes me, and we listen as footfalls approach and then fade down the hallway.

"We're going to miss the train," I say.

"There'll be another one."

"In nearly an hour."

"So we'll walk home," she says. "There are bigger things to worry about."

"Like what?" I say.

"Like that boy I saw you with on Friday night."

I'm suddenly aware of how small this space is, how warm the buzzing lightbulb is making it. "I don't know— What do you mean?"

"You aren't going to lie to me, are you?" she says. "You're the only person who isn't brimming over with just complete nonsense, and if I can't rely on you, I'll go crazy."

One of us is going crazy, all right, but it isn't her.

I stare at the door; I've never been in the academy when it's empty. It feels wrong. "What did you see?" I ask.

"You know what I saw. You were following a boy through the woods and then he told you to go home."

"You were in the cavern?" I say. "So late at night? What for?"

"Don't make this about me," she says. "The cavern is our safe house. Nothing that happens there leaves with us. Remember? The tonic we snuck from my mother's cabinet?"

I do remember. We were both sick for a whole day after that. Our parents still think it was a stomach virus.

"We aren't in the cavern. We're in a closet," I say. "And we've missed all the shuttles for sure."

Pen reaches for the cord, turns out the light. "Fine," she says, opening the door. "If that's what it's going to take, come on."

As we walk down the hallway, Pen fumbles through her satchel until she's found one of the day's assignment sheets. She waves it at the patrolman who opens the door for us, and she giggles and says something about being absentminded.

"About an hour until the next shuttle, ladies," he tells us. There's always a later shuttle for the staff members who stay after hours.

"We're walking," Pen tells him, tugging me along by the elbow. "My mother insists. She says I need the exercise if I'm going to fit into a wedding dress someday."

Before I turn away, I see the flustered look on the patrolman's face. This may have less to do with Pen's words and more to do with the wink she gives him as she goes.

She hugs her arms as she walks, as though fighting a chill, although the air is tepid. She's got that distance in her eyes again.

"My brother used to work with the engineers that man the scopes," I tell her. "They couldn't tell him much—only things that would help him in developing new medicines. But they told him that this time of year, the ground is covered with white dust."

"Dust?" she asks.

"Well, not dust exactly. More like ice shavings, I think. When the clouds send down water and it begins to freeze. It melts away in the long season."

"The ground is an absurd place," she says. "Imagine what their buildings must be made of to withstand all the things that fall down on them from the clouds."

"Maybe they don't care," I say. "They're probably always building new things. Why wouldn't they? They must have infinite resources."

"Nothing is infinite," Pen says. She doesn't want to hear me go on about the ground. I think she's angry with me for keeping secrets. But she brightens when the lake is in sight.

I look for signs that Judas might still be here, but of course there are none.

"If I were to build a house," Pen says, "it would be made of rock. In fact, maybe it would be underground."

I laugh. "Even if worms are dripping down from the ceiling?"

"Worms don't tell secrets," she says.

She ducks into the cavern ahead of me. When we were children, we were just barely able to stand if we kept our heads bowed, but now we have little room to do more than sit across from each other.

"Okay," Pen says, clasping her hands together so they form an arrow pointed at me. "Tell me everything. And I'll know if you're holding back."

"You won't believe me," I say. My heart is pounding in my ears, the way it did that night when I was tasting the blood on Judas's hand.

"Look at you, all red." Her eyes are suddenly serious. "Is it someone you're seeing behind Basil's back? Because, Morgan, it would mean a lot of trouble—"

"No!" The tips of my ears are burning. "Don't even joke about that. You'll get me whisked away to an attraction camp." I focus on a pebble on the ground. I thought I'd feel safer here than in the closet, but I keep imagining that the rocks will cave in on us.

"That boy you saw"—I take a deep breath, lower my voice—"that was Judas Hensley."

I can feel Pen staring at me. Painful seconds go by in silence, and then she bursts into laughter.

In answer, I meet her gaze with a guilty smile.

"Oh—" Her laughter subsides. "Oh. Morgan. Please tell me you're kidding."

"Nothing we say leaves here, right?"

She drags her finger over her heart in an *X*, sealing the promise, and I do the same.

I tell her everything, and as I say the words out loud, I realize how little there is to tell, how I've been obsessing over something that lasted for a handful of minutes. I don't tell her about the taste of his blood or the tantalizing sense of weightlessness. I don't tell her that in my dreams last night I followed him right to the edge of our floating city, and that the thing that called my brother to cross the tracks very well may be calling me.

"You're sure it was him?" she says breathlessly.

"I'm certain."

"Then—why hasn't there been a broadcast? Why did they just let us go to the academy and walk around the city while there's a murderer running free?"

"I don't know." I shake my head. "I didn't ask many questions. He said he'd kill me if I followed him."

"He didn't seem so big," Pen says. "We'll kill him first if he tries."

"I didn't believe him. I don't think he killed Daphne," I say. "I know it doesn't make much sense, but I'd much like to think I'd know a murderer if he was standing right in front of me."

"Well, we'd all like to think that," she says. She leans back against the rock wall, smirking. "You had a tryst with a murderer, you wicked thing."

"It wasn't a tryst!" My heated cheeks only fuel her delight. "And I don't think he did it. He was so . . . unassuming."

"He had you pinned to a tree."

"For a few seconds."

"Maybe he's still here," she says excitedly. "Maybe he's watching us."

I know it's absurd, but I've felt as though he's been watching me since we parted ways that night. "Of course he isn't," I say.

Pen grabs a pebble from the ground and scrapes it against one of the larger rocks, spelling out the words: "Are you a murderer?"

"There," she says. "When he comes back, he might answer us." She sets the pebble in the dirt with finality.

"Assuming he returns."

"He'll return," she says. "Internment is only as big as the king's fist. If you're going to hide, you have to circle the same places over and over again."

I wonder what makes her such an expert on hiding.

My mother is sitting by the window when I come home. She's wrapped in Lex's blanket, working on her sampler.

"I was starting to worry," she says, squinting as she

pokes the needle through the fabric. "You're home late."

"I was helping Pen look for an assignment she lost at the academy," I say. "We missed the shuttle and walked home instead." The lie has me averting my eyes, but she isn't looking at me anyway. Instead she asks me to warm the kettle and check on the bread she's got baking in the oven. The loaf, stuffed with roasted vegetables, is enough to feed a dozen. Half of it will probably go upstairs to Alice and Lex. My mother feeds them so often that Alice hardly bothers to cook anymore.

"It gets dark earlier now," my mother says. "Maybe it would be best if you didn't dawdle so much."

"I'm sorry," I say, pouring the tea and bringing it to her. She sets down her needlework. She works from her own patterns, and this one is of a cloud, and coming from the cloud is a peculiar flash of what I presume to be light. I run my finger along the strip of yellow.

I envy her talent for inventing strange and beautiful things the rest of us can't see. But I don't ask her about it; I think my questions frustrate her. Or, my lack of understanding frustrates her. She has one like-minded child, and he's on the verge of being declared irrational. Maybe he would have been by now, if Alice weren't so patient.

"The bread looks done," I say.

"Bring half upstairs for your brother and Alice. Tell her to be sure he eats something. He's getting too thin."

I don't know how she knows this; my brother lives right upstairs, but they never visit each other. The sight of him in this state is too much for her. Instead I'm their messenger, and most of my mother's messages are simply food.

Dutifully, I wrap half of the bread in a cloth.

My brother's door is locked again, and when I knock, it takes a long time for Alice to answer. She's still in her work clothes and her shoulders are drooping with exhaustion. She sees the bundle in my hands and gives a weary smile. "Come on in," she says, "but try to be quiet. He had a rough night and today isn't very much better."

On the kitchen table is the bag with the hospital logo that gets delivered to my brother every third week. It's still glued shut. He even opposes the headache elixirs our mother is so fond of, notwithstanding the fact that she began taking them after his incident.

"Again?" I frown. It's been several weeks since he had an episode, and I hoped they were going away for good.

"I wish he'd stop being so rock-headed," Alice says in a low voice. "I was up with him at dawn and he won't take a thing to ease the pain." She takes the bread from my hands and breathes deep the warm aroma as she unwraps it.

"Where is he?" I say.

"His office. The door's open. Step lightly and enter if you dare."

She's already slicing the bread. I doubt she's eaten today; when Lex is having a rough time, everything else fades away from her unless she's reminded.

I find my brother hunched on the floor in a corner of his dark office, wrapped in a blanket and shivering.

"What are you doing here, Little Sister?"

Worrying is what I'm doing.

"Can I come in?" I say.

"If you don't touch anything."

The transcriber is off; its rolls of paper stream out into a cavernous world of things he has imagined each night as I've slept in the room below. The smell of ink and the smoke of overheated wires are still in the air.

I step over and around his latest novel and kneel in front of him. The clock at his feet has a faulty second hand that goes forward and then back, and it is always twelve fifteen. He just likes the sound it makes; he carries it all around the apartment. If it's silent he begins to feel as though he's disappearing.

I put my hand over his fist. His knuckles are white with strain, his skin dry and cold. He drops his forehead to his knees. "Where does it hurt?" I say.

"Deep within the bones, there's marrow," he says. "And it's like the marrow has begun to expand, and my skeleton is splintering slowly from the pressure."

I want to wrap my arms around him. I want to give him my warmth and soften the marrow and make him better.

But he would push me away, remind me that I don't understand. I suppose it's hard for him to believe I'll ever be more than a child. The last time he saw me, I was thirteen years old.

All I can do is be still and not ask too many questions, not tell him how he scares me, never bring up all his years as a runner when he was so alive, and especially not talk about the medicine on the table. He'll die before he lets another elixir or tonic pass between his lips or get shot into his veins. Not that the pharmacy knows that; it's part of the king's policy that jumpers take the required medication in order to be considered nonthreatening to society. Alice will eventually pour them down the drain and report back to the pharmacy that she administered them to her husband in the correct order.

"Mom was working on an interesting sampler," I tell him. "It was"—I pause, trying to think of the right way to describe it—"color shooting out of a cloud. Sort of in a zigzag."

He's got his eyes squeezed shut. "A zigzag?"

I draw the shape on the back of his hand with my finger and repeat it several times. "It was strange. I wonder if she saw something in the clouds."

"She probably just thought it up."

"How do you do that?" I say. "How do you know something that doesn't exist to be known?"

Alice knocks on the doorframe. The smell of baked bread and warm vegetables permeates from the plate in her hand. "You need to put something in your stomach, love," she says. "You can argue if you like, but your sister will hold your arms if I have to force this down your throat myself." She winks at me.

"My stomach—" he begins.

"Is a cavern of fire, or whatever other poetic nonsense. I know," she says. "But this will help. Here." She sits beside me and sets the plate on his knees, forcing him to hold it.

She stares him down, and even though he can't see it, he knows, and he eats nearly half the slice.

"Happy now, dearest?"

"Ecstatic. How do you feel?"

"Wretched." But he says it with a bit of a smirk, and she wipes his lips with her sleeve.

I wonder if their marriage was always destined to be this way. I wish they could have had a happier go of things, but then, it doesn't seem as though they're wanting for anything more.

Except a child. But nobody talks about that.

Alice tries to coerce Lex to get into bed, or at the very least the couch, but he is immovable. She relents and brings him a pillow so that his neck won't get stiff. And it isn't long before he tells us to go away so that he can be with his thoughts.

Alice tells him that she'll be back with more food later.

When Alice has left and I've begun to follow her, Lex says, "Forget who you are." I pause in the doorway. "That's the answer to your question," he says. "Forget who you are and what you think is there, and you'll discover things that don't exist to be known."

"I don't understand," I say.

"Me either, Little Sister, but there you have it."

In the kitchen, Alice is rinsing plates at the sink, and all the muscles in her hourglass figure glide as she performs the most menial of tasks. Her burden of eyelashes flit up and down as she watches the water go down the drain. She is everything I've grown up wanting to be, and as the sunset steals through the curtain, it sets her hair ablaze with auburns and golds. She's unbreakable.

I want to tell her about Judas, and Ms. Harlan's card still stowed in my pocket. I want to ask her what I'm supposed to do about these fears I have of the edge, and how I'm supposed to be complacent within the train tracks when the world within them stops being enough. But she seems tired. My brother gives her so many reasons to worry, and I don't want to give her more. I take a rag from the counter and dry the dishes.

"Have you given any thought to your festival of stars gift?" she asks me.

"Not very much," I say, hoisting myself onto the counter once the last dish is dry. Alice goes about putting them into the cabinet beside me.

She puts her hand on her hip and studies me. "I still remember your sixth festival."

"My only request that year was for my front teeth to grow in so I didn't look like a building with broken windows."

She pinches my knee. "If I recall correctly, you also wanted a bowl of frosting."

My childhood is one long, muddled memory of bright blue happiness. Internment seemed bigger then, and the space on the other side of the tracks infinite.

"Maybe a necklace, then?" Alice says. "I saw one in the artisan shop that reminded me of birds in flight."

"That sounds lovely," I say. I stare at my lap. "Though, it feels wrong to ask for anything with all that's happened recently. I'd just like for there to be peace again, so we could all stop being so frightened."

Alice sits on the counter beside me. "You *are* getting older, aren't you?"

I lean against her and she wraps her arms around me. "Oh, Morgan," she sighs. "What's to be done?"

We've always been alike, Alice and I. We're fixers and messengers and helpers, and when things are greater than we can manage, we can't rest until all is right again.

Pen is sitting on the stairwell as I'm returning to my apartment. "There you are," she says, arranging her pleats as she stands. "I've been thinking about our friend the murderer."

"Not so loud," I hiss, tugging her toward my apartment and ushering her inside. "You're going to get us both declared irrational."

My mother is still curled on the window ledge with her sampler, but her head is bowed and she's snoring quietly.

"I thought we agreed that sort of talk would stay in the cavern," I say.

"It will," Pen assures, repeating the cross gesture over her heart. "I didn't say *what* I was thinking, just that I was thinking. We should go back there and discuss it in more detail." She raps on the wall with her knuckle. "Walls have ears. Rocks don't."

"Now?" I say. "It's dark."

"No, no. He'd be expecting that. We have to go when he thinks nobody would catch him. Like tomorrow afternoon."

"We'll be in academy," I say.

"Exactly what he'll be thinking," she says.

"We can't just walk out the academy door in the middle of lessons," I say.

She tugs the ends of my hair. "Don't think doors," she says. "Think windows."

10

Plenty of rules are laid out for us in our history book.
They were discovered by first being broken.

—"Intangible Gods," Daphne Leander, Year Ten

I bury my face in the curve of Basil's neck. I'm breathing in his smell of bottled redolence and crisp linen, telling myself that one day I'll be the one in charge of it. It'll be my job to keep his shirts pressed, to buy the soaps he likes.

He breathes in, and it sends a ripple through me. This is absolutely where I belong.

Why is it easier to realize this when we aren't face-to-face? Lately he looks at me and I avert my eyes. He says the sort of things he's always said, and my cheeks go warm. But when we're like this, standing on the shuttle, every dip and muscle of my body fits against him. In fewer than three years, we'll be married, and I hope I have all of this confusion settled by then.

Beside me, Pen is pushing Thomas against the window. "Must you always tug at my hair?"

"I'm just fascinated by your ringlets, dearest."

She hugs her arms to her chest and turns away.

Basil chuckles.

Pen clears her throat. When I look at her, she nods at the patrolman standing at the front of the shuttle who is tearing down the page that was attached to one of the windows. He crumples it and stuffs it into his pocket. Then he fixes a silver festival branch that he knocked askew.

I didn't get a very good look, but I know it was a passage from Daphne Leander's essay. I've reread it several times. I'd know it from a thousand paces away.

Basil sees it, too.

I turn my attention back to him. Back to where it's safe. "I won't be able to have lunch with you today," I tell him. "Pen and I have a literature project we're trying to catch up on."

"We're writing a play," she says.

"How artistic," Thomas says. "Ladies, I applaud you."

Pen rolls her eyes.

The shuttle jolts to a stop. The patrolman is telling us the usual: Keep it moving. Be safe.

The essay sits in his pocket, just another of the many secrets the patrolmen surely keep.

I hesitate.

Pen balances herself on the ladies' room sink and pushes on the window until it opens out. She frowns. "It doesn't open very far, but we'll be able to get through. I'll go first if you promise not to look up my skirt."

"I don't know about this," I say.

She stops pushing at the glass and stares down at me. "What's the worst that can happen?"

"We could get caught." I say.

"And then what? A few demerits? We're not doing anything wrong, you know. The king is the one letting us all go on in oblivion while a murderer is out there."

There's no sense trying to reason. She's made up her mind. "Stay if you want, but I'm going," she says pertly. "If I'm brutally murdered by Judas Hensley, it'll be because you weren't there to protect me."

Before I can say a word, she dives through the window.

I hear the swish of leaves as she lands in one of the hedges.

I hoist myself onto the sink and peek outside after her. "Did you die?" I ask.

"Like landing in a cloud," she says, tugging a leaf from her hair and flicking it away. "You coming?"

I think about Judas's white hair in the moonlight and his bleary eyes and the words Pen left for him in the cavern: "Are you a murderer?"

I push myself through the window.

Pen reaches up for my hands as I wriggle through and helps me accomplish a slightly better landing. And then we're both standing outside the academy in the middle of the day, while our classmates are at lunch and our betrotheds think we're writing a play. It seems as though something should stop us. The god of the sky himself should send a gust of wind in warning. But nothing happens at all.

Pen and I make our way along the stone fence that

divides the academy's property from the university's, and we step over a shallow river that trickles in a ravine at the base of the woods. If Internment were a clock, the section with our academy would be the six and the section with the park would be the twelve; it's a short walk.

Everything about this feels wrong, but I don't stop.

"Basil is going to be hurt if he finds out I lied to him," I say.

"He'll get over it. It isn't as though you won't still marry him in a couple of years."

My palms are sweating. My chest feels tight.

By the time we reach the cavern, the seams under my arms are damp with sweat and I can scarcely breathe. Pen looks into the cavern.

"Morgan!" she says. I crouch beside her and follow her gaze.

Her question has been smoothed away, and scrawled in its place: *Yes.*

Pen has her hand over her mouth, but by the swell in her cheeks I know that she's smiling.

I crawl into the cavern. He was here. That's all I can think. He was here.

"We should ask him something else," Pen says, wiping away his response.

All I'd like to ask is why he's lying. But I don't say that. Maybe I'll come back and ask him myself.

"We have to go," I say.

She turns a pebble in her hand, considering. I take it away and set it in the dirt, and continue, "We'll barely make it back before lunch is over if we leave now."

"Fine," she huffs. As we make our way back to the academy, she perks up at the sound of every snapped twig, every rustled leaf. It's a game to her. Our secret murderer stowed away in the trees, sending us messages.

I would tell her that what we're doing is wrong, but I like that we have a secret together, like the kinds we had when we were children. It's been so long since she's shared any secrets with me.

When we return to the academy, the window to the ladies' room seems a lot higher than either of us remember, and there's no sink out here for us to stand on. Pen tries using the hedge, but that proves impossible.

"Okay," she says, "if I hold my hands out, you could use them as a step and make it inside. Then you can pull me up after you."

"Or you ladies can enter through the proper door," Headmaster Vega says from behind us. "I'm more than happy to escort you. It seems we have some things to chat about in my office."

11

*Our bodies are burned when we die. All the good
in our soul lives on in the tributary, while all the
bad in us burns away forever. This frightens me.
Who decides what is good and what is bad? Who
decides what is saved and what is lost from our
souls?*

— "Intangible Gods," Daphne Leander, Year Ten

Pen has a powerful skill in going from

defiance to contrition. She is all "Yes, sir" and timid nods
the entire way down the hall. As the headmaster turns to
open his office door, she smirks at his bald spot.

"Ladies," he says, standing aside to let us in.

"Yes, sir," we murmur, heads down.

We file past the receptionist, who does nothing to hide
her surprise that among all the mischief makers she's seen in
this academy, we're the latest—a star student and a patrolman's daughter. The headmaster leads us to his office and
closes the door behind us.

"There now," he says. His chair creaks under his weight and he gestures for us to sit in the chairs on the other side of his desk. Pen fans her skirt daintily over her knees.

"The obvious question here is what you were both doing outside during academy hours. The second question—and I do believe this is the most important—is why you were trying to enter through a window rather than a door."

He waits for our answer. Pen glances at me, clears her throat. "We were talking," she says.

"Talking?"

She raises her shoulders, feigning embarrassment. "Female matters, sir. I'm a little more—seasoned—than Morgan and she was asking me for advice regarding a private conundrum with her betrothed."

Headmaster Vega clears his throat and straightens a stack of papers on his desk, clearly flummoxed. There's a bit of a blush across his dark face. "Why couldn't these matters be discussed during your lunch period?"

"Lack of privacy, sir," Pen says. My face is burning and I want to kick her, I want to kick her, I want to kick her. It isn't the lie she's telling so much as how much she's enjoying my reaction. At an age when intimacy between betrotheds is a distinct possibility, parents and academy officials try to stay uninvolved for the most part. It was the one topic she could broach without being challenged.

"We would have used the door, but Morgan didn't want her betrothed to know we'd left." As if taking a cue from a stage director, she looks at her lap and blushes. "We were trying to execute discretion. Sir."

Headmaster Vega clears his throat again. "I see. Given that this is a first offense for both of you, I see no need to summon your parents. I trust that from now on you'll keep your private affairs outside academy hours. This is an institute of formal learning."

"Yes, sir," she says.

"Sorry, sir," I say. My mouth has gone dry.

Headmaster Vega scrawls something onto a piece of paper and hands it to Pen. "You can head to your next class, Ms. Atmus. Stay for a moment, Ms. Stockhour."

Pen is just as perplexed by this as I am, but she doesn't question it. She squeezes my shoulder as she takes her leave, obeying the headmaster's signal to close the door behind her.

After the humiliation I've just endured, it is with great effort and embarrassment that I meet the headmaster's eyes. He picks up on my anxiety and says, "You aren't in any trouble, but I was hoping to speak with you."

"Yes, sir?"

"As you know, an academic record is kept of every student from their kinder years. In the last three years, your grades have faltered. You aren't struggling by any means, but when a record goes from flawless to flawed, it is noticeable."

This has nothing to do with being caught outside the academy. But that does nothing to quell my anxiety, because before the headmaster says another word,

I already can see where this is heading.

"Your family has had a rough go of things since your older brother's incident. I understand it left him disabled."

"Functionally disabled," I amend. There are those who have been dispatched after jumping from the edge damaged their cognitive functions. There are those who died on their own. "He's still able to contribute a trade." His identification card used to say he was a medical student. He threw it away after his incident, and Alice quietly retrieved it from the recycling. She keeps it hidden among her jewelry, and I've seen her take it out sometimes, turn it over and over in her palm. She loves my brother entirely, even the parts of him he'd like to forget.

I don't like talking about Lex to people I barely know. It isn't enough that I could have lost him, but what happened is a pall that will hang over my family for always. When it happened, my friends distanced themselves, one by one, until only Pen remained with that unwavering loyalty of hers. My father busied himself in his work, protecting Internment when his own son proved to be beyond protecting. My mother has been half herself.

Headmaster Vega attempts to smile. "I've only received happy reports from your instructors, and though one or two have said you're a bit of a daydreamer"—Newlan—"it's clear that you're a bright girl. I'm concerned that something is holding you back. I know that you met with the king's specialist, Ms. Harlan, and she informed me that she gave you a card with her home address, but that you haven't called on her."

"I didn't want to impose," I say. That's not true. I've been considering it. I came so close to telling Basil.

"I'd like you to meet with her," he says. "I gather that part of your hesitation comes from not wanting to burden your parents, am I right?"

Reluctantly I nod. It's the absolute truth.

"I don't think there's any reason to make them worry, then, provided you're willing to meet with Ms. Harlan during your lunch period. You may bring a cafeteria tray with you. How does that sound?"

He's asking, but it's not really a question. The headmaster is an authority figure, and authority figures don't make suggestions to students. They tell. Until we become the property of our spouses, we are the property of our educators.

"This matter will be met with discretion," he says. "There's nothing to worry about."

When I don't answer, he says, "This is a matter more common than you might think. Many students receive counseling for a number of different reasons, and it all turns out fine."

Fine. I mouth the word at my lap, desperate for the taste of it. What I wouldn't give for things to turn out fine.

"All right," I say.

He smiles, all the creases in his pudgy face curling like the wind the sky god conjures in my textbooks. "There will be no need to sneak off the premises to seek counsel from your classmates. I hope we have an understanding."

"We do, sir."

"Wonderful." He scribbles an excusatory note on a piece of paper and hands it to me. "You're dismissed. Have a pleasant afternoon."

After classes, Pen and I linger on the outskirts of the playing field, watching the athletes chase one another within the confines of the low stone wall that marks game territory. Basil and Thomas are on opposing teams, and I could swear they've turned their practice into a private competition to impress us. Thomas is about as tall as Basil, quick and lean while Basil is more solid. It could be anyone's win.

It's an especially windy day, which is common for the short season. I bunch my fists inside the sleeves of my red academy sweater as we sit and watch them.

"Look at that," Pen says. "If I were one of those poor, dumb, love-struck girls, I'd say there's nothing in the sky more fetching than that, our boys with their sleeves rolled up, going at each other like beasts."

I wonder if she knows her hand is to her chest. Her face goes flat. "Thomas doesn't look too bad from this distance, does he? What a disappointment to know he's not so exquisite up close."

"He's perfectly attractive," I say.

"He has a nose like a broken bridge."

"Oh, he doesn't," I say.

"You want him for yourself, is that it?" Pen says. "Have him. I'll trade you your day-old compost scraps. At least then I could use them to grow something I could stomach." She is smiling as she watches him, though. I watch the boys, too, trying to follow Basil across the field, the beads of sweat making his hair jagged when he doubles over to catch his breath.

I wrap my arms around Pen's shoulders and lean my head against hers. "I hope we live in apartments next door to each other once we're grown and married," I say.

"I'll be a mapmaker by then," she says, "penning maps by candlelight until all hours. Maybe I'll turn irrational. But not the bumbling, stupid irrational. The quiet sort, whispering things to glass jars as though they'll hold my secrets. No one will ever know."

There's a moment of silence before she snorts and giggles. I can never tell when she's being serious. She seems to prefer it that way.

"Hey," she says. "I have to get something from the art room. Come with me."

"I think Basil wanted to walk home with me."

"We'll be right back," she says, and tugs me to my feet. She leads me into the academy, up the stairs, to the art room.

There's a sort of eerie peace to an empty classroom. The easels display colorings like windows, each one a distorted view of Internment. I know which one is Pen's even before she has marched over to it. The easel's ledge is a mess of coloring pens, and bladder sacks haphazardly tied shut with twine, fat with colors. The bladders of small animals are the most common way of storing colors; paper wouldn't do the job, and collapsible metal was deemed too wasteful when an inventor proposed the idea a hundred years ago. The colors themselves are made from plants.

She's colored the glasslands the way they would look late in the afternoon, the domes and spires mirroring the orange sky and smoky clouds. She's memorized that place. Not only does her father work there as a sun engineer, but she has a perfect view of it from her bedroom window.

She frowns at her work. "My contribution to the festival," she says. "The instructor thinks it's quite good. She wants me to color it in the center of the clock tower canvas, assuming we get the king's approval."

"Really?" I say.

She shrugs.

Every year, a large canvas is prepared by the city's most talented artists. For the final week of December, the king allows the canvas to be wrapped around the clock tower. There's a final week of festivities under that canvas, and even the rarely seen prince and princess come out to mingle.

"Pen, that's a huge honor," I say. "Why don't you seem at all excited?"

In answer, she tears her coloring from the easel and crumples it in both hands. The colors are still wet, and oranges and grays stain her fingers. "It wasn't right," she says. Gritting her teeth, she pushes the balled paper together before yanking it into two pieces.

She drops the ruined project into a recycling tube, where it's immediately sucked away, leaving a smear of color on the rim.

"How could you say that?" I say. "It looked perfect."

"It was going to bother me all night knowing it was just sitting here all wrong," she says. "I'll make something better tomorrow. A portrait, maybe. You can be my model."

"I thought the assignment was to color the city," I say.

She shakes her head. "The assignment was to color something we love." She gestures to the easels, full of colorings. "Clearly, everyone loves Internment. But I've decided you're a more interesting part of my world than a bunch of buildings."

"Maybe you should color the clouds," I say.

"It's been done a thousand times," she says. "Really, Morgan. I'm disappointed in you."

"Forgive me," I say. "We aren't all creative geniuses."

We make it to the doorway before she runs back to her easel and takes the slenderest of the coloring pens. She wipes the bristles on a scrap of cloth and places it in her skirt pocket. "I'll work on it at home," she says.

I don't know very much about art—that has always been Pen's area—but I do believe that it is honesty at its core. I look at the smear of color on the recycling tube, and I worry that there's something Pen's trying to hide.

I can't sit in the apartment any longer. I can't listen to my mother's rasped breathing as she sleeps in Lex's blanket, and Alice's shoes upstairs. She has a pair of wooden shoes that Lex favors. They're loud and he always knows where she is when she's wearing them. Normally the sound doesn't bother me, but tonight I can't seem to concentrate on anything but those steps. Pacing this way and that.

Yes. That word keeps coming back to me.

Are you a murderer?

Yes.

Yes.

Alice moves across the common room.

I put on a sweater and leave the apartment.

A patrolman holds open the door for me, tells me to be safe. I hear that every day. Be safe. I wonder what the patrolmen are doing to catch the supposed murderer. I wonder what they're doing to catch the person who really killed Daphne Leander. There was some talk at the academy about a memorial service. It was held on Monday for family only. No friends were invited, if she had any friends—from what I've heard, she and Judas kept to themselves, a trait that gave them a reputation for being snobs. But I've learned not to take stock in what people say. I can only imagine what's been said about me since Lex's incident, and about Pen, who distances herself from all the high-ranking cliques at the cost of being my friend. "Who needs them?" she says.

The park is empty when I arrive. Little winged insects keep their chorus in the brush. I tread quietly, listening for patrolmen. Listening for Judas.

Only when I reach the cavern do I dare turn on my pocket light, angling it inside. But I find no messages written on the wall with a pebble. And I don't find Judas.

Instead, curled under a red academy sweater, I find Amy Leander fast asleep.

12

Elixirs. Pills. Specialists. Are they meant to help us, or to keep us compliant? I'm studying medicine because I've always felt it would be my calling to help others. But I wonder about that.

— "Intangible Gods," Daphne Leander, Year Ten

There's a strip of fabric tied around her wrist, the traditional mark of grieving after a loved one has been dusted to ashes and scattered. The academy sweater she uses as a blanket must have belonged to her sister.

Under the sharp blue-white glow of my pocket light, her face is young and troubled, her eyebrows pushed together. I've been watching her for only a few seconds before something moves behind me and an arm hooks around my throat.

Even before he has spoken, my heart is pounding up my spine, and I know the soft, measured breaths against my ear belong to Judas Hensley.

"Back away," he whispers. "Don't make a sound."

I suppose he means to be threatening, this boy who answered *yes*, but somehow I know he won't hurt me. He's only trying to protect the sleeping girl. I do as he instructs, until we're both standing outside the cavern. He lets go of my neck, circles around so that he's facing me.

"Are you having fun?" he hisses.

I focus on all the sharp angles of his face, neck, and collarbone. I can't help it; I've not seen anyone like him, the way he seems sculpted from shards of broken glass. "Bringing your academy friends here to play games and write messages?"

"Why did you lie?" I say. He stares in response, and I begin to worry that my instinct is wrong, that he did kill his betrothed and that he'll kill me, right here with no witnesses. Maybe Amy wasn't sleeping. Maybe she was dead, or dying. I try to remember if I saw her breathe.

But my instincts about people have never been wrong. Not even about Lex. The morning of his incident, he came into the room after my mother had finished coloring my cheeks with pink powder. I wasn't quite the right age for cosmetics to be acceptable, and I was holding a wet cloth, preparing to wipe it away before academy. We looked at each other in the mirror, Lex and I, and I had a terrible feeling like he was going to do something desperate. But he only asked our mother if she'd fixed the tear in Alice's pink dress.

"Lie?" Judas says at last. I try not to show my relief.

"My friend asked you if you were a murderer. You said yes."

"Not that it is any of your concern, but I didn't write that," he says. "I have a spy handling my correspondence."

I glance at the cavern, where Amy is asleep. "A little spy?" I ask. "Blond hair, blue eyes?"

Amy's presence, perplexing as it is, adds to my relief. She wouldn't be here if she thought Judas had murdered her sister.

"You should leave," Judas says. "Now."

And here comes the moment of decision, because I believe him. I believe that something permanent will change if I don't turn for those trees and return to my apartment and try to study to the sound of Alice's shoes. I don't know what will happen if I stay, and I don't know why I do.

When I don't take a step, he growls. Muscles move in his throat.

His eyes look better, not so swollen. His hands are no longer bleeding.

"Why isn't anyone looking for you?" I say. "How did you escape?"

He folds his arms, laughs in tandem with a breeze that comes through the leaves, the woods shaking around us like paper bells.

"Because no one can be smarter than a patrolman?" he says. "No one can be smarter than your father?"

This is meant to offend me, but it doesn't. I have seen my father concede to utter defeat in the hospital room. I've heard him choke on sobs and whisper angry things to the god of the sky when he thought I was asleep at Lex's bedside. I know that those uniforms are worn by men—only men.

"They are looking for me," he says. "The king probably doesn't want to announce that he was foolish enough to let a prisoner escape. Wouldn't want people to think he's lost control."

"The woods is the first place they'd look," I say.

"There's plenty of evidence elsewhere," he says. "And as I said, I have a spy."

"A little girl," I challenge. "And her parents must be looking for her."

His next laugh comes sadder. Something stirs in the cavern and we turn our heads.

Amy Leander is small as she crawls out into the starlight and shadows. She's wearing the red sweater now, and it falls halfway to her knees as she stands, her eyes trained warily on me.

"Your father's a patrolman," she says, the words something between an accusation and an observation. "Is that why you keep following me?"

"No," I say. "Is that why you ran away from me? You thought I'd turn you in for hanging up those essays?"

She stares at me a moment longer, then looks to Judas, who tells her, "Those were a bad idea. I told you they draw too much attention." He nods to me in indication.

"My father doesn't know I'm here," I say. "I'm not planning to tell him."

"What about your friend?" Amy asks. "The one with the curls."

"Keeps secrets better than anyone else I know," I assure.

Amy is wary; she stares at me with her dead sister's eyes.

There's no glitter this time. It's hard to reconcile that this girl, who can't be older than eleven, belongs to a jumper group, that a bag from the pharmacy arrives at her front door and that she had the gall to cross the train tracks and peer over the edge.

The feeling that overtakes me as I stare back at her, I realize, is envy.

But there's curiosity, too. She looks unscathed, but the edge always leaves its mark on those who dare to face it. She must have demons, too. She must recoil from society in agony on bad days.

"You know my brother, don't you?" I say. "Alexander Stockhour. Lex. He's in your group."

Her gaze shoots to the ground. "Has he said anything about me?" she mumbles.

Only that I should stay away.

Judas huffs impatiently. "You still haven't told us what you're doing here."

"I can go wherever I want," I fire back, surprised when the words come out so steadily.

"You were looking for me," he says.

"I—" I hesitate, because I can't come up with a lie fast enough. It's true, I was looking for him. I should be safe at home doing my assignments and preparing for bed, but instead I'm in the woods because—why? I'm looking for—what?

More. The answer is as confusing and as simple as that. I'm looking for more than what I know.

"I wanted to see if you were okay," I say. "That's standard

after saving someone from imprisonment, I think."

"I'm fantastic," he says. "You're free to leave now."

"Judas," Amy says quietly. His face softens for her. "She isn't going to tell anyone. She would have by now."

"I can bring food, if you like," I say. "My mother always makes too much. She still cooks like there are four of us at home, but really it's just me."

He doesn't answer.

"Will you be here?" I say. "Tomorrow night? If you're not, I can just leave it here for you."

"Maybe," is all he says, before he turns and begins pacing away.

Amy stands between us, gnawing her lip, as if deciding which of us should get her attention.

"Your parents must be worried," I tell her. "I'll walk you home."

"I told you, they won't know I'm missing," she says.

I open my mouth to tell her that she's wrong, of course they'll notice; how could parents who've lost one child not notice the absence of another? But then I remember my own apartment, my father who likely won't be home before midnight, if at all, and my mother coasting in the haze of her headache elixirs.

"We can just ride the train for a while first," I say. "Until we both get tired. That's what I do when I'm not ready to go straight home."

She's considering it. She runs her betrothal band back and forth along its chain, her mouth twisting one way and then the other.

Judas calls her from somewhere in the shadows and she turns her head.

He calls again, and she begins moving toward him.

"You can bring food tomorrow, if you want," she tells me, and then she breaks into a run and disappears into the darkness, after the boy accused of murdering her sister.

My father returns home long after I should be asleep. I've been lying in the dark, listening to the train and then the silence it leaves behind. It has gone by three times and I'm still awake.

I hear him pull out a chair, pour water for his tea. He moves down the hall, past my bedroom, and looks in on my mother. Soft words are spoken; the door closes again.

They were once wildly in love, my mother and father. Now they're just sort of together. Glued to each other by Lex and me and the blood in their rings.

The kettle whistles and then the sound dies away. The quiet becomes too thick; even Lex has stopped pacing in his office.

I slip out of bed and ruffle my hair with my fingers to make it seem as though I've been sleeping; my father will worry only if he knows I've been awake. Or at least, he used to worry about me. Before Lex's incident. Back when he still bothered to notice he had a daughter.

"Dad?" I say, stepping into the light of the kitchen.

He's got a stack of papers on the table, and he turns it over, hiding the words from me. "You're up late, heart," he says. "Couldn't sleep?"

"I heard you coming in," I say, wringing the hem of my flannel nightshirt.

"I didn't mean to be loud about it," he says.

"No," I say, taking the seat across from his. "I'm glad. I like knowing that you're home. It makes me feel better."

"Do you feel unsafe when I'm gone?" he asks. "This building is safe; you know that, don't you?"

I nod. "It's just that I worry for you," I say. "When you're home, I know you're okay. That's all."

He gives me a tired smile, reaches over the table and pats my hand. "Since you're awake, would you like some tea?" he says. "There's enough for two."

I shake my head. "Dad? What's going to happen to Jud—to the murderer?"

"What will happen?" my father says, shuffling his papers without turning them over. "That'll be up to the jury. I don't believe they've begun the selection process yet."

"Why haven't they?" I say. "Murder's a serious charge."

"I'm not involved with the politics of it," he says. "The king makes all of those decisions."

He isn't meeting my eyes now. He gulps his tea.

"Have you met him?" I press.

"The king?"

"The murderer. Of course you've met the king."

"I've seen him in the holding cell. I pass it when I'm turning in my reports each morning."

"So you saw him today?" I ask.

"I suppose so, yes."

He's lying. He's lying to me.

Maybe I'm lying, too, by keeping what I know from him. It doesn't make me feel any less betrayed.

"Do you think he's capable of murder?" I say. "I mean, a student my age?"

He clears his throat. "I've got a lot of work to contend with before I have any hope of sleeping tonight. And you have academy in the morning," he says. "We can talk about this later. You understand, don't you?"

"Yes," I murmur.

I understand. Later will never come.

Ms. Harlan taps her pen against her clipboard and tries to smile at me.

I concentrate on not fidgeting.

She asks me about classes and about my betrothed. She notes my reactions and makes direct eye contact when she isn't writing.

And then, when the lunch period is nearly over, she asks about my family. She wants to know if things have changed since the incident, if any of us have taken medication to cope. Something about the way she asks leads me to believe she already knows the answers and there's no sense lying.

"We were all medicated at first," I say. "But it interfered with my father's work. He has to be alert when he's called upon. And my parents didn't like how drowsy the elixirs made me, so I stopped taking them."

That isn't the whole truth. I had begun pouring my elixirs down the sink before they took me off them. I didn't like the heaviness of my limbs, the blackness of my dreams.

I didn't like how sterile they made the world around me seem; I couldn't think beyond what was in front of me, couldn't fathom that there was a ground below this floating city, couldn't wonder at the shapes in the clouds.

The only thing I liked about that awful time was going to the top floor of the hospital. Sometimes I wouldn't even visit my brother. I would just take the stairs up to the cafeteria on the top floor. That hospital is the second tallest building on Internment, and the cafeteria is made of windows. On an overcast day there's nothing to see but whiteness. Clouds turning and parting, revealing more clouds. It mesmerized me.

Ms. Harlan takes notes. "And your mother?"

"She suffers from headaches," I say. "She takes elixirs in the evening, so they won't interfere with her workday."

My answers are tidy. They are exactly what our medical records should reflect. Exactly what the king asks of families who've had a jumper. I may not know exactly what the king's specialist is fishing for, but I know that I need to protect my family. It's easy to give the right answers; all I need to do is pretend everything is as I want it to be.

"How is your relationship with your brother?" she asks.

"He lives upstairs," I say. "I check in on him sometimes, but his wife takes care of him. She makes sure he attends his support group and takes his prescriptions."

She smiles again, but these smiles only serve to unsettle me. There's something artificial about them.

"Are you opposed to medications?" she asks. And before I can answer, she's lifting a kettle from the portable

perfect ruin

sun warmer on her desk and pouring me a cup. "I'd like for you to try some of this," she says. "There's no medicine in it, but the herbs are said to have a soothing effect. If I can be blunt, Morgan, it sounds as though you're under quite a bit of stress."

I ran out to catch the train before I'd had a chance to touch my breakfast this morning, and I'm missing lunch for this meeting, which is perhaps why the spicy sweet smell of the tea seems so irresistible to me right now. She pours a cup for herself, blows into the steam and swirls the cup in her hands. I've taken only a sip when the bell rings.

Ms. Harlan looks as though she would like to ask another question as I grab my satchel from the floor. "I'm sorry," I say. "I have to go. I'll have only two minutes to get to class. Thank you for the tea."

"Tomorrow then," she says.

"Tomorrow."

Pen finds me in the hallway. "Sorry, sorry, sorry," she says, hanging on my shoulder as we walk. "It's my fault you're being punished. Can you ever forgive me?"

"I suppose you can carry my bag," I say.

She eagerly takes it.

"I was kidding," I say.

"So what happened?" she asks. "Did you have to write passages from *The History of Internment* a thousand times in slantscript?"

People haven't written in slantscript on a daily basis for more than a hundred years, but it's still taught in the middle-grade years as a form of history. The letters all curl into and around one another like ribbons; I couldn't read it, much less write it. Most students would call it torture, but Pen has a real talent for it.

I shake my head. "What did you tell Basil?"

"You were being tutored in math. It was the most convincing excuse I could come up with. You are atrocious with graphs."

I don't like the idea of lying to my betrothed. I can't imagine Lex and Alice ever lying to each other, and one day I want my marriage to be like theirs. Or, the way it used to be, at least.

But I can't tell Basil the whole truth—about my fascination with Judas and my wonderings about the edge, because in his protectiveness he may have me declared irrational. But lying is no way to handle things, either. That's what the edge does—it lures you away from those you care about. It ends your life even before your shoe has crumbled dirt into the atmosphere.

But how do I get rid of these thoughts? How do I become what I'm supposed to be?

I take my seat, giving Basil a smile from across the room. He does not smile back. There's something dire about his brown eyes today. He knows something is wrong with me.

Once class lets out, I manage to disappear in the crowd without speaking to him. And again after our last class of the day, while everyone is herding for the shuttles. I know that my missing the train will do nothing but add to Basil's suspicions, but I don't know what to do. The thought of riding the train is making it hard for me to breathe.

I hurry past the hedges and into the woods. I don't know if Judas will be here, or if he'll come out to see me either way. Amy will still be in academy. That is, if she's attending classes. Her family will be allowed another week of mourning before they're expected to return to society.

Still, I find myself heading for the cavern, longing for the days when it was just a fun hideaway, a pretend house where Pen and I served pretend tea.

Someone touches my shoulder, and I start.

Basil turns me around to face him.

"I didn't mean to scare you," he says.

My heart is pounding, less from being startled and more now from the weight and effort of keeping secrets from him. He always knows when something is amiss with me. I fight to keep my voice even, but it still comes out too breathy. "It's fine. I was just going for a walk."

"Alone?" he says.

"You can come if you want." I start moving away from the cavern, in the direction of the lake. It's bad enough that Judas saw Pen as an invasion; I don't want him to think I'm revealing his location to everyone I know.

"I didn't see you at lunch," Basil says. His knuckles touch mine, and somehow in the next instant we're holding hands. I don't think either of us initiated it—it just seems to happen. "Pen said you're struggling with math and had to get a tutor."

An amazing friend, Pen. Explaining one problem away with another.

I look at my shoes as I walk. I don't want to lie to him, so I keep silent.

"Morgan," he says. "It's going to be a quiet sixty years if you refuse to tell me things."

That's how long we have left—not quite sixty years, give or take a few months. At age seventy-five, we'll be dispatched in order to make room for new births. To live beyond our useful years would be selfish. That's how we show our gratitude to the god in the sky. We live our lives, and then when we have no more to give but our lives, that's what we do. We send our ashes up for the sky god to collect. The ashes become part of a current, a force, instead of just one body. It's called the tributary—a perfect harmony of souls. Until then, we're all living on borrowed time, on a floating city he allows in his domain with his clouds and his stars.

Long before our dispatch dates, though, we'll live in dodder housing. The dodder grows in thin yellow wisps and is bald of any leaves. It tends to twine itself around more viable plants, unable to fully thrive on its own. In our later years, once we've raised our children and given our vital years to our trade, we become like the dodder plant, and it's time for us to retire until our dispatch date.

I think about how long sixty years is. How long can Judas keep hiding? Even his confidante, Amy, will soon be old enough that her betrothed will be a priority. No more sneaking into caverns to keep Judas company.

He'll have to be caught. Internment is only as big as the king's fist, like Pen said. And then Judas will be executed because no jury is going to believe he's innocent. All I ever hear at the academy are whispers about the charges against him. That they found fire-starting materials in his apartment, bloody razors, angry letters. I've seen no proof, only words, but words can be powerful. Words can be what puts a boy to death.

"I've been thinking about the murderer, and about Daphne Leander," I admit. At least it's part of the truth.

I take another step, and at once I'm ensconced in a ray of light. Hot and blinding. "Basil?" I say. "Do you think Internment is what it seems?"

He moves closer, until he's in the same patch of sun. He tilts my chin, and when I raise my head to look at him, his eyes are marred with strands of gold. "I don't think anything is what it seems," he says.

I fall against him, wrap my arms around his neck. It feels good. It feels familiar and warm and right where I'm meant to be. Something as simple as his chin on the crown of my head makes me feel like a normal girl.

"Morgan?" he says. He feels the shudder that runs up my spine and he tightens his arms around my back. The moment couldn't last as it was. Being safe, being normal— it's only ever an act with me.

"I want to stay here," I say. "I don't want to move."

"Why?" His fingers are under my hair, the warmth against my neck raising the skin into little bumps.

Why? Because one day I'll be declared irrational. There's something wrong with my brother and me. The king's official knows it; that's why she took such an interest in me. I wonder if it was always this way, if there's something in our blood. When I was younger, all of my instructors had high expectations for me, being the little sister of one of their top students. But then he jumped, and as Lex became something different to everyone around him, so did I. There is no more high standard, only the worry that I'll fail too.

"I'm not—" My voice falters, or maybe I just lose my courage.

They'll fill me with elixirs until I'm somnambulating through the rest of my life, to numb this madness inside me that will surely progress.

"I'm not right. I don't want to lie to you anymore."

"You're shaking," he says, easing us down into the grass until we're facing each other. His hands move down the length of my arms and come to hold my wrists. "What have you been lying about?"

"Lex," is the first word I think to say. "I'm turning into Lex."

"You aren't making any sense," he says. "What do you mean you're turning into him?"

"I wasn't with a tutor at lunch," I say. "I was with the king's specialist. That lady who spoke with all of us after the broadcast about the murder. I don't know what she wanted with me. I don't know how she *knew*. She just kept asking all of these questions about my family, and she asked if I had thoughts about the edge. I lied, Basil. I told her that of course I didn't think about the edge. But I do. I dream about it. I want to know what will happen if I cross the tracks. I don't want to jump; I just want to look down.

I want to see what's down there with my own eyes, not through a scope."

I wait for Basil to pull me to my feet and drag me straight to the clock tower's affairs office to report all of this, but he only says, "Even if you were able to look over the edge without the winds hurting you, you wouldn't see much. It would just be patches of land. It wouldn't be any different from what's captured through the scope."

"What if I'm lured the way Lex was lured?" I say. "What if one day I can't stop myself and I walk right over the edge?"

"You didn't tell any of this to the specialist?"

I shake my head. "No."

"Did your parents ask her to meet with you?"

"They don't know," I say. "The headmaster thought it best that I don't bother them."

He seems angry, which reignites my nervousness. It takes so much to upset him.

"Don't tell this specialist any of what you told me," he says.

"I couldn't," I say. "I barely had the courage to tell you. I thought you'd say it was wrong."

He leans toward me until our foreheads are touching, our eyes downcast. "You aren't wrong, Morgan." Waves of coldness and heat bloom in my stomach. "Not at all."

I don't know how it happens. We move our faces at the same time, and then our lips are touching. I've lost my worries. Traded them in for the sun and the taste of his tongue and the thought that in sixty years we'll be ashes—we'll be tossed into the air and after a moment of weightlessness we'll be everywhere and nowhere. But for now there's quick breathing and the feeling like he has my heart in his palm as it beats outside my chest.

He knows that I'm not like the other girls—the normal ones—that a part of me is slipping off this floating city, and he doesn't care. He doesn't care.

Maybe we're both beyond saving.

13

Love should be a staple in our history book. Wasn't it an act of love when the god of the sky chose to keep us? Isn't love what makes living bearable, and unbearable?

— "Intangible Gods," Daphne Leander, Year Ten

The first kiss lingers. It travels away from the lips once it's over, and it breaks apart and settles in strange places. The stomach. Fingertips. Knees. It follows us along the cobbles and onto the train.

The train's rumbling rattles my ribs. It's late enough now that the train is crowded with workers on their evening commute, and the noise is like bugs that have gotten trapped inside the car, vaguely thrumming. I feel as though a layer of my skin has been peeled away, leaving me chilled, my senses heightened.

Basil keeps me fastened to his side, as though to protect me from the crowd. He kisses my temple, and I close my eyes, reveling in the sensation of it. Now that we've had that first kiss, the tension is severed. He can kiss me a thousand times. Ten thousand.

Then, too soon, the train rolls to a stop and his arm around me tenses to keep us steady for the final jolt. I stand with the feeling that I'm being awoken.

Alice told me that the first kiss would leave a girl feeling strange. I wasn't prepared for how right she was.

We take our time walking back to the apartment building. I watch a cloud swirl over the atmosphere. On very overcast days when the sky goes entirely white, it's like Internment is an inking on a piece of paper, and the rest has yet to be drawn.

"Do you have to see the specialist again?"

"Every day, until I hear otherwise," I say.

I see in his face that he's unhappy, but it isn't because of anything I've done; he's being protective. I'm glad I told him. I'd want him to tell me, if it were the other way around. "I'm not going to bother my parents with it," I say. "They'll worry. They'll think they've done wrong by us. First Lex and now me."

He stops me a few paces before the door to my building, takes my hands. "If you feel like going to the edge, come and find me," he says.

It takes me a moment to work up the courage to look at him. "What if you can't stop me?" I say. "What if I go mad and I jump?"

He squeezes my hands. "I won't let you go alone."

It may be the greatest thing anyone has ever said to me, and my smile is too small to express my gratitude.

"Shall we go inside?" Basil says.

"Not yet," I say, looking to the clouds again. This afternoon has been one long moment that I haven't wanted to end. I want Basil beside me a little longer. I want this warmth in my cheeks to stay.

He puts his hand on the small of my back, and I feel the current of my blood flowing under his touch. "You could walk with me to the playground," he says. "I'm supposed to find my brother before dinner."

"All right," I say.

The playground isn't far from the park, which means we're undoing our train ride by going there, but Basil doesn't seem to mind. Time is passing too quickly, though I keep willing for it to hold still.

There's only one child left on the playground, hanging by his knees from the dome of metal bars.

"Leland," Basil calls, and the boy topples clumsily to his feet.

"He's gotten better," I notice. "Last time he was falling on his head."

"He practices on the furniture," Basil says, and sighs.

"Is it dinnertime already?" Leland asks, dusting his knees as he ambles toward us. The necklace that holds his betrothal band has fallen against his collar so that the band is behind his neck. Basil stoops to fix it.

"Almost," Basil says. "Where's your tie?"

"I lost it."

"Lost it where?"

He shrugs. Leland has never been a child who can hold

on to things; he's careless even by the standards set by other seven-year-olds. He does his best to seem contrite for Basil's sake, an effort that's less than valiant. He scratches the bridge of his nose. "Hi, Morgan."

"Hi, kid," I say. I try not to laugh at Basil's fretful expression. "The tie will turn up somewhere," I say.

"It's the third one you've lost this year, Little Brother," Basil says.

"Or maybe it's been the same tie being found and reissued to me all along," Leland says, walking ahead. "We've never seen more than one at a time."

"Interesting theory," I say.

He beams. "Are you coming for dinner?"

"Another night," I say. Basil and I quicken our pace to keep up with him. Leland is all skips and twirls, always in motion. I think he'll become something theatrical, or at the very least some kind of athlete.

Or an explorer. The thought comes to me now and again, though I know it isn't logical. Explorers are for stories about the people of the ground. Explorers are for those who weren't born in a city that has been interned in the sky.

"There wasn't even a patrolman watching the playground," Basil says, quiet enough that his brother won't hear.

"There never used to be," I say. "When we were little, sometimes it was dark out by the time we went home for dinner."

"That was then," Basil says. Too late, he realizes the worried expression on his face and tries to smile for my sake.

I catch his arm and stop him from walking. "Nobody is going to hurt Leland," I say.

He locks his arms around the small of my back and draws me to his chest. I feel like a jar filled with lightbugs that have burst suddenly into flight. How can our little world be unsafe? How can it be anything but perfect?

Several paces ahead, Leland has made a game of leaping among the biggest cobblestones. He won't end up like Daphne; of course he won't. He is brimming with so much energy and life, not even death would be able to catch him as he skips toward the melting sun.

I wonder if the people of the ground ever feel that their children are too big for their world, too.

After dinner, my mother settles on the couch with her sampler. I sit on the floor with my homework spread out in front of me, but sometimes my gaze wanders to the underside of the fabric. I watch as the arches become stitched full with color. Whatever the colors mean, it has my mother in a good mood. She's humming.

But it doesn't take long, of course, for the headache elixir to exhaust her. She stoops down to kiss me before she goes to bed.

I finish up my equations sheet and wait for the soft snoring that means my mother is asleep, before I take my unfinished leftovers from the cold box and wrap them in a few sheets of water-soluble cloth. That way the evidence can be tossed into the lake. I don't know if I'm trying to protect Judas, or myself.

When I open the door, a slip of paper flutters from the

doorjamb. I unfold it, revealing Pen's swirling, flawless handwriting:

M—
I know where you're going.
Don't leave without me.
—P

My natural inclination is to include her, the way I've always included her. But Judas barely trusts me, and Amy is starting to—I can see it. Bringing Pen along would scare the both of them off. Amy is the one, after all, who answered Pen's question to indicate that we were dealing with a murderer.

For all the secrets Pen keeps for herself, surely she can allow me this one.

The cavern is empty when I arrive. Maybe Judas and Amy have decided not to trust me after all.

I leave the food anyway.

There are no further broadcasts, but news travels anyway. On the train the next morning, the word has spread that the jury selection for Judas Hensley has begun. Everyone is murmuring.

Pen isn't paying attention. She breathes onto the window and writes her name in the fog.

"Such a clear day," Thomas says. "We can almost see the ground."

I look over Pen's shoulder, and "almost" is the best way

to describe any notion of seeing the ground. All I see is the wooden fence that borders the train, and then the sky and Internment's uninhabited outskirts. If I were standing on the edge, then maybe I would see the patchwork of land that is captured by the scopes.

The thought of the edge has caused me to clench my fists. Basil touches my wrist.

Pen is someplace far away. With a flourish and a sigh, she rests her head against my shoulder and watches her name fill up with daylight in the window and then disappear.

Ms. Harlan pours us each a second cup of tea toward the end of our session.

I would love to believe that she's trying to help me, but her presence only serves to make me anxious. She asks how I'm sleeping and how frequently my mother takes her elixirs. She asks about my brother and even about Alice. Stoic Alice who never flinches even when things are at their worst. Even when she was on the verge of becoming a loner forever.

"I understand your sister-in-law underwent a termination procedure," Ms. Harlan says.

I stare at the bell that's near the ceiling, willing it to ring.

"Yes," I say. "Three years ago."

"Was she ill afterward?" Ms. Harlan asks.

"I don't know," I say. "I was too young to have paid much attention." This is a lie. I remember everything about the weeks to follow. I remember wondering how it was that Alice could be physically healthy, while it seemed so very possible the grief alone could kill her.

"I understand that you were young. Thirteen, was it?" Ms. Harlan says. "But do you remember anything at all about her or your brother being angry with the king? Questioning the rules that keep Internment functioning?"

"No." Also a lie. I had never seen Lex so angry in my life.

"It's all right. They aren't going to be in any trouble," Ms. Harlan says. "Questions are normal after procedures like that."

"I really wouldn't know," I say.

Procedures. Like "incident," this is another word that covers a broad range of unpleasant things. There is the termination procedure. The dispatch procedure. The dusting procedure that reduces bodies to ash. The mercy procedure that dispatches the infants who are born unwell. Lex wrestled with these things constantly as a pharmacist. I would never hope to know the things he has seen.

Mercifully, the bell rings. I'm gone even before the tea has had a chance to cool.

Basil is waiting for me outside the headmaster's office, and immediately I go under his waiting arm, and he steers me away from Ms. Harlan and her questions. It's Friday, but the thought that I'll have two days free of questioning does little to settle me.

"What did she say?" Basil asks.

"She knows," I say softly. "I don't know what it is, but it's something about my family."

After class, Pen and I walk to Brass Beans Trinket Shop. It's a little toy store modeled after a storybook castle, complete with a balcony atop a tower. We don't actually have castles—they're too large and impractical—but the notion of them has existed for as long as Internment has been above the ground, like a secret we were never meant to have. Or maybe the stories of castles on the ground are untrue, and we dreamed them up for ourselves. Even the princess has said she longs to live in one; our centuries-old clock tower is as close as she'll come to that.

Pen and I fell in love with the trinket shop when we were toddlers and never quite outgrew it. We have an annual tradition of picking out our festival of stars gifts here and exchanging them early.

Though the people of Internment don't exchange gifts for birthdays, Pen's and my festival gifts also double as late birthday presents, because it marks the anniversary of our friendship. Her birthday is only a handful of days after mine; in fact, that's how our mothers met and how we came to be friends. She was part of an October batch of due dates, while I was to be part of a November group, right along with Basil. But in late October, my mother was rushed to a hospital room with early labor pains, just as Pen's mother was being dismissed from it with false labor. We were both eventually born that week—I too eager, and Pen too hesitant.

"Do you suppose we'll come here even when we're in dodder housing?" I ask.

"I intend to die young," Pen says, tapping at each in a

row of tiny wooden princes and princesses. "Tragically, I hope. You're immortalized if that's how you go."

"Be serious," I say.

"This is no place for that," she says. She hoists a small metal insect in the palm of her hand. She squints at its tail, reading the tiny label affixed to it. It's modeled after a quartet flutterling, if the four wings and long tail are any indication. I see them by the water, mostly.

Pen tugs at a tiny thread on its back, and with a mechanical whine it takes flight, spiraling busily around our heads. She squeaks with delight.

She intends to die young, she says. I think she'd make a brilliant old woman, though, surrounded by toys and tonics, saying crude things and flinging water balls at the young lovers holding hands.

The quartet flutterling lands on her shoulder. "I want this," she says. "Think how much more fun it'll be when we're drunk off tonic." It has happened only a handful of times, and mostly in the year following Lex's incident. Pen would bring a bottle of her mother's spirits to our cavern and tell me it would take the sting out. For a couple of hours it did, I suppose, but my life was still waiting for me in the morning, and I'd have to face it with a headache.

"I want you to have a gift you can enjoy while you're sober," I say.

She hugs the flutterling protectively to her shoulder. "I will. Do you see anything you'd like?"

I stare at a row of bound journals. Like all other books on Internment, the blank pages in those journals are recycled. They'll be mostly white, but there will be shadowy flecks, bits of someone else's handwriting, fragments of old images. Pure white pages are expensive and rare; my brother has the scrolls for his transcriber only because they're considered necessary for the blind, and the words are printed with indents so he can feel them, which is why the paper must be unblemished.

I saw him rip apart a manuscript in a fit of frustration one afternoon, and I wanted to scream.

"Not yet," I say.

"We could try upstairs," Pen says, petting her new toy. "Do you need to get something for Lex?"

"No," I say. "He says the best gift I can give him any year is peace and quiet. He says I snore and it disturbs his writing."

"You don't snore," Pen assures. "He just loves to tease you."

"You're lucky you're an only child," I say.

We move up the creaky wooden steps, through a tunneling stairwell that's lit by flame lanterns on the wall.

For no logical reason at all, I think of Judas, all angles in the moonlight, and of Basil, who kissed me when I told him I feared going crazy. I'm only just beginning to feel for him the way that Alice feels for Lex, the way my mother feels for my father. It's an injustice that Judas's betrothed is dead at any age, but especially at this one.

Did they ever kiss? Were they in love, or will Judas spend the rest of his life never getting to know what that feels like?

"You're being quiet," Pen pouts. We reach the top of the staircase and she tugs the thread, setting the flutterling in the air again.

"Basil kissed me," I say.

The flutterling lands in her palm.

"At last," she says. "I was beginning to wonder about his sexuality. You've no idea how close I was to grabbing a brochure from the infirmary about those natural attraction classes."

I feel my face go warm. "You were not."

"How was it?" she says.

I'm looking at my shoes, and I don't have to say anything, because my smile tells her everything she needs to know.

She wraps her arm around my shoulders, leading me toward shelves of water balls, dirt candies, and other assorted pranks. "Let's find you something childish, quick, before you grow up completely."

The food is gone when I check the cavern again.

If Judas is lurking nearby, Amy won't be with him. The jumper group meets tonight.

"I'm leaving this here," I say to the trees as I set another package in the same spot as before. "It's apple cinnamon bread. It's my favorite. My mother bakes it because she says it reminds her of when I was little and it was the only thing I'd ask to eat."

After a while, a voice above me answers, "Your mother's an excellent cook." The branches rustle overhead as a shadow jumps from them to land before me. "All mine ever makes is soup, and it isn't very good soup at that."

I cant my head. "Is that where you were hiding last night?" I ask.

"If I told you, I wouldn't be a very good hider," Judas says, ducking into the cavern.

I follow after him, and then set my pocket light between us as we sit on the dirt. It doesn't have much of a glow, but at least he can see the food package.

He eats, and I try not to bother him. I don't want to scare him away, but I'm brimming with questions and confessions. I want to tell him about the talk on the train of jurors, and the specialist questioning me about my family. I want to ask him about Daphne—what he knows about her death, if he misses her, if he loved her.

He looks at me and stops chewing, mouth full, and says, "What?"

I realize I'm staring and look at my lap. "How is Amy so . . ." I try to find the right word. "Together?"

"Together?" He takes another bite.

"It's just that my brother is a jumper, too, and I've seen enough of them to know that it leaves scars. But she seems fine."

He watches me a moment, considering whether or not I'm one to trust. Or maybe he thinks me too stupid to understand the enormity. "She's a strange girl," he says. "Always has been, always will be. She somehow made it to the edge all by herself when she was seven. Wandered off during outdoor recreation at the academy."

Seven?

"She was unconscious when the patrolman found her. It's been a matter of debate whether or not she knew what she was doing. Her parents will say that she just wandered off, and that she didn't understand and wasn't paying attention. She liked bugs. Flutterlings and bramble flies— anything with wings, she'd chase. They said she must have gone after something and lost track of where she'd wandered."

"But you think otherwise?" I ask.

"I do," he says. "But she doesn't remember why she did it. That's the thing. When she woke up, she didn't seem injured, but her mind wasn't quite right. She forgets things. She has fits where her eyes go back and no amount of calling will get her to hear you, and she senses things. Says she knows when someone is being dispatched and can hear their thoughts floating away on the wind. Her grandmother died of the sun disease, and Amy dreams about her all the time. Says she's being haunted by her ghost. Her parents took her to a specialist for a while."

I don't say that I'm meeting with a specialist myself. "Did it help?" I ask.

"Sure," Judas says. "It taught her to be a better liar."

Amy's mind hasn't been quite right.

Judas's words stay with me on the walk home. Maybe that's why she's so trusting of Judas. Maybe he did murder Daphne.

If something is wrong with her, then it's wrong with me

as well, because I don't believe Judas had anything to do with Daphne's death.

Pen is perched on the stairwell when I get home. She's wearing a flannel nightgown and her hair is plaited to set her curls when she sleeps. "You left without me," she says.

She looks exhausted, or just sad.

"I know," I say. "I'm sorry. I didn't want to scare him off. Give me some time and then I'll introduce you."

She shakes her head. She's looking at the floor. "No you won't," she says. "You're keeping him for yourself. I'll only get in your way."

I don't know which hurts more—that she thinks this of me, or that I realize there may be some truth to that.

"Pen . . ."

"Don't." She stands and is already climbing the stairs as she says, "I'm going to bed."

I start after her, and when we reach the door to her landing, she turns to face me. Her eyes are dull. I hate to think I'm the cause.

"Wait," I say.

"Why?" she says, shouldering her way through the small opening in the doorway. "You wouldn't wait for me."

14

Last year, my betrothed asked me to marry him, as
we lay in the grass musing over shapes in the clouds.
I laughed. I told him that of course I would. We were
promised to each other, weren't we? He said, "Pre-
tend we aren't. Will you marry me?"

—"Intangible Gods," Daphne Leander, Year Ten

I think about Daphne's slashed wrists and Judas in the trees and Pen's words. We've argued before, but I can't remember the last time she looked so wounded. I can't remember the last time I felt like such a terrible friend. I'm sneaking out behind her back to meet with an accused murderer and a girl who talks to ghosts.

The floorboards creak above me as my brother moves about his office. Insomniacs, the pair of us.

I get out of bed and climb the staircase to my brother's and Alice's apartment. I use my copy of the key to open the front door so my knocking doesn't wake Alice. She's a light sleeper, always on high alert in case Lex breaks something or hurts himself or has an episode. My father has bitterly said that Lex is the child she'll never have. He hasn't forgiven Lex, and, like my mother, has trouble just looking at him. But he finds excuses to come upstairs because he adores Alice, wants to make sure she's okay. Even Alice's parents don't visit anymore; they're too embarrassed to be associated with a jumper.

The apartment is dark, but the sparse furniture makes it easy for me to navigate to my brother's office. Softly I knock on his door.

As he paces about the room, the transcriber's wheels follow the sound of his voice, spitting out a reel of paper with his words printed onto it. The clattering sound of the transcriber comes to a halt, as do his murmurings.

"Lex?" I whisper.

He opens the door, and it's a devastating shame that he cannot see the paper lantern moon that shows from the open window. Alice was right; it does seem as though I could reach right out and touch it.

"Morgan? What's the matter?"

"I couldn't sleep," I say. "Sorry to interrupt your writing."

"I needed to stop anyway," he says. "None of the pieces are fitting right. Sometimes you have to ignore it until it decides to be agreeable again."

He sits in his favorite corner, turning the broken clock around and around in his long fingers.

I sit across from him and close my eyes. I pretend his darkness is the same as mine. I do my best to ignore the presence of the moon that eavesdrops at the window.

"What is the story about?" I say.

"Terrible things," he says.

"Ghosts?" I say.

"Ghosts aren't terrible," he says. "They aren't real. They're a fantasy we've concocted to tell ourselves this life isn't the only one we get. Even at their worst, ghosts are doing us some good."

For someone with such a vivid imagination, my brother is prone to fits of logic.

I draw my knees to my chest, and in the darkness of my eyelids I try to find the courage to ask what I'd like to know. I pretend that my brother and I are in the same place, that we're riding the train in an oval with no set destination, chasing the thoughts we never shared even with each other.

What comes out isn't a question, and as I'm saying it, I realize it's because I've known this for a while. "You and Dad have seen things the rest of us aren't supposed to. That's why you're so obsessed with terrible things."

Lex says nothing.

"You've seen others like the irrational woman who used to live downstairs, and the infants that aren't strong enough, and the people who have reached dispatch age." I pause. "And Alice."

After a long moment, he says, "Especially Alice."

I think I've made him angry with me, and that he's going to shut me out, tell me to go back to bed, and then tomorrow carry on as though none of this ever happened.

What he says is, "So?"

"So," I say, feeling a little bolder now, "is that why you went to the edge?"

When he doesn't answer right away, I open my eyes and see his cheek in a patch of moonlight. We have the same round face. Right up until his incident, he looked young. Now he's so much older, like a man who somehow exceeded his dispatch date. I understand why my mother has such trouble looking at him; it's impossible not to search for traces of that youth.

"You're full of questions tonight," he says, pulling at a loose thread coming from his sleeve. He's forever tugging at his shirts, winding threads around his fingers. I've heard Alice complain about all the mending she's left to do.

"I don't mean to be," I say. "I mean to stay out of everyone's way, but sometimes I can't stop . . . asking. I never seem to run out of things I want to know."

"It's your way," he says. "When you were little, you were like a question mark with eyes."

"Your tone makes it sound like a bad thing," I say.

"This floating city is all you'll ever have," he says. "It's enough for some, but not for people like you and me. It saddens me that you'll have to learn that, just like I had to."

All this time I've been unnerved by my fascination with the ground; I've wondered and worried and thought about the same things over and over, and just like the train that speeds past us now, my wonder has taken me to no new destination. I know he's right, but I haven't given up my search for something more, even if that something is within the train tracks.

"I've always been like you in that sense, haven't I?" I say. He shakes his head. "No way. You've always been you."

"Lex?"

I don't know if it's the moonlight or the stillness as everyone else in our family sleeps. Or it could be that my own restlessness is driving me mad, but I want to tell him about the specialist, and about Judas and Amy. I want to tell him the things I can't stand to admit to myself—that I miss the way it was before, and that when things are at their worst, I think it's his fault that our mother sleeps all day and our father is never home. He doesn't need them anymore, but I do. And I have to pretend that I don't, because of what he did.

Lex leans back against the wall and I realize he's not waiting for me to speak. He knows I'm not going to. He reaches out in the darkness and bumps my knee with his fist. "Get some sleep, Little Sister. I've got more terrible things to brood about."

In the morning, there's a knock at my bedroom door.

"Come in," I say.

I'm still trying to wake myself up when Pen peeks into the room. "You're not sleeping naked, are you?" she says.

I push myself upright, blinking away the drowsiness. "I had a dream about you," I say. "We were climbing a ladder into the clouds."

She sits on the end of my bed and folds her legs. "Was I on top or on the bottom?"

"Next to me. It was a peculiarly wide ladder."

She looks thoughtful.

"You were mad at me the whole way up," I say.

"About that," she says, dropping her hands into her lap. "Morgan, I'm sorry. I was being a child. I shouldn't have been so vicious."

"I shouldn't have left without telling you," I say.

"No, I understand. You didn't want the competition when you met up with your secret Prince Wonderful."

I throw my pillow at her and we burst into giggles.

Pen glances at my opened door, as though to be certain my mother isn't nearby listening. Very quietly, she says, "What's he like? Judas."

"He's . . ." I fall back against the mattress, considering. "Untrusting. And he seems sad."

"Can't imagine what about," she says, caustic.

"I don't believe he killed her," I say. "I just don't."

"Well, you were alone with him in the cavern and you didn't return hacked into bits, so there's something to that," Pen says. "Does Basil know?"

"Of course not. He'd never allow it."

At the mention of my betrothed, I feel guilty. He proved trustworthy with my secrets the other day, and it's wrong to keep things from him. I know this. But Judas isn't my secret to keep. Telling Basil could hurt Judas more than it would hurt me.

"Maybe I'll tell Basil once it's safe," I say. "When Judas is proven innocent."

Pen laughs. "When will that be? According to what

163

we're supposed to know, he's locked up in the courthouse right now while the jury selection begins. The king obviously has men searching for him. He's going to be found and then he's going to be found guilty."

"Maybe not," I say. "Maybe the real murderer will be caught."

Pen crawls onto the bed and lies beside me, knocking her head gently against mine.

"Just be safe. You're the only friend I've got."

"You could make replacement friends," I say. "Lots of people like you."

"Awful beasts, the whole lot of them." She wraps her arm around mine and squeezes.

"I'll have to be careful, then," I say.

"If anything happens to you," she says, "I'll kill him."

I'm struck by the edge in her tone.

"Anyway," she says, "I'm glad we're not angry with each other anymore. In lieu of a festival of stars present, Thomas just wants to drag me around the city today. I was hoping you'd share in my misery. We can wear shell hats like the princess." The king's daughter is known for her sense of fashion.

"If we're playing princess, we have to act as though we're better than everyone," I say.

"We *are* better than everyone," she says. "Unlike the princess." She shoulders me toward the edge of the bed. "Come on, get dressed. I'll help you pick out an outfit. How you dress is a reflection on me."

I end up borrowing her purple shell hat with synthetic

fibers pinned to one side that are meant to mimic bird plumage. Basil stares at them while we're pressed together on the train.

"You don't like it?" I say.

"It's just, I didn't know birds could have pink feathers."

"Birds are white, silly," Pen says. "It's just a decoration."

"The birds we've seen through the scope are white," Thomas says. "But I've read stories in which there were all sorts of species. Maybe there are pink birds in a different region. The ground has all sorts of climates."

Pen huffs a pale blond curl away from her face. The train stops with a jolt and she breezes ahead of him, tugging me along. "Such an insufferable know-it-all," she mutters. But I swear there's a hint of a smile to go with the words.

The boys catch up to us and take our arms in tandem. Thomas kisses Pen's cheek as she pertly raises her chin to accept. "It's your day," she tells him. "Where are we going?"

"The library first," he says. "They're having a sale."

Most books on Internment aren't for sale; we can borrow them from the library, and as the years go on and the spines begin to crack and the pages yellow, new editions are printed and the old ones are sold. When I was little, I was the first to borrow a newly printed library book and I hid it under my mattress. I wanted to know what it was like to own a new book for myself. One that hadn't been worn down by someone else's hands, with pages that hadn't absorbed someone else's spills.

After a week, guilt made me return it. I never borrowed

that book again; I couldn't bear to see it the victim of a stranger's hands.

As we walk, Thomas and Pen gradually move a few paces ahead of Basil and me. Thomas whispers something to her, and she throws her head back and laughs. The shadows of clouds pass over them, and whatever Thomas was going to say to her next has been forgotten as he watches her. She's a revelation in the sun, dazzling everywhere the light touches her. And not just today. Even when she's sad, even when she sings off-key.

Basil touches one of the feathers. "Careful," I say. "It doesn't belong to me."

"I didn't think so. It's not very you."

I try to smile, but I'm still thinking about last night. I'm still thinking about the ground and if there are different kinds of birds. If things down there are mostly good or mostly bad. If they ever wonder about us.

Basil steals a kiss to my jaw, and I smile at my feet.

"There you are," he says.

"I don't mean to be distant," I say, hooking my arm around his.

He stops our walking, and I realize that Pen and Thomas have stopped too. We've just passed the theater, and at the end of the block we can see what used to be the flower shop. It's gray and splintered. The roof has caved in, and there's a makeshift wire fence surrounding it now, with signs cautioning us not to approach.

Other passersby are staring at it, too.

"It's depressing," Basil says.

"Alice used to bring me here on the weekends when I was little," I say. "It was one of her favorite places."

Things aren't the same. The patrolmen and this ruined building are proof of that.

After a few seconds, Thomas and Pen start walking again and we follow them. We go to the library and then to a tea shop. The day is full of light breezes and sweet aromas, but I cannot rid my hair of the smell of ash.

15

Each of us has a betrothed so that we won't have to
spend our lives alone. It leads me to wonder to whom
the gods are married. The elements, perhaps. Or do
they know something that we don't about solitude?
— "Intangible Gods," Daphne Leander, Year Ten

After classes on Monday, Basil and I
spend time trying to skip stones on the lake. We don't talk
much; somehow that has stopped feeling so necessary.

As we sit on the grass, I watch the sunlight catch bits of
gold in his hair and I think that he's more handsome than
the prince. The prince, like his sister, is always at the height
of fashion. He's always polished and there are rumors that
he wears cosmetics in his images. But there's nothing more
real than sunlight on skin.

Feeling brave, I push forward and kiss him. He pulls me
on top of him, and, laughing, we fall into the grass.

I rest my forehead on his, trying to line up our noses
and mouths so we're at a perfect parallel. He slides his

hands up my sleeves and I have the distant sense that Judas is watching us. I wonder if he and Daphne were ever like this.

I try to dismiss the thought, but too late I'm thinking of her body on the train tracks and how awful her final moments must have been.

"Kiss me?" I say, and he does. It's so easy now. It roots me to this place, makes me feel at home.

I rest my arms on his chest and draw back so I can look at him. He pushes my hair behind my ears and says, "You look worried."

"I'm only thinking about what sort of person I am," I say.

"What sort of person?" he says.

"It's something my brother said. He told me that I'm the sort of person who doesn't think Internment is enough." It sounds crazy now that I've said it aloud, but I trust Basil now with the things that make me sound unhinged.

"He's right. Internment isn't enough for you," Basil says, surprising me. "Neither is the ground. Neither is the sky."

I smile. "Being betrothed to me has made you lose your mind," I say.

He looks around us to be certain we're alone, and then he says, "With all that's happened lately, I'm beginning to understand why you'd fantasize about the ground."

I roll over so that I'm lying beside him. "Maybe I wouldn't even like the ground. Maybe it would be cruel or ugly. Maybe it would be exactly like here. I just want to know."

"It wouldn't be like here," Basil says. "Think of how much land there must be."

"That's just it. I can't even imagine it." I hold my arms over my head, watching the way the sunlight fills the spaces between my fingers. "All my life, the more I've been told not to think about it, the more I can't resist. It's like . . . like . . ."

"Like being in love," Basil suggests.

I turn my head to look at him. "I think you may be right."

He looks back at me.

"I can stop talking about it so much," I say. "The ground, I mean. If it bothers you."

"I do think we should be careful what we say, and where," Basil says. "There's too much fear right now, and I worry."

He turns his face skyward and shields his eyes from the sun, but I think he's just trying to hide from my stare.

"Worry about what?"

"About what will happen to you," he says. "Even when we were children, I thought that something like what happened to Daphne could happen to you. One day you'd say something that upset the wrong person, and— We're supposed to keep each other safe. That's what I'm trying to do."

"Basil." I move his hand away from his eyes. I want to tell him there's nothing to be afraid of, but after the honesty he has just given me, I can only give him the same.

"We have each other, and we always will, whatever happens. And if someone does murder me, you needn't worry, because I'll come haunt you."

He smirks. "Rattling the windows and tipping glasses and things?"

"I'd say nice things while you slept so you'd have good dreams," I say. "Or maybe mean things if I get jealous." I shove his shoulder.

"But we aren't ghosts," he says.

"No," I say. "Not for a long time."

"Sixty years," he says.

"A thousand," I counter, and tug him by the collar until he's kissing me, and anything we believe is true, and everything in the world is ours.

The short season takes more light from each day. Judas is scarce. I haven't seen him at all this week, but Amy will still meet me in the cavern. She says he's hiding in the farm and mining section. She says he has a plan. When I ask her what this plan could be, she tells me that he won't tell her. It's too important and she's too unpredictable.

And one night, I find her sitting out in the starlight at the mouth of the cavern. She's toying with the strips of cloth tied around her wrists.

"Amy?" I say.

She doesn't answer, and when I kneel in front of her I see the sheen of tears on her cheeks.

"Suppose it was painful," she whispers. "All that broken skin."

She has been so steely that I could almost forget she's in mourning. She's never talked about what happened to her sister. Barely mentioned Daphne at all.

"She was going to do something important." Her voice cracks. "She wasn't there yet, but it was happening. The things she wrote and the thoughts she had. She was going to prove things are wrong on Internment, and someone didn't want that, and that's why she was killed." She uses the cloth to dab at her eyes. "And now she's gone, and no one will ever get to hear what she had to say."

Gently, I ask, "Is that why you were putting up her essay?"

She nods. "It was a draft she didn't turn in. Instead, our parents made her write about the ecosystem and turn that in. But I had to give her a voice. My parents blamed Judas for her thoughts and the things she said. Before her death, my parents went to the king asking for Daphne and Judas's betrothal to be undone. They would have preferred that she be alone—rather than tied to him."

"I didn't think undoing a betrothal was possible," I say.

"It isn't." She swipes the heel of her hand against her nose, sniffling. "That's probably why they blame him so much. They were practically the first in line to have him arrested once she was killed. But it doesn't matter anymore."

"Why doesn't it matter?" I say.

She looks at me, eyes glistening in the moonlight. I see a girl who has been to the edge, and who has nothing left to fear. "Because I'm going to finish what my sister helped start. I'm going to find a way off of this place."

I can't help the pitying expression that surely comes over me. She raises her chin in defiance. "I can't tell you everything," she says. "But you'll hear about it, and when you do, I'll already be gone."

She doesn't have anything to say to me after that. She gets up and busies herself trying to climb one of the trees.

"You like to climb?" I say.

"I'm not allowed," she says. "I can get away with it only when Judas isn't around."

I can't imagine why he would worry about Amy climbing trees. She appears to be quite good at it.

"When I was little," I say, "I used to climb trees, too. It took me months before I could reach the top of the highest tree I could find here in the woods. And once I'd climbed it I realized there was nowhere else to go."

Amy's expression is thoughtful. "Did you ever think about what it would be like to climb in the opposite direction? Instead of going above Internment, to go beneath it?"

"Like a tunnel," I say. "Yes, I think so, now that you mention it. I could burrow along the roots that go all the way to the bottom of the city, and then I'd be dangling high above the ground."

"You're kind of strange," Amy says, swinging from a low branch.

"You are, too," I say.

Before she hoists herself up to the next branch, she smiles at me. "Go away now," she says. "I have important things to consider."

I leave her to her ascent for the stars.

Somewhere around the block, I hear a sweeper. They always come sometime after dinner. Men driving machines propelled by giant round brushes, gathering all the debris from the street so that it can be recycled.

I pass my apartment, not ready to go home, and keep walking until I reach the border of my city: the train tracks.

And I'm not alone. There is a patrolman at the far end of the platform where the doors will open when the train arrives. And Pen, sitting on the steps of the platform in the light of a street lantern. Paper lanterns hang from the lantern's post, decorated with slantscript requests.

Under Pen's long red coat I can see the hems of her pinstripe pajamas and her wool slippers. She grins at me. "Have a fun tryst?" she asks.

"What are you doing out without your shoes?" I say. I think back on what she said about killing Judas if anything ever happened to me, and I wonder if she followed me.

She looks over her shoulder and nods at the silver branches, lanterns, and charms that decorate the train platform. "Thinking about this year's request," she says.

I sit beside her. "It's strange to see Internment so afraid, especially this time of year," I say.

"It's important that the festival of stars goes on, no matter what happens," Pen says. "The fear will pass eventually, as unhappy things always do." She smiles at the sky, but offers a little nod toward me. "Do you remember how excited we used to get when we were little, and we would try to sneak away with whatever treats your mother was baking for the festival?"

"She knew what we were up to, and she let us get away with our pockets full of mini pastries anyway," I say.

Pen sighs wistfully.

"I still do love the city this time of year," I say. "I love the way it looks, the way it feels. I just don't get excited about the requests anymore."

"The requesting part is more fun when you're a child anyway," Pen says. "Children ask for simple things."

When I was young I asked for a flutterling farm in a jar, and the next year, for my brother to be nicer to me. Lex struck the match for me both times, never knowing what I'd asked for, and together we watched our papers fly up into a sky of burning stars. My mother bought me the farm, but my brother's patience with me grows thinner every year. From that festival on, I began to suspect that by being born I disturbed something in his fragile world. I gave him someone to worry about, and he would never forgive me for it.

"The god of the sky has never answered my most important requests," I say. "Do you suppose it's because I was never very good at slantscript?"

"No," Pen says. "I'm rather good at slantscript, and my requests go unanswered lately, too."

"Maybe this year I'll offer up a request on Judas's behalf."

Pen shakes her head. "Don't waste your request. There isn't much that can be done for him now."

"Do you think Daphne's essay is right?" I ask.

"All that whatnot about the gods being a myth that we dreamed up to add meaning to our lives?" she says. "It goes against everything we've been taught. We're living on a big rock floating in the sky. How many explanations can there be for that?"

"Maybe there's a science to it," I say.

"Medicine is a science," she says. "Electricity, colors, mapmaking. Those are things that can be crafted. What kind of science could explain how we got here or even why we exist? Of course there are gods."

"Daphne said the gods are a theory," I say. "Theories can't be proven."

"Daphne is dead, may I remind you," she says. "You need to get your head back up in the sky with the rest of us. You're always so fixated on what's beyond the city. Whatever there is, it isn't for us. We've been interned."

She's impassioned by her faith, yet another reason Instructor Newlan adores her. Her next breath moves the hair from her brow. "We didn't make ourselves," she says. "We aren't the greatest things to exist. I can't believe that. I won't believe that. We have too many faults."

"I didn't mean to get you so riled," I say.

"I'm not riled, Morgan. Not at all. I'm just concerned that one of these days your daydreaming will go entirely too far." She fidgets with the hem of her glove.

"I was just discussing."

She talks of staying in the sky. Yet sometimes she is her own floating city, drifting farther away from me.

"You should think more about the things you choose to discuss aloud," she says. "Maybe the specialist will leave you alone then." She was subjected to one of the king's specialists in third year, when her mother's tonic addiction prevented her mother from working. That was the year Pen learned to set her own curls.

"I haven't talked to the specialist about it," I say. "I don't like her. She makes me uneasy."

Pen hugs her arms. "Just lie like the rest of us," she says as the train approaches. The train's roar nearly swallows her voice when she says, "And if you must escape, escape here in the city. There are so many places for it."

The train door opens with a mechanical whine. No one disembarks. The shops are all closed and there's hardly anyone out at this hour on a weeknight unless they work for the hospital or the king's patrol. And still, the trains run, keeping vigil over those who dream of leaving the safe world within the tracks.

"I don't need to escape," I say.

She leans back on her elbows and looks at the stars. "That's good," she says, starting to smile. "See that? You are an apt liar after all."

The train pulls away from us.

I frown and put my hand over hers. "Please don't be angry," I say. I don't understand her when she gets like this, and it frightens me.

She shakes her head. "I'm not. Really."

"Were you waiting for me?" I say.

"You aren't the only one who can sneak off into the night

177

to meet mysterious men," she says, raising her chin. "It just so happens that I am having a starlit picnic tonight."

The clock tower strikes its first chime of the tenth hour, and I see a figure in the distance. The figure removes its bowler hat and spins it on its finger. I recognize the sharp click of those shoes on the cobblestones. Thomas moves into the light of a street lantern. This shocks me more than a mysterious man would have.

"Hello," he says, nodding to the both of us. "I didn't realize I'd be graced with both of your companies tonight."

"Morgan's leaving," Pen says, squeezing my hand before rising.

"I thought you were having a picnic," I say. "You didn't pack any food?"

Thomas smiles in his theatrical way. "Tonight, we're feasting on the words of dead poets," he says.

Pen narrows her eyes. "Must you be so cloying?"

But she descends the platform steps with him, though not letting him wrap his arm around her shoulders when he reaches out.

"Good night, Morgan," she tells me. She picks the lint from her coat sleeve and tosses it away, blithely unaware of the way Thomas looks at her—as though he has no purpose at all but to love her.

16

Death is the end of some things. Not everything.
— "Intangible Gods," Daphne Leander, Year Ten

In the morning on the way to the academy, Pen can't seem to stay awake. Not that she's trying. She has her head on my shoulder and her eyes are closed.

The crowded train car forced Thomas and Basil to take seats elsewhere.

"Out late with Thomas?" I ask.

"You don't have to sound so hopeful about it," she says.

"It's just nice to see the two of you getting along," I say.

"I suppose I should get used to him," she says, and sighs. "But we weren't out very late. I was working on my coloring for the festival after I came home. The art instructor was furious when she realized I'd crumbled my portrait of the glasslands."

"You shouldn't have done it," I say.

She sits up, blinking lazily. "Artistic license." She yawns. "You wouldn't understand."

"Not a talentless commoner like me," I say.

She pats my cheek. "We all have our own skills," she says. "I can color still life and scrub tonic stains out of the furniture. And you are a professional diplomat."

"Am I?" I say.

"To a fault," she says. "For example, you're always kind to your brother, even though he's been picking on you since day one. Most little siblings are brats. I'm so relieved my parents never entered the queue after I was born."

The train slows to stop. "If I'm such a diplomat, why aren't I at all popular?"

"To everyone who matters, you are," she says.

While she's adjusting her satchel over her shoulder and standing, the light catches her face and I see the cosmetic powder around her eyes. She never wears cosmetics unless she's trying to hide something, like that she's been crying. It would do no good to ask; she would only take her own advice and lie.

"You didn't need a sibling, anyway," I say. "You've always had me."

"Yes." She hooks her arm around mine and leads me down the aisle. "After so many years, we're rather stuck with each other now. We're like a double birth."

A double birth is when two children are born from the same womb at one time, and sometimes they're even identical. There's a story in the history book about one such pair. Their names were Odette and Olive. But while they wore the same face, they couldn't have been more different. Odette was content with her life, while Olive was restless and ever unhappy. She seduced Odette's betrothed by pretending to be her; Olive fell so in love with being her sister that she drowned Odette and assumed her identity. Years went on, and Olive, pretending to be Odette, married her sister's betrothed and bore numerous children, all of which were born dead. Convinced that she was being punished by the god in the sky, and driven mad by grief, Olive confessed what she had done.

Double births were banned after that. If two were to be born of the same womb, the first was allowed to live, while the second was drowned before it finished its first cry. It was believed that the second child was Olive, always Olive, trying to be reborn once again as someone new.

Within the last hundred years, medicine has progressed enough that double births never need to happen.

It would frighten me to share a face with someone else, but that's one of Pen's favorite chapters in the history book. She says it's poetic that one soul could bear so much sadness that it tries again and again to come into the world as someone else.

Lex and Alice aren't speaking. Alice swore to me she wasn't angry, but she's slamming the cabinets as she puts things away. Down the hall, my brother is talking to his transcriber and he has just knocked something over. When he's flustered, he forgets where things are placed.

I don't know what this is about. Basil and I missed the worst of it. My mother has just sent us upstairs with dinner, but dinner doesn't seem to be in the immediate future here.

Alice wants to leave, I can tell. She wants to put on a pretty dress and go for a walk. Men who are unaccompanied by their betrotheds would wink at her, tip their hats, and smile the way they always do, and she'd tug on her earrings and look away. A little flirting is harmless, she's told me. But she could never be the sort to commit an irrational act out of lust or greed. Such things have had people declared irrational, ruined their family's reputations, and affected their chances of entering the queue. But Alice's loyalty to my brother isn't rooted in fear. She always hurries straight home from work to be with him, and she won't go as far as the market unless I'm nearby to check on him. She loves him completely and without complaint.

"I'm sorry, Morgan," she tells me, taking the plate from my hands and bringing it to the cold box. "Now isn't a good time. Tell your mother we say thank you."

"Is everything okay?" I say. Basil touches my arm and guides me toward the door.

"As much as things will ever be," she sighs, and closes the door behind us.

I hear her high heels pacing about the kitchen, disappearing down the hall.

I frown. "I wonder what Lex has done this time."

"I'm sure it's nothing to worry about," Basil says. "They argue all the time. They argued on their wedding day. Do you remember?"

"Yes," I say, and force a rather unconvincing laugh.

"What's the matter?" Basil says.

Everyone seems to be falling to pieces around me. Alice and Lex are struggling in the aftermath of Lex's incident with the edge, even all these years later. I don't know what is the matter with Pen—destroying her art and hoarding her secrets; and I cannot stop thinking about Judas Hensley and his dead betrothed.

But none of these things are mine to share, not even with Basil. So I say, "It's nothing." No need to burden him with the burden of others. Perhaps Pen is right, and I am diplomatic to a fault.

"Come on," Basil says, hooking his elbow around mine. "We can go for a walk."

He's trying to distract me so I don't go sullen on him. Boys get nervous when girls are sullen.

"Not to the lake," I say, too quickly. It's after dark now and Judas might be lurking; Amy said he's been drifting through the labor sections, where there will be nobody but the food animals at night, but there's no telling with him. I swear I feel his eyes on me in the afternoons sometimes.

Basil raises an eyebrow as he holds the stairwell door open for me. "No?"

"I'm still hungry," I amend. "Maybe we could try the tea shop near the theater. They have desserts."

"You know it's near where the flower shop burned down," he says. "We'll have to pass by it."

"I know." Maybe if I keep seeing it, it won't be so scary. There are no patrolmen to hold open the lobby doors for us tonight. Security seems to be lessening, and I wonder if it's to perpetuate the illusion of safety or so that there will be more men secretly looking for Judas.

I have my answer before we make it to the shuttle station. A crowd has gathered, and patrolmen are pacing with their arms out, saying "Get back, get back" while nobody seems to be listening.

A flutter of a white bow gets my attention, resting atop a short blond ponytail. Amy. I break free of Basil's arm and run toward her.

"Morgan, wait!" Basil says.

"Amy!" People are moving around her like the angry waves the god of the earth cast to drown his people in the history book.

She doesn't move. Doesn't even turn her head. As I get closer I see that a boy is holding on to her hand, the pair of them like statues. Why won't they move?

I muscle my way through the crowd, and when I reach her I can see that she's trembling. Her face has gone pale and her eyes are rimmed with red. The boy at her side is staring too.

"Amy?"

A whimper.

Basil catches up to me. He's got his arm around my waist and he's trying to tug me away, but I'm resisting. "Come on," he says. "Don't look."

"What?" I say. And even though he has told me not to, I can't help following Amy's gaze.

The crowd has gathered here to see something.

I don't understand at first. Through the crowd I can see a boy who has fallen on the cobbles. Some other part of me knows what's happening, though, because I'm already frozen still when I see the university crest on the rich purple vest, and I realize that he hasn't simply fallen down.

His eyes are like the eyes of the trout my mother buys at the market on weekends. Peel back the paper and there are those eyes, bloodshot, glassy, and lifeless.

His dark skin is glistening wet, clothes plastered to his shape like a body emerging from water for air. But air means nothing to him now; he isn't going to breathe.

The crowd has parted to make room for the medical vehicle, which has arrived too late.

Basil tugs my arm, and once again I hear the patrolmen shouting for us to get back. Someone crashes into me. "Amy," I gasp, and finally she looks at me. There's still that defiance in her eyes, but there's fear too, because she's a child and her parents don't notice her absence and she needs someone. She needs somewhere to go. I grab her hand and she follows me as I follow Basil, and the boy holding on to Amy's other hand follows too.

In the lobby of my apartment building, nobody knows what has happened yet. It's a different world in here. We file into the stairwell and up the stairs. One step and then the next, I move, incapable of focusing on anything more. Breaths are hard to come by.

"The flower shop," Amy blurts, stepping hard. "And Daphne." Step. "And now Quince."

"Stop," the boy says. Amy breaks away from me and sits on a step and buries her forehead in her knees.

We all stop to look at her.

The boy sits beside her and asks if she needs her pill. She shakes her head.

"I need off," she whispers, to no one in particular. "I need to get off this place."

"You have to take one," the boy says. He fumbles through her satchel until he finds the pharmacy bag of yellow pills. "You'll have a fit."

"Get Alice," I whisper to Basil.

I sit next to Amy, and in resisting the pill the boy holds out, she looks at me. "One at a time," she says. "He's going to kill every last one of us. We're all going to die and I'm one of the people to blame."

She looks so breakable.

The boy grabs her chin, forces the pill into her mouth. She flails and struggles, but the pill goes down. She touches her throat and growls at him.

"You know I had to," he says.

"It was a mistake bringing you anywhere with me," she says. "You're just like them. I can't believe I'll have to marry you; this year my request is going to be that Internment drops out of the sky before that day comes."

"Go on then," he says. "The way things are going, it may come true." He hardly seems wounded. He's done what the doctor has advised him to do. Jumpers need their medication.

Lex told me to stay away from Amy. Was he right?

Does she have something to do with what I just saw? Does Judas? I hid him in the lake. I saved him from arrest. Am I involved in whatever this is?

One story up, the door bursts open and footsteps are pounding. Alice has taken off her heels and she runs barefooted down the steps. "Come on," she's saying, in that urgent way she uses when Lex crashes to the ground overcome with sudden pain. "Come on, it's going to be okay. Let's get you kids upstairs."

She has to tug Amy up from under the arms and nudge her before she begins to move.

By the time I've made it to my brother's and Alice's apartment, something is happening to me. My mind is beginning to remember details, like the boy's eyes that were staring at the stars, not blinking as patrolmen stepped over him. The flash of medic lights animating his shadow.

My knees are shaking and I sit in a kitchen chair before I fall instead. Basil stands behind me, holding my shoulders.

Alice leans on the table before me, tilts my chin so that our eyes meet. "Did you see the body?" she asks.

I nod.

"Oh. Oh, Morgan."

I'm not ready for sympathy. I'm not ready to understand what I just saw, but the images persist.

Down the hall, Lex is calling for Alice because he's heard footsteps and voices, and he doesn't like people in his home unannounced. He won't leave the safety of his office while they're here.

Amy raises her head at the sound of his voice, but she doesn't speak. "Look at me," the boy says. "Do you feel dizzy? Does it feel like a fit is coming on?"

He touches her forehead, and she slaps him away. "I'm not an irrational, Wesley."

Lex is calling for me now. "Sister," he's saying, hissing the way he would when I was young and I'd made him angry. "Morgan, get over here."

I rise to my feet, pretending the floor isn't tilting. I move methodically until I'm down the hall, in the doorway to Lex's office.

Alice follows me and turns on the light for once; it's strange to see all of my brother's shadowy things colored orange by the glow. He's standing with his clock in his hands. For a moment I envy his blindness. I want to curl up in that darkness and have the city disappear around me. I want to be in a place where awful things are never seen and never known, and there's only the whirr of the transcriber as the paper fills with fiction.

"What did you see?" he asks.

"A body," I say. "Dripping wet, although we weren't near the lake. Patrolmen were holding us back."

"What did it *look* like?" he insists. Alice touches his arm to calm him down. I can't understand why it should matter to him. If it's someone he knows, it wouldn't be by the sight of them.

"A university student in uniform. A boy," I say. I remember the dark skin and the open eyes, and the name that Amy said in the stairwell. Quince. My voice is unsteady when I get to the end of the sentence.

Lex moves closer. I foolishly think he's going to hug me, but instead he leans close and says, "Go downstairs. Pretend that none of this ever happened. Get into bed."

"But—"

"Listen to me, Morgan. Dad will be hurrying home to check on you. You can't let him know what you saw. You have to pretend you've been asleep."

I look to Alice for reason, but she only gives me a sympathetic nod of assent.

"But Basil and the others," I say.

"Take Basil with you. He's been in your room doing homework. Neither of you have any idea what's going on outside. I'll take care of the others. Go. Don't screw it up."

He reaches for my hands, but hesitates and pushes me for the door instead.

In my bed, I close my eyes and try to be still while Basil pretends to study by the light of the lantern that swings over my desk. My bedroom has an overhead light, a luxury, as many of the less updated apartment buildings have electrical fixtures only in the main living areas. But I prefer the soft glow of the flame lantern anyway.

Basil turns a page.

"I keep seeing the body and then it becomes you, or Pen, or my family," I say.

"I see it, too," he says. "It could have been any of us."

I open one eye and watch his shoulders move as he slouches over the textbook. Maybe he really is trying to study.

"Basil," I say. "Internment isn't very big. The person who did this could be anywhere. Could live in this building."

"One person did this," he says, "but there are dozens of patrolmen. The good outweighs the bad." Still, he doesn't sound so certain. He's trying to be brave for my sake, but he's scared too.

"Can you lie down with me for a little while?" I ask.

"Of course."

I open the blanket to him, and when he gets beside me, I rest my head in the curve of his neck and I try to imagine a life without a betrothed. Try to imagine Judas breathing Daphne's ashes as they're released into the tributary.

Basil squeezes his arm around me.

"Do you really believe the good outweighs the bad?" I say.

"It has to." He sees how little this consoles me, and he nudges my forehead with his chin. "I'll always be here to make sure you're safe."

He's strong; one of the most promising athletes in the academy. I've seen him lift weights half as heavy as I am, and he can climb a rope in record time. But what is all of that worth, really? Can it protect against something that steals you away and leaves your dead eyes gaping at the moon?

"I'll always be here to make sure you're safe, too," I say. "Even if you are the one who's stronger."

"You're strong," he says. "Believe me about that."

His fingers weave between mine, and if I were bolder,

I'd bring his hand to my heart so that he could feel what he's doing to it.

He kisses my temple and I feel his breath on my forehead and I nearly feel safe.

Nearly, though not nearly enough.

"Sometimes," I say, "I want the world that was promised to us when we were small. Uncomplicated and nonviolent."

He shakes his head. "You wouldn't be happy with that."

"I'm not happy with the way things are now," I say. "I don't want to be scared that every time I leave my apartment I'll find a dead body or see a building catch fire."

"I'm not certain what's to become of the city," he says. "But I know we'll be able to face it."

"I wish I had your courage," I say.

"I'm drawing it from you," he says. He bumps my shoulder. I don't know how he's able to make me feel better in the darkest moments.

"I have a thought," I say. "The two of us running into the sky and disappearing."

He closes his eyes to see it too.

Outside my bedroom, I hear my father's patrolman shoes on the kitchen floor. The entire apartment shudders with the authority of them. Basil takes his place at my desk, and my body goes cold where he was holding me. My door creaks open and I close my eyes. As Lex promised, my father is here to check on me. And as promised, I pretend to be asleep. Basil kisses my forehead and whispers "Good night" before he leaves.

I stay very still as the university student dies a thousand deaths behind my eyelids.

17

*We have our long seasons and our short seasons, but
every day on Internment looks about the same. I've
heard of water and ice falling onto the ground. Would
the people of the ground think Internment is a para-
dise, or a punishment?*

— "Intangible Gods," Daphne Leander, Year Ten

I don't sleep. While I was pretending to, though,
my father escorted Basil home. I didn't move when Basil
blew out the lantern and kissed my forehead in good-bye.
I didn't get to tell him to be safe.

Now the sunlight is giving me a new day. And guilt-
ily I take it. I'm craving the brightness, and I stand before
the mirror studying desperately the highlights in my hair
and the shadows cast by the rounds of my shoulders. I am
where the sun can find me, I tell myself. I am safe.

"So much like a woman," my mother says. I don't
know how long she's been watching me from the doorway, but a smile swells the cheeks under her sad eyes. I

can't tell if she's admiring or mourning me.

"I was just about to get ready," I say.

"There's no class today, heart," she says. "Come have breakfast; I've baked some blackberries."

No classes. Internment is back to its state of panic, then. I wonder if there was a broadcast last night that nobody told me about. It doesn't seem so. Over breakfast, my mother tries to tell me about the body that was found at the shuttle station, but her voice keeps trailing off. Her head is down, and all she manages to say is that a university student was killed and that the king has asked everyone to stay inside their apartment buildings until further notice.

The blackberries are flavorless. The sunlight has dimmed and everything is like a grainy image.

"Mom?" I say. "Was the city like this after the murder that happened when you were young?"

She clears the plates from the table without asking if I'm done, and she touches my head as she moves to the sink.

"No," she says.

Pen and I sit on the staircase in our apartment building's lobby. We can't go outside, but younger children in the building have gathered nearby and are playing games. Pen stares through the window of the image recorder her father gave her last year for her festival of stars gift, not taking any images. He makes more money than most do for his work in the glasslands, but Pen hardly ever uses the expensive things he buys her; this is the first time I've even seen that thing out from under her bed. Through the bubble of glass, she watches tiny versions of the children run, all of them shrieking with laugher.

"Why do we scream when we're excited?" she says. "Why is it always the most graphic, violent things with us?"

The clouds have grown especially heavy as the day goes on, coloring the sky white through the windows.

I keep my voice low so the children won't hear me ask, "Do you suppose the university student screamed? And Daphne?"

She blows a curl from her eye. "Nobody heard them, that's for sure." She grunts. "Thomas is going to be unbearably clingy tomorrow."

"He only wants you to be safe," I say.

"Only so he doesn't have to be alone in life if I get killed," she says. But we both know there's more to it than that. He adores her. Most of us are content to love our betrothed. But Pen does have a point. Is there anything worse than being alone in life? Alone like Judas. Alone like the murdered university student's betrothed.

She stares into her image recorder again, but still she doesn't capture any images. There's nothing about this day she wishes to remember.

"I'm going to get drunk now, I think," she says, standing. "You're welcome to join me."

I grab her wrist and pull her back down beside me. "Now's not the time for that," I say.

"On the contrary, the timing is ideal. We're both miserable, aren't we?"

"Yes," I say. "We promised to sneak tonic bottles only when we're looking to have fun. This wouldn't be fun. It would just be sad."

She opens her mouth but doesn't argue.

I worry about Pen adopting her mother's habits, but I know better than to tell her this.

Last year, when she fell ill during class, I was the one to ride with her on the train and be sure she made it home safely. Sallow and stumbling, she insisted the whole way to her bed that it was a stomach virus. But I could smell the tonic in her bedroom. It was heady and stagnant, and I felt that I was returning her to a bad memory that no one should face alone. So I didn't go back to the academy like I was supposed to. I helped her into pajamas, tucked the blanket around her shivering body, and read aloud from her class textbook about the life cycle of insects.

By the time Thomas came to see her, she was asleep. He sat on the edge of the bed, holding her clammy hand and frowning as he traced her knuckles. "We'll have to be more vigilant," he said. "Especially you. She tells you more things."

"Not when it comes to this," I said.

There are many afflictions on Internment—viruses, sores, infections, diseases—but what's to be done when the affliction is the remedy itself? Tonic is a peculiar medication I will never understand. I've asked Lex and he says it makes conmen of anyone it affects. I suppose he's right. I am inconspicuous when I check for the scent of it on her clothes and on her breath on the days when she's especially morose. She doesn't see that I peek into her satchel on the train. And when she brings tonic into the cavern, I don't fight her. I come along, entertaining her jokes to keep her spirits high. I make sure she gets home safely.

Thomas has argued with me about this. He tells me I should take the bottle away. But I know that if I did, she would only avoid me the way she avoids Thomas when she feels smothered. I wish she would stay away from her mother's tonic, but if she must have it, I would prefer she isn't alone. I never judge her.

"Let's stay here," I say.

I rest my head on her shoulder and watch the world through her recorder.

Even in a city so high up that the weather hardly changes, a fog has settled here. I've passed at least three pharmacists that are scurrying around the building this morning, delivering pharmacy bags to the apartments of those who need a pill to calm them. My mother was one such delivery, answering the door in her work clothes, her hair still rumpled, her eyes bleary. She grabbed my arm as I passed her, pulled me a step back, and kissed my forehead. She hates that I'm going to class today. She hates relinquishing me to this city that has become so unsafe.

The students are escorted single file to the shuttles. Pen and I hold hands, saying nothing as we're nudged up the train platform by a patrolman. Pen glares over her shoulder at him, though.

We meet up with Thomas and Basil while we're looking

for empty seats, and despite Pen's complaining about Thomas yesterday, she seems glad to have his arm around her shoulders now. The boys sit on either side of us, and I let myself pretend it means we're safe.

"What do our instructors expect us to learn today?" Thomas finally says, his whisper loud in the car of somber students.

"There's a screening room," Basil says. "Maybe there's going to be a broadcast."

"We could have watched a broadcast from home," Pen says to the clouds. Even her hair is paler than usual today. Internment has a history of kings and queens with fair hair and light eyes, because it was believed that fairer complexions caused sun disease and that they were too delicate for outdoor labor. And for that reason they used to be a trait that distinguished the upper class, back when Internment practiced such rankings. Because of Pen's fair hair, two hundred years ago, she would have been able to commission a girl like me to do her laundry. We used to tease each other about it when we were children; she would demand that I lace her shoes, and I would throw one of them at her.

"Maybe it's just going to be a normal day," I say.

Please let it be a normal day.

Pen pats my cheek.

The train stops and we're all escorted right to the academy's doors.

The headmaster is standing on a chair in the lobby, waving his arms, telling us all to face him and be quiet. There are seconds of murmuring before a hush falls over the room.

It's a wonder the way students are programmed to obey, when as individuals we have trouble just sitting still. Basil holds one hand and Pen holds the other, and all around us, others are finding ways to cling to their betrothed and their friends. It never used to be this way. Closeness never came from fear.

"In a moment, you will proceed to your scheduled classrooms," the headmaster says. "The king has been kind enough to lend us a few of his specialists, and they will be speaking with you in lieu of your instructors today. I'll expect your best behavior. That is all. As you were. Move on."

Pen and I turn to our betrotheds for a quick good-bye, and then the boys have to leave us for their classrooms.

"Morgan?" Pen says.

"Mm?"

"It's going to be all right. Isn't it?"

"Of course it will," I say. "How's your mother holding up with all of this?" My mother has a penchant for head-ache elixirs, and everyone knows that a tonic addiction is far worse. Inebriation is a sleep from which one cannot awaken; it steals the will to return to the waking world. The eyes will still be open, but the stare will be vacant.

"She's out of her senses, of course," Pen blurts, like it's nothing. "This will knock her right off the edge. She's convinced I'll be snatched from the cobbles."

I've known Pen all my life, and when it comes to her mother, I can never tell if it's all as nonchalant as she makes it seem. When common sense would dictate that she's hurting, that's when she turns indecipherably glib.

I tug at one of her curls and she smirks. "Don't get sullen on me now," I say.

"Now, who could be sullen looking at your pretty face? It's why Basil is about the happiest boy alive."

She hears it right after she says it. Alive. There is something about a citywide tragedy that makes us remember how strong certain words are.

The specialist standing in our instructor's place is as dull as death, though. He stands tall and pencil straight, except for his hand, which waves at us so we'll take our seats. Some of the students seize the opportunity to change the seating arrangement to be near their friends.

"Who here knows what treason is?" For such a slight man, the specialist has a harsh way of speaking. We all look to one another uncertainly. Of course we know what it means—the first years could boast that—but none of us has the wherewithal to answer.

"It's disloyalty," he answers for us. "In more barbaric times, the punishment was decapitation. We're more civilized now, of course. We don't even use the word 'treason' much these days. That's because we've lived in relative peace for several decades.

"These murders and the fire in the flower shop were acts of treason," he says. "The king has had his finest patrolmen investigating these incidents, and the finding has been that the betrothed of one victim, whom as you all know has been incarcerated and is awaiting trial"—Judas—"did not act alone. There is a group of rebels spreading blasphemous propaganda. Perhaps you've seen the literature posted about the city." He must mean Daphne's essay. "The king's patrolmen believe that there is a group of rebels slaying our own as part of a blasphemous ritual. They won't stop until all teachings of the god of the sky have been stopped. The king has received demands from this group that a ladder be built that will lead us to the ground. This is clearly impossible. The air beyond our atmosphere is too thin to breathe. These are the workings of madmen."

The room is silent, and the specialist's hard, enunciated words strike chord after chord within me. It's too much to comprehend at once. I think of my brother warning me to stay away from Amy, and then I think of Amy wearing a hair ribbon and sticking her dead sister's essays to the water room mirrors. There's nothing evil about her. There's nothing dangerous in Daphne's essay. The only danger lies in what happened to Daphne after she wrote it.

This isn't adding up. Not at all. And the way the specialist talks reminds me of the way my father spoke to me in the kitchen when he said that Judas was still locked away. He was lying, and I suspect everything this specialist tells me is a lie as well.

And then I begin to worry about Amy, who hides in the darkness and whose parents don't miss her when she's gone. Is she in danger? I can't let myself think about what will happen to Judas when he's found. If he's found.

The hallway is quiet as we make our way to our next class. Pen and I are forced in different directions.

When a hand touches my shoulder, I assume Basil has

found me. But this isn't his grip tightening around my fore-arm, and when I turn, I'm faced with Ms. Harlan.

"Morgan," she says. "I was hoping I'd run into you."

She already knows so much about me, it wouldn't be a stretch to assume she has access to my class schedule. "You found me, then," I say. "But I'm going to be late to class."

"Never mind class," she says. "With all that's happened, we should talk."

Students are herding past me, like animals to slaughter, as Thomas would say. They don't so much as turn their heads to me, they're so lost in their worries. Or perhaps they don't see me; it has been so long since any of them acknowledged me. There's a stigma about the children and siblings of jumpers. I realize now that Daphne faced it her-self with her little sister.

I wish we had known each other. This is a persistent regret of late. I would have talked to her, or at the very least smiled when we passed in the hallway. Something to show that she had done nothing to feel sorry for, and neither had our siblings.

I know what it is to be the reason a crowded cafeteria falls silent when I walk by. I have endured looks of pity and disapproval for an action taken by my brother. Pen would never say as much, but there was a time when Thomas had trouble meeting my eyes, and I suspect he discouraged Pen's and my friendship.

I'll never share this with Ms. Harlan, and I avert my eyes so she won't try to read what I'm thinking.

"There you are," Basil says. He's beside me in an instant. "We're going to be late for class."

We don't have our next class together.

"Actually, I was going to borrow our Ms. Stockhour for a bit," Ms. Harlan says.

"What for?" Basil says. "Has she done anything wrong?"

His tone is pleasant, but I see the clench in his jaw and I feel his biceps tighten against my arm.

"Not at all," Ms. Harlan says. "We only need to discuss her struggles with geography as we've been doing for a while now. It's important to maintain a sense of normalcy even in times of chaos. Go on ahead to class. She'll be with you shortly."

Basil is looking into her eyes, unhappy, untrusting.

"It's all right," I tell him. What I don't say is "Thank you." Thank you for knowing that this is not right, and for trying to protect me. What I don't say is that I want him to leave before he causes any trouble for himself.

He knows me well, though, and he understands.

"I hope you're able to bring that grade up," he says, kissing my cheek. Then he's gone, and Ms. Harlan is smiling theatrically as she holds her door open for me.

I push past her, betraying no anxiety. I think of what Lex told me after I saw the university student's body. I saw nothing. I was in bed, getting ready for sleep.

Ms. Harlan doesn't ask about the university student, though. Strangely, there is nothing accusatory or suspicious about the way she sits across from me and pours two cups of tea. There is also a glass bottle on her desk, filled with a molten gold liquid with flecks that catch the sunlight. Sweetgold; it was a rare treat in my home, because everyone knows that its sugars are terrible for the teeth. Ms. Harlan uncorks the bottle and spoons a bit of it into my tea, causing an oily ghost in the liquid before the sweetgold sinks to the bottom.

"I thought we'd be indulgent today," she says, her glasses misting briefly as she takes a sip from her own cup. "These are trying times, you know? My grandmother used to keep a bottle of sweetgold in her cabinet for the hard times. Not that there were many hard times when I was a girl."

"Times will get better," I say, sounding sincere, because it's only after I've already said the words that I realize I don't mean them.

"Did you know that at the end of the warm season, the sweetgold is at its peak? Something about the stress of the pending cold worries the bramble flies, causes a chemical reaction."

"I don't know much about bramble flies," I say. "Only that they sting when they feel threatened, and that their stings leave a nasty welt." This isn't everything. I also know that they feature prominently in my mother's old sketches, and that Alice can calm them by humming; she encounters them a lot, working with plants as she does.

"The venom in the stinger is also an ingredient in many healing elixirs," Ms. Harlan muses. "Curious things, really."

She's watching me, so I sip my tea. The sweetgold glides along my throat, and warms my stomach the instant it's down.

I'm waiting for the inevitable. To be asked what I saw. Maybe she even knows, somehow, that I saw the university student myself, that I know his name is Quince, and because Amy knew him, I suspect he was a friend to my brother's jumper group. But Ms. Harlan is not as menacing or as suspicious as usual today. She only smiles at me in a sad way and says, "Your family must love you very much."

It wasn't a question, but I feel oddly compelled to say, "Yes."

"And your betrothed, Basil Cowl."

It worries me that she has taken the time to learn his full name.

My muscles tense. I say nothing. I finish my tea.

Still glancing at me, Ms. Harlan scribbles on a piece of paper and then slides it across the desk. "You should be going back to class now," she says.

The rest of the day is as foggy as the morning felt. I don't eat a thing off my lunch tray. Basil thumbs patterns along my thigh under the table. Thomas coaxes Pen to nibble some of her apple. Her eyes are sunken, the lids mapped by tiny purple veins. She's the most spirited person I know, and as vivacious as she is most days, that's how dark she is other days. I believe her broken spirit has more to do with the pall that hangs over the city than the university student's death alone. She loves Internment more than anyone I've ever met, and when it's miserable, she's miserable.

I should be saying something to cheer her, but I can't bring myself to open my mouth. The entire cafeteria is quiet.

I can still taste the sweetgold, but it has gone sour on my tongue.

The boys try to strike up a conversation. Basil says there have been a lot of clouds, and Thomas says this is always the case in the short season. It has more to do with the weather patterns on the ground than with us.

I think of the white, frozen dust that falls from the clouds and covers the ground. How green and new the world must be when the sun melts it all away.

18

We accept gods that don't speak to us. We accept gods that would place us in a world filled with injustices and do nothing as we struggle. It's easier than accepting that there's nothing out there at all, and that, in our darkest moments, we are truly alone.

— "Intangible Gods," Daphne Leander, Year Ten

After class, Thomas has somehow persuaded Pen to come home with him. "I suppose I'm not much in the mood for my mother's inebriated weeping anyway," she sighs, letting him tug her away with him once we've gotten off the train.

Basil and I walk to my building, make our way past the patrolman who is there to hold open the door now that another murder has occurred, and climb the staircase leading to my apartment.

"My mother will probably be asleep," I tell him, working my key into the doorknob. We never used to bother with locks before Daphne's murder. "But I'm sure she left dinner if you're hungry."

Only, there is no dinner waiting for me in the kitchen. The stove is cold. My mother didn't even bother with a light, and with the sun nearly set, the apartment is full of shadows.

Basil catches my frown when I see the pharmacy bag on the table. "Maybe she just isn't feeling well," he says.

"She's getting worse," I say. It's because my father works so much. She'll deny it, but I know that's part of it.

I peer into her bedroom and can just make out her form. The blinds are, as always, drawn. She's on top of the covers, curled away from me. I frown and close the door. I wonder if she went to work at all today. Workers are granted only two missed days a month before they are required to be medically evaluated.

When I return to the kitchen, without breaking stride I go straight into Basil's arms, defeated. What a spectacular mess he's betrothed to. But our home will never be like this. He will never leave for days at a time and I will never go back to the malaise of those elixirs. I'll jump off the edge of this city, I'll go mad, I'll go blind before I let our home be like this. There will always be dinner waiting for our children and they'll always feel safe. Whether or not safety exists. "I just had a silly thought," I murmur against his chest. "Us sitting at a table eating dinner with our children, and outside, the city is burning down."

"You're warm," Basil says, pressing his chin and then his wrist against my forehead. He draws back to look at me. "How do you feel?"

"A little light-headed," I admit. "All I've had today is tea."

His fingers brush against the tips of my ears and there's a moment of dizziness, but that clears away when I feel a stab of pain in my stomach. All the pleasant lightness is being stolen away by this new pain that has me tasting something like blood where I tasted sweetgold earlier today.

Basil is leading me to a kitchen chair, but I don't quite make it before my knees buckle.

"Morgan!" He catches me under my arms. He calls for my mother, but of course she doesn't hear him, lost in her dreams under tree roots and in old colorings of children she's never met.

I double forward onto my hands. Something is happening. Something is very wrong. The floorboards are blurring and my stomach is all knives, organs bleeding into my lungs.

"I'm taking you to the callbox," Basil says. It's a machine in every building that can be used to contact the hospital in an emergency.

I can barely get the breath to say, "No. Take me to Lex." My brother could fix anything—stings and scrapes and odd afflictions were his specialty before he began sewing quilts. We always knew he'd go into medicine; as a child he was fascinated with healing.

When Basil lifts me into his arms, I cry out in pain. He has never moved so fast. I blink and we're at my brother's door, and Basil is kicking at it because it's locked, and I want to tell him not to make such a commotion—what has

.

possessed him?—but the motion has made me too dizzy to speak.

The door swings open, and Alice greets us with her hair done up high on her head, woven into and into itself like the pages from Lex's transcriber.

They're saying words I can't catch as Basil hurries me through the kitchen. I see the unlit candles and the dishes laid out sparkling clean, before they're pushed away with a chorus of awful shattering sounds, and then Basil is laying me down on the table. There's the warm smell of something cooking, and all I can think is that on one of the rare nights when Alice has cooked dinner, I've ruined it. But she doesn't care. She's kicking the shards out of the way to get to me, and yelling for Lex.

I close my eyes, but then Basil says, "No, Morgan. Look at me," and I do. Somehow I know that this is important.

"What's happening to me?" I say.

"I don't know," he says. "I don't know, but we'll fix it."

Time is playing out before me like the scope slides we're shown in class. One image, blackness, then another.

In the next slide, Lex is standing over me and his face is serious, detached. He presses his fingers against my neck to take my pulse. Alice tells him the things he cannot see. "Her skin is flushed but not sweaty. Her lips and tongue are pale. Her pupils are dilated."

He touches my forehead. "Get the storage container that's under the water room sink," he tells her. "It's full of corked vials." His voice is short, almost angry.

She's gone.

"Morgan?" He's leaning over me now. There's a little of the blue that was in his eyes before the edge faded them to gray. "Tell me where it hurts," he says. My answer is a shuddering whimper when he kneads into my stomach.

Alice is back with the vials and she sets them on the counter and says, "Tell me what to do." Her voice is steady. Her eyes are red.

"I need to know what I'm dealing with before anyone does anything," he says. "Talk to me, Little Sister. I need your voice. Describe what you're feeling."

"I don't know," I manage. "It's like my stomach is burning, and everything is spinning a little."

"She said she didn't eat anything today," Basil offers.

Lex pushes into my stomach again. He's in medic mode; he would have to be in order to touch me. Some months into his blindness, he began shirking away if my arm so much as brushed his. Alice said I was at the age when girls change overnight, and it made him feel that I was a stranger. I was no longer as he'd last seen me. I had barely noticed the differences in myself until she said it. It took a lot of insistence to reacquaint him with my hands. He didn't know how to trust what he couldn't see.

"Did you have anything at all?" he says.

"My pill," I say, cringing.

"New prescription?"

"No," I say. "And tea. At lunch."

I hesitate for only a beat, but Basil knows what I'm thinking. Recognition and anger fill his eyes. "You were with that specialist at lunch," he says.

"Basil," I snap.

"Could she have done this to you?"

"Specialist?" Lex says. "You've been talking with a specialist?"

I hesitate.

"Tell him," Basil says.

"Her name is Ms. Harlan," I say. "She's been asking me things, mostly about our family; I didn't tell her anything. I swear."

I expect my brother to be angry—he hates when anyone who works for the king starts nosing into our affairs—but he doesn't ask me to elaborate. Something about that name has made a crumble in his calm veneer, and there's a quiver in his voice when he tells Alice, "There's an orange liquid and a blue. Do you see them?"

"Yes."

"And a measuring bottle."

"Have that."

"Lex?" I say. "Do you know her? Who is she?"

"No one you should be dealing with. Alice, I need you to measure something out for me."

My brother may have abandoned his trade, but his trade has clearly not abandoned him. He has all those bottles memorized. Alice is his eyes, quickly reading the names on the labels he touches, measuring the exact amounts he tells her to.

"Is there something I can do?" Basil asks.

"Just keep holding her hand," Alice says. "You did good bringing her here; she wouldn't have made it to the hospital."

The train speeds past and I feel as though I'm going to fall from the table as the vibration rattles it.

Basil will never be allowed to love another girl if he loses me now. It's forbidden. You get one partner and it's your job to take care of each other. Loners are loners for life.

I don't want to leave him. I don't want him to be broken the way that Judas is broken.

"I don't want you to be charged with my murder," I say.

Basil touches my cheek. "You aren't going to die," he says.

Lex says, "You're delirious, Sister."

"I'm not," I say, although the ceiling is blurring. "Pen is right. You're forever picking on me."

"Talk all the nonsense you want if it helps to keep you conscious," he says.

I look at Basil's eyes, and I see what he'll be like in his dodder years. I see his skin wrinkled, his expression still soft and kind. I want to live to grow old with him, and I feel that future being drained out of me as though someone has cut a hole in my skin.

Across the kitchen, Alice is holding the measuring bottle up to the light to see that the elixirs form the richness Lex is describing.

They're talking softly. I don't hear Alice's question, only Lex telling her, "I can't neutralize something if I don't know what it is. I have to force it out."

He comes back to my side. "Morgan? Staying awake?"

"Yes," I say.

"This is going to make you sick," he says. "But you have to drink all of it."

That's the only explanation I get before Alice is emptying a vial down my throat. It fizzes and burns. Her hand covers my mouth so I can't cough it up.

It's not long before the concoction takes effect. Basil holds back my hair when I vomit into the bowl Alice is holding before me.

Lex is at a distance now, trying to stay in his medic frame of mind, but wincing at the sounds I make.

"How does she look?" he asks.

I slump against Basil, gasping to catch my breath.

"Still flushed. Sweaty," Alice says. She grabs my chin, looks right through me. "Pupils are still dilated."

"Sweat is good, at least," Lex says, taking my pulse again. My heart is pounding, and from the way his bottom lip juts, it's got him concerned. "Are you certain all you had today was that tea? Nothing else, not even a headache elixir or a study aide?"

"There was a pharmacy bag on the counter when I got home, but I didn't take anything," I say, finding it's easier to get my breath now. The sharp pains in my stomach are less frequent. "Must have been delivered this morning."

"Opened?" There's an edge to the word. He's wary of medicine, but this means something more to him, and it compels me to be honest.

"Yes. Mom always takes them after work," I say. "She didn't want you to know."

"Did you see her?" he presses. "Talk to her?"

"She was sleeping when I came home."

"I'll get her," Alice says. And before another word can be said, she's out the door. I'd like to know what's going on, but speaking would bring the nausea back.

Lex feels the vials in the container and then holds one of them up to us.

"Is this green?" he asks.

"Yes," Basil says.

He uncorks it. "I need you to mix this in a glass with two parts water."

Basil is only away from my side for seconds, and then he's feeding me a glass of pale green liquid. In contrast to the other concoction, this is minty and smooth and I don't have to choke it down.

"It almost tastes good," I murmur.

"Your pulse is rapid. This will slow it back down," Lex says. "Let's see if we can stop this from spreading."

"Stop what?" I say. "What is it?" The words are thick; my tongue and cheeks feel numb.

He doesn't answer.

My body goes heavy. I lie back against the table and fight to keep my eyes open.

The walls are murmuring. My mind is hovering outside my skull.

Lex is pacing, pacing. He rubs his hand along his cheek, hard. I hate to see him so worried about me.

Basil is stroking my forehead and whispering some nice words that don't quite reach me.

Alice comes back. Her steps are slow. I don't understand

why my mother isn't with her, but I can't muster the strength to ask.

She steers Lex into a corner and I try to focus on them, but my vision is tunneling. I have no choice but to give in to this feeling of weightlessness.

I close my eyes and at last Basil's words find me.

He was saying, "I love you."

19

I cannot say for certain whether we would be stronger without the notion of gods, or weaker.
— "Intangible Gods," Daphne Leander, Year Ten

The darkness is empty of dreams. There are stabs of red pain, hands pushing back my hair. I'm going to spend all of sixty years in this darkness, clawing at moments of awareness. I'll never be free until I've become ashes.

Something burns in my throat and I struggle. "We're here with you, love, we're here," Alice says, somewhere high above the surface of the black. But then I'm alone again.

Her voice was so sad.

Another voice finds me. If anyone could reach me here, it'd be my brother. He knows his way through every kind of darkness.

"Let her pull through," he whispers. I think he's talking

to the god in the sky. He doesn't even believe there is a god anymore. "I haven't requested anything for three years. You owe me."

The last time I heard my brother talk to the god in the sky, it was when I was seven or eight. He was supposed to be watching me, and I was sour that he was more interested in his writing, so I hid in a tree that surrounded the pond so that he'd be forced to look for me.

I waited for him to notice I was gone. When he did, he called my name. His voice changed each time he said it. It became more afraid. He didn't consider that I might be hiding in the trees. He ran to the lake first, where I'd been setting leaves on the surface and watching them float when he last saw me.

Uniform and all, he dove into the green water. Pages of his manuscript were scattering in the wind and grass. But he didn't call to them—he called to me.

I couldn't answer. His fear had me paralyzed.

I'd only wanted to make him care. Just for a little bit. That was all. But I wasn't prepared for the power of what I'd done.

Please, he'd said.

"Please," he says now.

I'm a little girl in the trees. I can't find the footholds to return down to him. I can't go back to that day and undo it.

I'm sorry. I didn't want to hurt you. I'm sorry.

20

As a child, I trusted the god in the sky with decisions like life and death. It wasn't until I began studying medicine that I learned these are decisions made by humans. Flawed humans—as though there were any other kind.

—"Intangible Gods," Daphne Leander, Year Ten

A moment before I open my eyes, I hear Ms. Harlan's words:

Your family must love you very much.

It's a warm thought. I have a family. This floating city is filled with people, but I belong to only a small number of them.

Then the thought breaks apart, is replaced by shadows and lantern light.

"Morgan?" Alice's voice is eager.

There's a smell like metal, sickness, and candle wax.

I don't know where I am. The lantern on the ceiling is swinging, swinging, making the room jolt. Alice reaches up and steadies it.

"Is she awake?" Lex asks. His voice is hoarse. He's slouched in a corner, but the room is so tiny that it's nearly impossible not to be in a corner.

"I think so. Her eyes are open again." Alice is kneeling in her dress, leaning over me. Her copper earrings catch the light; her hair is coming unwoven.

And I remember that I ruined the dinner she and my brother were going to have before Basil burst through the door carrying me, and everything was swept from the table.

I'm not on the table anymore. I'm lying on some kind of mattress on the ground. It feels as though it's stuffed with sheep shavings. This room is unfamiliar, and as my mind slowly clears, I become certain that the walls and low ceiling are made of metal.

"Morgan?" Alice says again, pushing the hair from my eyes. My skin feels so tender that the touch gives me chills. "Are you back with us?"

I open my mouth and remember the sick taste on my tongue. Ghosts of my earlier agony are webbed between my ribs, and they stir the moment I move to sit up. "What happened?" I ask.

My eyes go to Lex. His leg is shaking, causing a shuddering in his entire body that makes his chin move as though he's nodding. He seems small. His eyes are open but there's nothing there. Nothing but faded blue.

"You were poisoned," he says. "I don't know what exactly it was, but it was wicked. I thought giving you something to sleep would help numb the pain, but it didn't do any good. You've been crying out for hours."

Was I crying out? I recall twisted dreams and bits of light.

My tongue still feels strange. "Poisoned?"

The compassion on Alice's face gives way to a moment of anger. My brother is tearing at his thumbnail.

"Why?" I say.

After a long moment, Lex says, "That Harlan woman— Basil said you've been speaking with her often."

I can't untangle myself from the drowsiness, not fully. I want to close my eyes, but I've no desire to claw my way up from that fitful blackness again.

I try again to sit up, and this time Alice helps me, propping the rough pillow against the wall so I can lean into it.

"Ms. Harlan did this?" I ask. I never trusted her and never understood what she wanted with me, but I didn't think she wanted me dead. Now that I think on it, the sweetgold she gave me was peculiarly rich.

"She was just a pawn following orders," Lex says. "I'm sure she asked you plenty of questions and figured out you were innocent in all of this. You weren't involved."

I press the heel of my hand to my forehead. "I don't understand."

Lex raises his head, and it's as though he's seeing me. I can tell that he wants to. "The king is the one who wanted you to die. Your only crime was being a part of this family. He intended to have us all killed. You, me, our parents, even Alice."

"A pharmacy bag arrived for us this morning," Alice

says. "We didn't take them, or we'd have been poisoned as well." The king would have no reason to suspect they wouldn't take their dosages. Alice doesn't like to lie, even on the pharmacy reports, but she owes no loyalty to the king and the government that stole her child. She would suffer the sadness of that termination procedure a thousand times before she'd take the pills meant to leave her numb.

"Where are Mom and Dad, then?" I say.

My brother turns his face to the floor again, as though to look away. Alice sits back on her heels and smoothes the wool blanket that's covering my legs. My question goes unanswered.

"Lex. Where are Mom and Dad?"

There is a moment of perfect silence. Of oblivion. In that moment I can build a house out of my memories and I can be safe there, with walls and windows that are sealed tight, no room for reality to sneak in. And then he says, "They're dead."

The poison returns to my system, blooming and twisting through my bloodstream, winding around my lungs. My vision is tunneling. The heaviness on my chest is like the weight of Internment itself.

"That can't be right," I whisper.

"It was too late," Lex says. "There was nothing I could do. I don't know why it took so long for the poison to affect you, but you were the only one I could do anything for."

I think of my mother on the bed, turned away from

me when I checked on her. I was sure she was sleeping. I wouldn't have thought to listen for her breathing. "That's the real reason you put me to sleep when Alice went downstairs, isn't it? You didn't want me to find out?"

He doesn't deny it. "You were ill, Morgan. Barely hanging on. You wouldn't have been able to handle knowing."

"We very nearly lost you too," Alice says.

"You're the first person I've known who survived that woman's poisonings," Lex says. "I knew she was responsible the moment you said her name. She's done it before. She works for the king."

"Why—why would they want us dead?"

Lex is wringing his shirt in his hands now. He doesn't answer.

Finally Alice says, "Tell her."

Lex shakes his head. "She can't be hearing these things right now. She needs rest."

I'd like to argue, but I can't muster the strength. My throat is dry and it hurts to breathe. Tears won't come. Shouldn't there be tears? Nothing about me has ever been right. I have done all I could to be complacent on this floating city, and still I've been restless. I've taken all the right pills and said the right things, and I have never been satisfied. Now, when I should be crying, all I can think of is the ground. Of those faded, wonderful patches of earth, each color a different city. All the people who must be down there. How easy to be lost. Not like here, where you can run only so far before everything finds you.

I wonder if, surrounded by so many others on the ground, they marry in dozens and droves. I wonder if their capacity to love stretches out further. I wonder if it would seem silly to them that there's only one person I want to comfort me now.

"Where's Basil?" Too late, I have the thought that he's dead too.

"He's been by your side all night," Alice says. "But it looked like you were waking up, so I asked him to wait outside. I didn't want you to get overwhelmed."

"Overwhelmed . . ." My voice trails off. I've just been told I was poisoned and my parents are dead, and she didn't want me to get overwhelmed.

"I want him," I say, wresting away from her attempt to console me.

Her lips barely move. "Okay." She stands, and I can see that I've hurt her. She touches Lex's arm and he doesn't resist when she pulls him toward the door. They leave me alone.

When Basil comes to the doorway, his eyes are bleary, his hair disheveled. His mouth moves to speak, but I say, "Don't. I've had my fill of words just now."

He's at my bedside in an instant, his arms fitting around me just so, because we were made for each other. Paired up the day he was born, one month after me. Our betrothal was planned months before we were born, and we were supposed to be born the same week, but I was early. I could never get anything right even from the start, but that never mattered to him. Even if I'm all wrong, even if I'm broken and filled with delusions of the ground, even if I'm orphaned, he wants me.

I don't make a sound. I never thought grief could be so silent. I'm sure I'm not processing the news of my parents properly. When Alice came to the hospital and she saw Lex confined to a bed by wires, with his eyelids taped shut and his breaths coming through a tube, she ran to the water room and I followed her. Through the door I heard her scream; only it was more than a scream; it was a cry that must have shot through the heart of the sky god himself. If he has a heart. If he even exists.

"I knew you'd be okay," Basil says. "But it was a very long night."

"I didn't feel any of it," I say. I felt nothing but dreams. I wish I could go back to them. Even the darkest nightmare holds the hope that I'll awaken in my own bed. Not so here. I don't even know where I am.

There are no city sounds. It's quiet, save for our breathing. Basil and I are so close, collarbone to cheek, chin to crown. But there are questions between us, words dripping down our skin. I'm afraid to ask them. I'm afraid to even let go of his shirt.

But I know that I have to. I can't let my parents die without my knowing what happened. I can't sink back under this blanket and go back to dreaming.

"Where are we?" I ask.

"We're underground," Basil says.

"In a basement?" I say, drawing back to look at him. He doesn't look at me with pity, and I'm grateful for that. He knows me even better than I could have hoped.

"It's . . ." He looks up as though the answer is on the metal ceiling. "More like a body," he says. "The others explained it to me last night, but it was hard to pay attention with you lying there in pain."

"Others?" I say.

"They're waiting outside," he says. "Morgan." He takes my hands. "Whatever you decide, I want you to know that I'll stand behind it. I said I'd follow you off the edge, and I meant it. I'd jump into the sky with you. Wherever you go, you won't have to go alone. Even if you want to go back."

The words are wonderful, but I'm not sure what he's trying to tell me. I know that I'm about to find out.

"It's going to be a long story," he says. "Are you up to hearing it yet?"

"Yes," I say. I won't want to hear what the others have to say, but I have to. I stretch my legs off the makeshift mattress. There's no time left for resting, and no room for dreams. It's time to wake up.

I ignore the dizziness as I rise to my feet. There's a low ceiling; Basil can just about stand at full height. The floor is made of wooden planks that are crudely finished, full of knots and nicks; they shudder and creak under my steps. Basil opens the door; its green color is chipped, the wood splintered and aged. The entire room seems to be made of pieces of different buildings. Beyond it, there's a

perfect ruin

narrow hallway. I hear voices murmuring from a room at
the end of it, where lantern light is flickering through an
open door.

The murmurs cease when Basil and I enter the room.
There are tattered couches and cushions arranged in a half
circle on the floor. Lex is of course on the floor, with Alice
beside him.

Judas's and Amy's eyes are on me immediately. I tug
the sleeves of my red sweater over my hands. My necktie
is missing, but I'm still in my academy uniform. It feels
more like a game of make-believe to wear it now. One look
around this room, and I'm sure my days of being a schoolgirl are done.

Amy is looking at me like we have loss in common. Or
maybe I'm imagining that.

"Sit down," Lex says.

Basil and I share a paisley green cushion that once
belonged to what I'm sure was a hideous couch.

"I'm sitting," I tell him. "Maybe you'd like to tell me
what sort of place I'm sitting in."

"It's a machine," he says. "Or, if you prefer, we're in the
chest of a giant metal bird."

What a thing to say. I wonder if our parents' deaths have
driven him mad.

Madder still is that, with all that has happened, it isn't
the hardest thing I'm made to believe today.

"It's far more extraordinary than a bird," says an older
man, likely near his dispatch age; as though to keep track
of his remaining time, there's a copper clock on a chain

227

clipped to his pocket. He's short and round with tufts of hair that at one glance seem white, but at the next a sort of yellow. "It doesn't simply fly; it can also burrow like a dirt warren."

I try to reconcile this. Dirt warrens are small black creatures that burrow in the ground and eat worms and things. Birds, from what I understand, are known only for flying. "How can it be both?" I ask.

The clock man opens his mouth to speak, but my brother interrupts. "First," he says, "you should know the reason you're here."

21

Fear is more dangerous than blasphemy.
—"Intangible Gods," Daphne Leander, Year Ten

When my brother jumped from the edge of Internment, my father said it was because he had a lot of demons. But long before my brother was a jumper, when he and I were children, my father began collecting demons of his own.

As a patrolman, he fitted anklets on people who had turned irrational. He took part in the quiet dispatches of those who had committed crimes, their deaths later made to seem accidental. He was made to participate and even choreograph ugly things on the promise that these things would keep us all safe. And in the evening he would come home to his happy children and his loving wife and try to reconcile his role as one of the king's elite.

Lex isn't sure when our father began to tell my mother of the things that were happening behind the peoples' backs, but my parents began to talk of changing things. There were other patrolmen and wives who felt the same way, and they began to meet in secret. At first they wondered whether they could persuade the king to change his methods. But this is a king who has ways of killing those who disrupt the order of his city. And the talk soon turned to rebellion. When they met Professor Finnian Leander, who taught technology courses at the university, he introduced the idea that they could leave Internment. Fly away on the wings of a metal bird.

Finnian Leander turned his blueprints and ideas into stories for his granddaughters—Amy and Daphne. "I could never take credit for their imaginations," Professor Leander interrupts, smoothing his fingers over the face of his clock. "Their minds stretched farther than Internment long before my silly stories."

"So Daphne became a part of it," I say. I look to Lex. "What about you? When did Mom and Dad tell you all of this?"

"It was after I jumped," he says. "At first Dad would whisper about it in the hospital, when he thought I was too far gone to hear him. My eyes were taped shut. He would apologize and say he should have realized the things I'd been seeing as a pharmacist. He should have told me everything sooner. He blamed himself."

My brother speaks so coolly about it, as though he's talking of people he's never met, but I see the way his fingers are fidgeting with the hem of his shirt. This is all hard for him to say.

I finish for him, "And you became a part of it, too."

He nods. "But I had suspected something like it for a long time," he says. "I didn't realize they'd actually built the bird, but I wasn't surprised."

He never got to see this place, I realize. Dad told him about it after the incident that blinded him.

"And that's why they're dead?" I say. "Because the king found out about it? And Daphne, and the university student?"

"Quince," Amy says softly.

"Others, too," Lex says. "There are plenty of deaths that nobody thinks twice about. The king can do away with anyone and make the cause appear to be anything he pleases."

"Then why was Daphne's death so public?" I say. I try not to think of the brutality of her demise. It was more than doing away with a nuisance—it was too violent and cruel to be anything but personal. Did the king do it himself, or did he have someone do the dirty work? Was it the prince, with his firm jaw and sparkling eyes?

"The king is trying to make a point now," Professor Leander says. "He doesn't know about the bird for certain, but he knows that there is unrest. He knows about the plans to leave the city. We have our suspicions about who may have betrayed our secret. It may have been done under duress. And now not only does the king want to stop us, but he wants to frighten everyone else into thinking that leaving the city is an act of evil. He wants them to think that we're deranged and violent, so that they'll fear us and seek his protection."

Basil presses the back of his hand to my forehead and frowns. I lean into his touch before he draws his hand away. I'm glad he's here, still by my side after all the trouble I've caused him.

"So all of you had this secret," I say to Lex, an edge to my tone, "and nobody thought it'd be a good idea to tell me?"

"You weren't burdened by it," he says. "You didn't carry the things that we did, and we didn't want that for you."

"So—what, you were all going to fly off Internment in a metal bird and just leave me home with a note saying that dinner was in the stove and you wouldn't be coming back?"

"Don't be stupid," he says. "There was no sense putting you at risk before anything was certain. We never would have left you behind."

I think of the night my father came to my room after Daphne's murder. *You're getting old enough now to see life for exactly what it is.* That's what he said. He must have come so close to telling me before he lost his nerve about it.

I realize I'm shaking. The metal walls are caving in, and

all these eyes are on me and it's getting hard to breathe.

"I need air," I say.

"You can't leave," Alice says, sympathetic. "It isn't safe for you. The king will have men looking for you."

"Why?" I say. "None of this has anything to do with me. You all made sure of that."

Lex laughs bitterly, and it takes all my strength not to hit him. "I guess that specialist saw something in you anyway," he says. "There are extraordinary things in that head of yours. You don't even realize the sorts of things you say."

I try to recall the things I said to Ms. Harlan that might have made me stand out, but there's nothing. I remember her accusatory stares and her suspicions, but I never betrayed a single thought. I lied each time she asked me about the ground.

I've been told I'm a terrible liar, though. There's that.

Basil tries to put an arm around me, but I pull away. I rise to my feet. I wouldn't know how to get out of this place even if I could, so when I hurry from the room, I go straight back to the tiny bunk. The green door closes behind me with a slam.

I hear Alice, as practical as ever, saying, "Let her be."

I pull the blanket over my head and listen to the rush of blood in my ears. I have never been so aware of all my bones, and how heavy my limbs are, and how much effort it takes to breathe in and out.

A little bit of light peeks through the weave in the

blanket, and it's like the stars gleaming in a sky I might never see again.

The quiet here isn't perfect. It's filled with clinks and groans, as though I've been shrunk down and imprisoned in the engine of some machine. I suppose the truth isn't far from that.

The doorknob turns eventually. A bit of light reaches me when a piece of the blanket is lifted just enough for Amy to stick her head under. "Hey," she says.

I just stare at her.

"They told me to leave you alone."

"And you thought this would be the best way to do that," I say.

"Move over," she says, and crawls under the blanket with me. The blanket between us is tented by our shoulders, and in the darkness her eyes are very round. I wonder what it's like for her, looking so much like a dead girl. When she grows older, she'll be very nearly a perfect replica of her sister.

"You can't be afraid," she tells me. "You can be sad if you like. You can be angry. But it's the fear that'll freeze you in place."

"They think you wandered to the edge accidentally," I say. "But I think you knew what you were doing, especially when you go saying things like that."

"Nobody knows what they're doing at the edge," she says. "You don't know what you'll find there; it's just that you've had your fill of *not* knowing."

"What was it like?" I say.

"Windy," she says. "Theory is, the wind is what keeps you from going over the edge. You hear it roaring, and you can't see anything but sky and bits of the ground through the clouds, and you think you could jump and then you'd be like the birds, sailing down and down until you land in one of those colorful patches. But when you jump, everything goes black, and when you wake up, you're still here."

This rivals the news of my parents' deaths as the saddest thing I've heard today.

"There are a lot of dead bugs, too," she says, her teeth showing as she smiles. She looks like a little girl for once.

"Bugs?" I say.

"Hundreds of them all around the edge, just thrown back onto the grass when they tried to fly off."

She laughs and I laugh too. I don't even know why. Maybe I'm in shock.

When we're quiet again, she says, "I'm sorry your parents are dead."

I say, "I'm sorry your sister is dead."

"It won't be for nothing," she says. "I'm glad you survived. You'll get to see what your parents and my sister were working for."

"Even if we do make it to the ground," I say, "who's to say it's any better? What if there's another king no less corrupt than ours? Or what if the ground is just another city floating over an even bigger one, and so on?"

"Then at least we'll be the wiser," she says. "I'd rather be disappointed than oblivious."

"Would you now?" I say.

Her smile is back. "But I bet the people down there will be fascinated by us. I bet they'll feed us their delicacies and give us crowns and ask us all about our city."

Her notions are as good as mine, I suppose.

"I'd much like for you to be right," I say.

22

We are promised many things on Internment, but change isn't among them. One generation's king and queen birth the next generation's king and queen.

—"Intangible Gods," Daphne Leander, Year Ten

I decline all offers to partake in a tour of the metal bird.

I realize that this is a phenomenal place, but I'm not in the right mind to appreciate it. I spend the rest of the evening reliving the memory of mother turned away from me on the bed, and the night I sat at the kitchen table with my father as he lied about Judas. He was trying to protect me. If I knew nothing, he thought I wouldn't be a target. I see that now.

I don't say very much. Basil worries. Lex has Alice check the dilation of my pupils and he pays close attention to my temperature, asks me to describe any stomach cramps or dizziness. I tell him that I don't feel much of anything. He has nothing to say to that. He was never very good with emotions. It's staggering to think he's the only family I have left.

There are probably patrolmen in the apartment now, rifling through our drawers and looking for signs of treason to justify the murder of an entire family. When they get to my bedroom they'll find an open textbook at the desk, and the wooden marionette Pen bought for my festival of stars gift. They'll find blue bedsheets and a closet full of uniforms and a feather headband draped over the mirror. They'll find pieces of a girl who followed the rules.

That girl is gone now.

There's no daylight here. There are no clouds. I hear a rumbling that I think is the train up above us. I lie with my face in the mattress, and Basil rubs circles on my back. He says nice things and he stoops down to kiss the back of my neck. Despite this hollowness inside me, the feel of his lips raises bumps in my skin.

I hear the door open, and Alice calls my name.

When I don't answer, Basil says, "I think she's fallen asleep."

Alice doesn't believe it. When I was younger, there were nights when my parents still went out together, when they would be gone long into the starlit hours, only to return with giggles and whispers, shushing each other as they slammed doors and stumbled off to bed. While they were gone, Alice would look in on me. She would know if I was pretending to sleep, and she would tickle my feet.

She doesn't touch me now. She only says, "We'll sort this out, love." She doesn't say my name, but I know the words are for me. "You aren't alone."

The door closes.

"She's been crying," Basil says, lying down beside me.

After a few seconds, I raise my face from the mattress to look at him.

"I don't want to talk," I say. I feel like I can't get the words out in time. They spin angrily in my brain but disappear on my tongue.

"Okay," he says, and wipes at a streak of my tears with his thumb. "You don't need to say a word."

"Never again?" I say.

"Not if you don't want to. I'll just read your expressions. Everywhere we go, I'll speak so you don't have to."

I know he isn't being serious, but it's a nice thought. Him always at my side, always knowing what I'm thinking until our dodder days are over and we're dispatched.

Only I don't know if we'll be allowed in dodder housing. I don't know what's going to happen or where I'll go if Internment is too dangerous for me.

I close my eyes.

"Want me to turn out the light?" he says.

I shake my head. He tucks the blanket over both of us. It's rough and unfamiliar, so I wrap my arm around Basil. The boy I'm supposed to spend forever with. He still feels and smells like home.

"What about your parents and brother?" I say.

"They'll be safer if I don't try to find them now," he

says. "They had nothing to do with any politics. I can't imagine they'd be a target."

He doesn't sound very sure about that. Their son is betrothed to a girl the king tried to kill, after all.

"You must want to see them," I say.

"I can't," he says, and his voice falters, and I know he's trying to be strong for my sake. "You heard what they said. It would put everyone at risk—them, you, me, everyone on this bird. My family will understand. They know that my place is with you. I was going to have to leave home eventually."

I think of Leland running along the cobbles the day we picked him up after class. He's disappearing in the sunlight and I can't bring him back.

"But not like this," I say. "You shouldn't have to leave home like this."

"You'll be killed if the king finds you," he says. "It was my worst fear that something would happen to you, and I won't chance it again. If you're leaving Internment, I'm leaving, too."

"If I were nobler, I'd beg you to stay with your family," I say.

"It wouldn't change that we're meant to stay together."

"What if we get to the ground in this flying bird some-how, and there are no rules like that? What would keep us together then?"

"The same thing that's keeping us together now," he says.

It's quiet after that, and I'm left to remember that

beautiful, strange thing he said to me before the medicine pulled me under.

I love you.

Is this what love means? That the rules aren't the reason you stay together?

Buried away from the clock tower's chimes, I rely on Basil's wristwatch to know the hour. When he falls asleep, just after midnight, I slide out from under his arm.

"Morgan?"

One foot off the mattress, I freeze. His eyes don't open, though, and I realize he's only talking in his sleep.

Carefully I slide the rest of the way out of bed and kneel before him to be sure he's really asleep. "I'll be back soon," I whisper. "I'm sorry."

I close the door behind me when I leave.

The hallway contains a few other bunk rooms like mine. I hear voices behind the closed doors. Professor Leander means for this to be a sort of house if it lands on the ground; his intentions lie in the faucets and electrical fittings that don't work as of yet.

There's a spiral staircase that leads me down into a kitchen. It's mostly dark, save for a little lantern hanging from the ceiling. I walk as softly as I can to avoid creaking floorboards. If the upstairs is the chest, then I wonder what part of the bird this is; the stomach, I suppose.

The lantern lights only a small bit of the room, allowing me to see outlines of cabinets, a stove, and a cold box. There's also a chandelier hanging over a table on the far end, but I haven't seen any evidence of working electricity on this bird. It has all been flame lanterns.

No matter, though. I'm able to find the drawers easily enough, and it doesn't take much rummaging for me to find a knife.

"I hope you weren't looking to fix a midnight snack. There's not much food." Judas's voice throws my heart into my throat. My shoulders go stiff. He hops onto the counter in front of me and stares at the open drawer. "The professor had big dreams of making this place a second home, but by now he's accepted that we'll all be lucky enough if it gets us to the ground without killing us. A one-way journey to be sure." He eyes the knife in my hand. "May I see?"

I hold the knife out but don't let him grab it. "There, you've seen," I say, lowering it again.

"A serrated blade," he says. "Great for slicing bread or potatoes." He narrows his eyes. "Not so great as an assassination tool, though. You'd want a paring blade for that. Short, easy to conceal, and a pointed edge that would go right to the vital organs."

"I can't imagine what you're getting at," I say.

"You know," he says, "if you try to take the king's life to avenge your parents, you're likely to get killed by his security before you've made it halfway up the clock tower."

He knows what I'm up to, then. There's no sense pretending. He reaches into the drawer and selects a paring knife, which he graciously holds out for me to grasp by the handle.

"Are you going to tell the others?" I say.

"They were your parents," he says, "and this is your decision. I'd advise you to revisit it later with a clearer head, but it's not my place to stop you."

"You can come with me, you know," I say. "The king had a hand in your betrothed's death. You've just as much a right to this grudge as I do."

"No thanks," he says. "Believe me, I've wanted to. I hate that she's dead while he's still breathing. But that isn't what Daphne was about."

I wrap the blade in a cloth napkin and tuck it into the waistband of my skirt. "Suit yourself," I say. "How do I get out of here?"

It's too dark to be sure, but I think he's grinning when he points to a door across from us. "There's a ladder that'll take you down and out of the bird. We're pretty far underground, though. Let me go with you and show you how the pulley works."

He grabs the lantern from the ceiling hook and leads me to the exit. We scale the ladder down a tunnel that leads to a metal door.

"The bird's all rickety inside," he says, "but it's airtight. The professor says the air is thin beyond our atmosphere. He says we'd suffocate on our way down if there were so much as a crack in this thing."

If my parents were still alive, all of this would fascinate me. I would have questions and I would be certain that I was dreaming, so spoiled would I feel at the idea of the ground being a possibility.

Now the idea of sailing to the ground in a metal bird only stirs a rivulet of blood in my stomach where there should be excitement. I can't quite bring myself to care. The colors have all dulled around me.

I was a different girl yesterday. I also possessed more patience and sanity.

Judas opens the metal door and bows with a flourish of his arm, the lantern raised to light the way. "After you," he says. "Watch that first step."

Beyond the bird, there's nothing but dirt and rocks. "How far below the surface are we?" I ask.

"Not as far down as you'd think," he says, hopping from the bird to stand beside me. "The first time I came down here, I thought we were too deep, and that if we kept digging we'd fall right through the bottom of Internment itself."

I used to think something like this when I was little. I would watch worms wriggle into the dirt and I would imagine that at the bottom of the city there were clumps of worms falling away with pebbles and crumbs.

Judas hands me the lantern. "Here, hold this."

Holding up the light, I follow him to what appears to be a wooden crate and a series of ropes.

"Your betrothed carried you all the way down here in this thing, you know," he says. "Can't have been easy. It's hard maintaining balance when it's in motion."

"He's strong," I say.

"It would be a shame for his efforts to go to waste," Judas says. "It did seem like he wanted you to live."

He's so certain I'll get myself killed. I say nothing as I climb into the rickety makeshift lift. Judas tugs at one of the ropes, and as he pulls, we begin to ascend the tunnel in the earth.

The light catches the freckles of sweat on his throat. "What was she about?" I say.

He tugs at the rope with both hands. "Sorry?" he says.

"You said murdering the king isn't what Daphne was about," I say. "What was she like, then?"

He cants his head back, smiles ruefully at the darkness. "She was mad, for starters," he says. "Everything she stood for revolved around that."

I envy a dead girl for the look this boy gives her memory. "She must have been something to see," I say.

"She was going to do big things," Judas says. He doesn't sound at all sad about it. "I don't have her spark, but I'll have to do in her absence."

"My friend Pen says Daphne's essay was a bunch of whatnot. She says we need to keep our heads in the sky where they belong."

"Your friend Pen is afraid," he says.

It's hard to reconcile Pen being afraid of anything.

Judas goes on pulling the rope. "What kind of a name is 'Pen' anyway?" he asks. "No way it's on the naming list."

There is a list of approved names that is specific about spelling. Because of that, it isn't uncommon for people to adopt nicknames later on. There are no rules about those. "She doesn't like her real name," I say. "When we were in kinder year, there were three other Margarets in our class, and the instructor started calling her Pen because she always had coloring pens in her dress pockets. I suppose she preferred it after a while."

I peer over the edge of the crate; it's hard to see how high we are, and in the darkness I can just about see the metal slope of the bird. I can't tell if it actually looks like a bird. "And anyway, she isn't afraid," I say. "She just has a lot of faith in the way things are."

"That's the way the king would like it, to be sure," Judas says.

"Why? If he's so corrupt and he kills anyone who proves to be a nuisance, why wouldn't he just let us go soaring down to the ground and die?"

"Because he's the most afraid," Judas says. "He gets to play ruler over this floating rock and nobody challenges him. But if transport between Internment and the ground were easy, his ways would be challenged. He might be overthrown. You're only proving that point. You already want him dead, and you're just one person; imagine if everyone knew what he was doing. There'd be a riot."

"There shouldn't be a riot," I say. "He should die quietly, and in pain. He should have someone he's wronged standing in the doorway, watching to be sure he's dead. That person should be the last thing he sees."

"You know that his death will only mean the prince is crowned the next day," Judas says. "I don't believe he'll be any better."

"Then I'll murder the prince, too."

Judas makes a sound that could be a snicker, but by the time I hold the lantern to his face, his smirk is gone.

We reach the top of the tunnel and Judas goes about tying the ropes to keep the rickety crate in place. "You know I'd be a horrible person if I let you go through with this," he says. "Not to mention it'll be my head when everyone realizes you're gone."

"How do I open this?" I fumble with the wooden door overhead. Judas undoes a series of elaborate and rusty latches. With a hard shove, he throws the door up into the blackness and I'm hit with the smell of ash and something else I can't quite place.

"After you," he says cordially, taking the lantern from my fist.

There's a small ladder leading up to the opening, wobbly and rustier than the latches were. Flecks of copper dirt crumble under my feet. I'm still wearing my uniform, right down to the polished black shoes.

"Careful not to slip on the mold," Judas says, climbing up behind me. "All the moisture underground makes for unpleasantness. A lot of people think our lakes are replenished by the sky god, but spend some time underground and you'll come to favor the theory that we absorb water from the clouds."

Absorbing water from the clouds would make more sense than believing our lakes are a gift from the sky god. But when presented with the evidence, I see how much more terrifying it is to think we're on our own.

I cough on the ashes and crawl onto the gritty ground.

I'm back on the surface of Internment, but I don't know where. I can't see a thing because Judas has blown out the lantern.

"What'd you do that for?" I say.

"We can't let anyone know we're here," Judas says. "It'll look suspicious, a light escaping through the cracks."

I'm about to ask where we are, but then I can identify that other smell beneath all the ashes. It used to fill my brother's apartment whenever Alice was in the room. Flowers.

"We're in the flower shop," I gasp.

"Or what used to be the flower shop," Judas says. "The king didn't know exactly what we were up to, thankfully. But he knew we met here. He had the place burned down as a message to us, I'm sure."

Amy's face when I chased her down the street and she saw the fire takes on a whole new meaning now.

The train speeds by, and as the ground rumbles, I drop to my knees, fingertips dusting wilted petals and stems.

"This is home," I say to them.

"Look. Morgan." There's a rustling noise as Judas crouches beside me. "I don't know you very well, but based on our previous exchanges, you seem pretty . . . not stupid."

"I know I can't kill the king," I finally admit. "Thank you for letting me have the illusion as long as you did."

"No assassinations," he says. "And you know that you can't return home. So, short of that, what are you really after?"

"A message," I say.

"A message?"

"For Pen. Just to let her know that I'm okay. I could write something in our cavern with a rock; it could be as cryptic as it needs to be—she'll know I was there."

Judas hesitates. "It's dangerous."

"She would do it for me," I say. "She'd never leave without a good-bye. And don't tell me it isn't possible to sneak out there. You've had patrolmen looking for you for a long time and you've snuck around plenty."

"I'm not saying it isn't possible," he says. "But it's not safe."

"Lead the way," I say. "If I get caught, leave me behind."

"You don't believe I'll leave you behind," he says.

"Don't tell me what I believe," I say, standing. "You have no idea."

I think I hear a laugh on his breath as he moves past me.

"We can't use the front door," he says. "But there's a board that we can pry away from this window. It's brittle, so be careful not to break it. We have to put it back exactly."

He pries the board away from the window frame, and there's the light of the half-moon spilling into the alleyway. "After you," he says, whispering now. "But be quiet about it. I don't know where the patrolmen are."

We aren't very far from my apartment, and I know this section very well, but that doesn't stop it from feeling different now. I suppose I was hoping that I could get to the surface and it would all be like before. If I were to leave the alleyway and look to the right, I'd see the lights from my building and force myself not to think of my parents.

I would be a minute's walking distance from the train that would take me there.

But I don't look for my building. I make no movement toward the train. I watch Judas climb out beside me and secure the board back in place. He turns to me, a finger over his lips, then cants his head in the direction of the shadows beyond the street lanterns.

I follow him. Our footsteps are more silent than I would have thought possible.

I try not to pay attention to the cobbles, or the smell of the grass, or the chill in the air that always leads me to think it must be dusting on the ground. But I can't stop myself from thinking of how that frozen dust must look. Does it melt at the warm touch of human skin? The world must be so ethereal, all its cracked walkways and worn buildings covered by perfect white.

Judas moves expertly between the trees, and I do my best to follow in his footsteps. My brother said that some of the patrolmen were part of this secret plan to leave Internment, and now I wonder if the reason Judas hasn't been caught is because there are patrolmen on his side.

"What do we call this?" I whisper.

"Call what?" Judas says.

"This—plan. To leave Internment. Is it treason?"

He doesn't stop walking, all stealth, but he looks back. His lips are chapped and deep red when he smiles. "It's a rebellion."

I don't understand why my heart leaps onto my tongue. It's more than that mere word causing my skin to prickle, my cheeks to go warm. It's the way he said it. It's him, moving in the darkness, something pulling me to follow.

He stops walking and holds out his hand to keep me from taking another step. We're in sight of the cavern now, and I can see a figure kneeling at its mouth, head in hands.

"There's someone," he whispers.

"Pen!"

He tries to keep me from going forward, but I push past him, and by the time she's turned her head, Judas has disappeared into the shadows.

"Morgan? Morgan!" She runs and doesn't stop until she's crashed into me and I'm toppling backward. Her tears are smeared onto my face when her cheek brushes mine.

"Pen?" I say. She's sobbing, gripping at the back of my shirt. "Breathe," I say. "You're scaring me."

"You—" She chokes on a sob and draws back. "You're scared? What a thing to say. You had me thinking you were dead." She claps her hands against my cheeks, staring through the darkness, making sure it's really me. Her eyes reach mine and she loses what little composure she mustered, and she pulls me to her chest.

I've never seen her this way. Wouldn't have thought it possible.

"Don't cry, silly girl," I say. "I'm right here."

I bring her to sit at the mouth of the cavern with me, and after many quivering breaths, she tells me what happened. With all the sorrow and the chaos after the university student's death, the pharmacy was overflowing with orders for elixirs to calm the nerves. They were ill prepared for so much action, and some batches were improperly measured. At least a dozen deaths were reported from a tainted batch, my family among them. Lex, Alice, my parents—all of us.

So that's what they're telling everyone.

She smiles, wipes a tear from her cheek. "But you're okay. It was a mistake. I should have known better than to listen to my mother; she has one foot in a fantasy novel at all times. What really happened? Did you have to go to the hospital to get looked at? Like when Carmilla Tilmaker swallowed a dead bramble fly in kinder year."

What really happened?

Now it's my turn to be somber. I am too exhausted to cry. Is that normal? To be orphaned and not grasp the magnitude of such a word, let alone expend any emotion over it? "I was ill, but I'm okay now. Lex and Alice are fine."

She plays with a lock of my hair, waiting for me to go on.

"Pen?" I stare at her knees and mine. "What if there

were a way off this city, and I told you I was going to take it? Would you file to have me declared irrational?"

She doesn't answer. There's no way she could already know about the mechanical bird or the conspiracy or any of those things, but she knows me. She knows that something is coming.

"I can't stay here," I say. "I wasn't even supposed to come out, but I had to"—say good-bye—"see the stars again." I can't imagine they'll be this pretty from the ground. On the ground, the history book says, the humans have infinite land to fill with buildings; and the scopes show us that they make their own lights, and the stars mean nothing to them. But up here, we see them, as clear as lightbugs that float in the air around our heads.

Pen and I raise our heads and look at each other. "Come out from where?" she asks.

I listen for some sign that Judas is still nearby, but though I know he's watching me, he's silent. It's as though I can feel him willing me not to say another word about it.

And he needn't worry. I won't tell. But it isn't to protect the metal bird or the rebellion. It's because of what she said that night on the train platform. She told me I needed to stop thinking about the ground. She said that she didn't want to know what was beyond Internment.

We aren't the greatest things to exist. I can't believe that. I won't believe that.

This is her home. I can't take it away from her. Instead, all I can do is stare at her—this lovely, lovely girl who might have been nobility in another time with that hair and those eyes. If I never see her again after this moment, I'll have enough memories of her to carry for every day of the rest of my life. But no matter how vivid those memories, they will all end here, now, her eyes glimmering in the starlight, and the feel of the blade pressed to my hip.

I won't even get to see her wedding, I realize. She'll have so many years to float in the sky, and my days here are coming to an end.

"I have to leave now," I say.

She says, "Where are you going?"

"To murder the king," I say. I know it isn't possible, but I just want to know how it feels to say the words out loud. They feel perfect. My blood swirls and swirls with delicious warmth at the fantasy of it. "I'm going to creep into the clock tower," I say, "and climb every last stair until I get up to the king's apartment. I'm going to sneak into his bedroom while he's sleeping and cut open his throat. I think that's how I'll do it. I'd like that."

Pen would laugh at the absurdity on a normal day, but she's looking into my eyes.

"Morgan—" She grips my arm, stands, and tugs me into the shadow of heavy leaves as though to protect me from what I've said. "You can't be blurting out things like that right now. It's treason. What if someone hears?"

"Nobody is listening," I say. "Nobody ever listens to us. We're all milling around pretending that what we do is important, that *we're* important, but the king will do away with anyone he'd like."

There's a bright moon tonight, split to pieces by branches. It's an organ with veins and arteries. A non-beating heart. If there's a god at all, he's dead in his sky.

Pen holds my face in her hands. Her thumb brushes at my cheek over and over. "This isn't like you at all," she says. "What's happened?"

I've said ugly things, but she doesn't flinch.

"You asked what really happened," I say. "My parents are dead."

I stare at her collarbone that's framed with lace, the hollow of her throat, her shoulders that rise with the weight of her next breath. We're fragile things. Our bones show through our skin. What would any god want with us?

Some sound escapes her lips, but I can't comprehend it. All I know for sure is that I have to leave. I can't face her like this. "I've said too much," I say, and take a step away. I'm just about to run, when she grabs my wrist. I struggle. For the first time in my life I struggle to get away from her, but she's too strong for it. I pull with all I've got, and her shoes dig into the earth, her legs don't even move. She's rooted, hardly a grunt for her efforts.

All the fight goes out of me. She lets go only when she's sure I won't run.

"They're dead," I say, and sink into the dirt. She kneels beside me.

When her mother became addicted to tonic, Pen was the victim of too many well wishes and sympathies. She has told me before that she's had her fill of them for a lifetime no matter the tragedy, and that holds true. She says nothing.

"I can't tell you the rest," I say. "I would if the whole story belonged to me, but it isn't all mine to tell. That's the only part that matters to me, anyway. They're dead, and I can't stay. This all sounds so incredible that I wouldn't expect you to believe it."

"I believe you," she says.

Of course she does. She's out of her mind, the only girl left in the academy who'd still want to have anything to do with me. We're the same sort. We always have been.

As I'm rising to a stand, there's a stab of pain in the side of my neck, and I can't move a muscle. The dart that's just hit Pen's shoulder is the only explanation. We've just been attacked. Something moves in the trees, and I'm falling back into someone's waiting arms.

23

*My grandmother succumbed to the sun disease long
before her dispatch date. Before she was to be given
to the tributary, my sister and I were brought in to see
her. I had seen death in my medical texts before, but
never up close. Her body was silent and screaming at
once, the same question over and over: Is this it?*

—"Intangible Gods," Daphne Leander, Year Ten

You're a lousy shot," the girl huffs. "You
almost completely missed her neck. Papa would have never
let you hear the end of that."

"I am doing our father a favor, might I remind you,"
the boy says, grunting as he hoists Pen over his shoulder.
"We've just done more work in five seconds than his incom-
petent staff has done since that girl's murder. Honestly.
Letting fugitives run about this city like it's a giant floating
tea party."

"I've always loved your analogies, Brother," the girl
says as she drags me from under the arms. I recognize her

long hair, half of it braided around her head like a crown. The girls in my class have all tried to imitate that braid, with little success. It can be worn this perfectly by only one girl—the king's only daughter, Princess Celeste.

The boy holding Pen can only be Prince Azure, then. Not that I can move to look at him. With some effort I'm just able to blink.

"He'd thank us if he knew," the prince says.

The princess smells like cinnamon and something else, something I'd find pleasant if it were wafting out of a teahouse or spilling from one of the many bottles on Alice's dresser. Now it just nauseates me.

Blackness is clouding my vision, and I fight it. I've already been poisoned once; I refuse to succumb so easily again.

I cling to the words the prince and princess are saying. They provide no answers, but they're keeping me conscious.

"Mine is heavy," he complains.

"Weakling," she says. "It'll be a wonder to me when you inherit this city."

"I don't see you carrying yours over your shoulder," he says.

"About that, you should be more careful," the princess says. "Maybe she's our prisoner, but that's no reason to destroy such a lovely dress."

Despite the circumstances, all the girls of Internment would hate Pen if they knew that her dress had caught the attention of the princess. It was among the many presents from Pen's mother. "Compensation for inebriation," Pen calls them.

"I don't know why we need both of them, anyway," the prince says. "The patrolman's daughter is the one we need."

"Can't leave witnesses," the princess says. "So I'll thank you to quit moaning about it."

Can't leave witnesses. I hope they've overlooked Judas, but there's no indication that he's nearby. With horror I wonder if he returned to the flower shop to give Pen and me a chance to say our good-byes. He might have no idea what just happened.

My heart should be pounding—I'm frightened enough— but my body won't work. Perhaps the dart was meant to render me unconscious and I'm fighting it somehow. Or perhaps they want me to have my awareness when they torture me.

I have plenty of time to worry and speculate. The prince and princess trudge through the woods for what feels like forever, arguing the whole way.

"Would you be quiet now?" the princess says. There's a heavy thud, and then the prince is flinging me into a wagon beside Pen. Just as he's about to cover us with a large cloth, he stoops forward and brings his face close to mine. His breath is cinnamon, too. His eyes are clear, reflecting two perfect little skies full of stars.

"I think your dart killed her," he says. "Her eyes are open."

I will myself not to blink.

The princess brings herself close, her white rabbit fur cuffs sweeping across my forehead as she clears the hair from my face. Only the king's family wears white fur, because they spend most all their time indoors, and it's supposed to symbolize their purity of spirit. The rest of us would never be able to keep it clean.

The princess's hand hovers over my mouth for a few seconds. "No, she's definitely breathing."

"It's creepy," the prince says. "It's like she's staring at me."

I feel the fur cuff against my face again as the princess brushes my eyelids closed. "There. Happy?"

"Yes. Lovely."

There's darkness, the weight of the cloth covering me completely.

We're taken a bit farther, and then a voice says, "Your mother has asked that you not hunt in your best clothes."

"We're sorry," the prince says. "We've caught a deer this time, though. We'll send it to the food factory once Celeste has sawed the antlers for her jewelry collection."

Meat is a rare delicacy, mostly reserved for the festival of stars, and hunting is restricted to those who work in the food factories, but apparently those rules don't apply to the king's family.

There are the sounds of doors closing. I can feel Pen's limp body jostling against mine as the wagon is steered through a series of turns, and then I think we're being hoisted down a flight of stairs. I try to open my eyes, but my eyelids are heavy. The prince and princess are whispering now, and their words are lost to the throb of blood in my ears. I'm still fighting for consciousness when the wagon goes still. There's the smell much like the one underground when Judas led me outside from the metal bird.

"Do you think it would be too mean of me to steal that dress?" the princess says. "It's so lovely."

"You're ridiculous," the prince says. "You can't leave her naked."

"You should be thanking me for the opportunity," she says.

He says something in return, but it's as though they're talking underwater. The words make no sense. The blackness takes over.

It's the chime that wakes me, so close that the sound is caught between my teeth. Internment feels as though it's shaking.

Another chime. Another.

"It's three o'clock," Pen says.

I open my eyes to the light of a single candle flickering in a sconce on the stone wall. Pen is slumped under it, arms behind her back, staring where the light doesn't reach.

"We're in the clock tower," she adds. "In case you haven't guessed."

She doesn't sound angry or frightened, just exhausted.

I realize my hands are tied behind my back with twine, but I manage to push myself up against the wall.

"Can you reach against my hip?" I say. "There's a knife. I don't know if it'll be enough to cut through the twine, but it's something."

"Oh, good," Pen says, attempting to reach it. "If Princess Whatsit unbuttons a single button of this dress, I'll cut her face."

"You heard them talking as they dragged us in here, too?" I ask.

"Yes, but I couldn't move." She manages to dislodge the knife from my waistband. There's a clatter as it hits the floor when it falls from the cloth. "Hold still."

"I'm sorry about all this," I say.

"We're both having a bad night," she says. "And now the king's freak children are probably going to try to murder us and hang our heads on their walls. What else could we expect from a girl who collects deer antlers?"

I think of Basil, warm and asleep in the metal bird. It seems an act of insanity that I left him. I'd give anything to crawl back under that blanket.

Footsteps echo somewhere in the blackness. Pen drops the knife, and she isn't able to hide it before there's the creaking of a door.

"I knew we should have checked for weapons," the princess whispers angrily. "See that? They've got a knife."

"How was I supposed to know schoolgirls walk

around with hidden knives?" the prince says.

"No matter," the princess says, swishing her hair behind her shoulders. She strides over to us, stomps her glittering white slipper onto the knife, and slides the knife toward her. "I'll be keeping this," she says to us. "Can't have you trying to kill us."

"You wouldn't have to worry," Pen snaps, "if you hadn't kidnapped us and tied us up like wild animals."

"You aren't fooling me," the princess says, walking backward toward her brother. She gestures to me with the knife. "You threatened to kill our father."

"We heard you," the prince says. "You said you'd cut his throat."

They're both nodding importantly.

"Your father killed my parents," I say, unaware until I've spoken them that I have the bravery for words. I always thought that if I ever spoke to the famous duo, I'd be nervous. They seemed so unattainable on the broadcasts and in their images. But up close, they're only people. Dressed in frilly pajamas with lace at the cuffs and collars, but people nonetheless. I can't remember why I thought there was anything to fuss over.

"Your family committed treason," the prince says.

"How would you know?" I say. "How would you know anything that happens on Internment? You never come down from your clock tower. Do you know what treason even is?"

"Of course they don't," Pen says, trying to soothe me.

"They're idiotic, Morgan; you can't expect them to understand what they've done."

"Fancy words," the princess says, "considering we've got weapons and you've got your hands behind your backs. We were going to bring you something to eat, but forget it now."

"Just kill us if that's what you're going to do," Pen says.

The princess seems to be considering it. But she lowers the knife and smoothes her nightgown against her hips. "We're still deciding whether or not to tell our father we've captured you, Morgan Stockhour. He's got patrolmen out looking for you, you know, and they've been ordered to bring you to him. Alive or dead." She sings those last three words, twirling her long hair around the knife.

"And it never occurred to you that that's insane?" Pen says. "The king giving orders to kill a harmless girl your own age? Killing her family and then chasing after her — that's good leadership to you?"

The princess is looking at my eyes, and maybe Pen's words have reached her, but then she blinks them away and covers her mouth with her hair as she murmurs something to her brother. He stares at us. Despite his round face, there's fierceness in his eyes that are framed by brows a shade too dark for his hair.

It's too much, that stare. I feel everything crashing down, as though Internment has fallen from the sky and broken into pieces on top of me.

I'll never see my parents again. I'll never go home again. Instead I'm staring at the eyes of this heartless boy. He is a symbol of the city that has betrayed me.

Pen sees the change in me. She brings her mouth close to my ear. "Don't do it," she whispers. "Don't you cry in front of them. Dig your nails into your palm. Hold your breath."

I do what she says, and it helps.

The prince covers his mouth and says something to his sister. I focus on the pain in my palms.

"We've decided to let you live," the princess says. "For now. If we killed you tonight, it would be an awful lot of blood; we'd be up until dawn with the cleaning, and we have lessons in the morning."

"But we aren't going to untie you," the prince says. "It's in your interest to be quiet."

"You don't want someone else to find you," the princess says.

"They won't be as generous as us," the prince says.

It makes my mind spin, the way they together seem to be speaking one long sentence.

They back into the darkness until I can't see them, and then there's the sound of a door closing and latches being latched.

I unclench my fists.

"You were very brave," Pen says, allowing me to drop my head in her lap. I'm free at last to cry, but the tears won't come.

"What a mess I've made of things," I say. "For both of us."

"I've spent the entire day thinking you were dead," she says. "If the price of having you alive is being locked in the clock tower, I cheerfully accept. I didn't have anything better to do with my night."

And despite that, I can smell no trace of tonic. She endured the news of my supposed death while sober. I'm proud of her for that.

"Maybe they'll let you go when they realize you have nothing to do with all of this," I say.

"You don't have anything to do with this either," Pen says. "They're warped. You don't deserve this any more than I do."

I close my eyes.

"Was that true?" she asks. "What you said about the king killing your parents?"

"He had a hand in it," I say. "My parents and Lex—they knew things they weren't supposed to know. They were planning something he didn't like."

"Whatever it was, it can't have been worth murdering them over," Pen says.

Struggling without the use of my hands, I sit up and look at her. "They were planning to leave Internment. I don't mean jumping over the edge, but actually flying away properly."

She stares at me, trying to decide what to make of this, and then she laughs with uncertainty. "And the king believed them? Lots of people fantasize about that."

"They built a machine," I say. "It's hidden where the king can't find it, so he's tried to stop the plans they laid out. Those deaths today weren't because of tainted pharmaceuticals."

I wasn't going to tell her all of this, but now that she's trapped here with me, she deserves to know what for.

"It's like Micah and the boat of stars," she says, speaking of a chapter in *The History of Internment*. "When he saw a constellation in the shape of a boat, he thought the sky god was speaking to him, so he built one just like it."

Pen knows all of the chapters. She can make them a parable for any situation, she's so adamant about her faith.

"You remember how that story ended," she says.

I do. Micah took his boat to the edge of Internment, and when he tried to sail into the sky, the boat splintered apart, impaling him. He became the first jumper. "I don't think this is like that," I say.

"Nobody can leave," Pen says. "The sky god won't allow it. The king knows that. I don't understand why he would kill anyone for trying when they'll only see for themselves."

"Maybe that's wrong," I say. "Maybe there is a way off Internment, and we're right on the verge of discovering it, and it frightens him."

She looks sympathetic. "I know how much you want to believe that, especially now, but—"

"I *wanted* to believe it before," I say. "Now I have no choice. My parents died for this, and I have to see it through. Even if it ends like Micah and the boat of stars."

If I ever get out of here, that is.

We don't speak after that.

The walls shake as the clock chimes the fourth hour.

24

So many of the things I've always wanted are the things I've been taught to fear.
— "Intangible Gods," Daphne Leander, Year Ten

The main floor of the clock tower holds the affairs office, where neighbor disputes are settled, weekly wages are collected, and couples apply for marriage certificates and enter the birth queue—things of that nature. And in the main hallway, right by the entrance, there's a machine on the wall where patrolmen enter their ID numbers at the start and end of their shifts.

There's also a room full of courthouse paperwork, some of which would be used in Judas's trial if they knew where to find him.

At the end of the seventh chime, I'm thinking of all the patrolmen reporting for duty, my father not among them.

When I was little, my father would bring Lex and me along to collect his and my mother's wages sometimes. He would talk to the woman who sat at the lockboxes, and Lex would let me stand on his shoes so I could peer over the counter. I liked being there. I liked when my father told the woman our last name and she would search for our envelopes in the box marked *S*. *S* for "Stockhour," because that name meant we all belonged together.

I never would have imagined that the clock tower could be such a miserable place, underneath all that.

The candle over our heads is nearly extinguished. Pen is eyeing it.

"A shame stones don't catch fire," Pen says, gnawing at the twine binding her wrists. After much struggling, she was able to curl herself into a ball and maneuver her arms in front of her. "I'd burn this whole place down."

Wearily, I try to imagine Internment without the clock tower, and find I'm having trouble picturing the city at all. All I can see is the metal bird.

Basil must be worried sick. And Alice, too. Lex will be angry; I'm always screwing things up—that's what he says.

He can be as angry as he pleases. I'm angry with him, too. And my parents, for that matter, for never saying a word to me about the metal bird or the things happening in the city. They were trying to protect me, I know that, but every good memory feels like a lie now.

Pen's hands are shaking. She bites angrily at the twine, but if it has any effect, it's minimal. She growls. "I'm going to need a water room soon," she says.

I've needed one since the chimes marked the sixth hour, but I don't say that. I have no right to complain when I'm the one who caused this.

Pen tries grating the twine against the heel of her shoe. The water room has been her only complaint. No mention of her own parents, who are undoubtedly worried by now. Her needy mother, and her stern father. I think she's trying to spare my feelings.

After a few minutes, she gives her arms a rest and leans back. "Thomas is probably writing bad poetry about my absence by now," she says. "'My lovely Pen / Disappeared from maps / Eaten by a deer perhaps.'"

Neither of us is in the mood for laughing at her joke.

"What do you suppose he thinks happened to me?" she says. "Let's play twenty guesses."

This is a game we made up when we were children. It began one day when I lost my shoe playing dress-up at her house and we began guessing what had happened to it, each guess more absurd than the one before.

"He thinks you really were eaten by a deer," I say.

"He thinks my mother swallowed me whole like one of her pills," she says.

The candle goes out.

My eyes struggle to adapt, but the blackness is perfect. Pen pushes herself against me and fits her head into the curve of my neck. Her curls have gone frizzy and flat, but they still smell lovely, as though to defy the musty air of this room.

"He thinks you built a machine and sailed into the sky," I say.

"That's a good one," she says. "Let's stop now. I'll never top that."

Neither of us speaks after that. We stay close together, tensing at each sound we think we hear. Waiting.

We hear the latches sometime after the ninth chime. Pen draws a sharp breath, waking from a frail sleep.

The door opens with a slow creak, candlelight stealing through the gap.

Princess Celeste is alone this time, holding a silver tray in one hand and a flame lantern in the other.

"I've brought grapes," she says, setting the tray on the ground and nudging it toward us. "And I figured the candle would have gone out, so I've got a new one.

Pen and I say nothing. The princess raises her eyebrow. I think she was expecting us to move away from the sconce so she could replace the candle. When we don't, she takes several tentative steps toward us, touches the new candle to the flame in her lantern, and then sets the candle into place.

She jumps away from us as though we'll bite. Her skirt swishes against my knee and for a moment I feel the cool purple silk. She's wearing a plum uniform; plum is a game that involves rackets spun with twine and a ball the size of a plum that gets hit back and forth.

Now I realize that the twine binding our wrists is probably from a plum racket.

She stands back, staring at us. When she puts her hands on her hips, I see the perspiration marks under her arms, indicating she has just finished a rigorous game.

"Well?" she says. "Aren't you going to eat?"

"We don't want your poison grapes, thanks," Pen says. "But a water room would be nice."

The princess gnaws her lip, cants her head. "Oh, a water room. I hadn't thought about that. I've never had hostages before. I kept a rabbit hidden in my bathtub for a while, once. It just went where it pleased."

"We aren't rabbits," Pen says.

"Right. Well, if you eat the grapes, you can use the bowl to—you know."

I try to see what's beyond the semi-open door. I can see no daylight and no lanterns, nothing but blackness. We're hidden so deep in the clock tower that there aren't even lights to guide the way.

Basil must be frantic. Being unable to reach him is impossibly frustrating. I can only hope he doesn't think the king has succeeded in murdering me. Not that being right under the king's nose is much safer.

The prince enters, out of breath, in his plum uniform, a ring of sweat around the collar. "I told you not to come here without me," he says, grabbing the princess by the arm and pulling her away from us. "What if they overpowered you?"

"And what would you have done to protect me?" she says. "You can't even shoot a dart properly."

They turn their backs to us, talking softly, stealing glances at us over their shoulders. Pen squirms uncomfortably. I don't know how she can manage it; I'm so stiff that even the thought of moving is painful.

"You," the prince says, turning to Pen. "Come with me."

I don't know what this means. I don't know if he's going

to let her go or try to kill her. She must be thinking the same thing because she doesn't move, instead looks at me.

The prince grabs her arm, yanks her to her feet. Her legs have gone numb and she stumbles. "It would be unwise to scream, either of you," he says. "It's an old building. Voices carry. We're the nicest people you're likely to encounter. Maybe you were clever enough to get your hands in front of you, but you're no match for the people a scream will summon."

Pen jerks away when he tries to touch her hair. Her lips are pursed and I think she's going to scream just because she was told not to, but she doesn't. As he drags her toward the door, she looks back at me and mouths, "I'll be fine."

The door closes. My heart pounds. Breathing gets harder. The princess stands at an arm's length, twisting her hips, her skirt swishing over her knees.

"He took her to the water room," she says. "The only danger she's in would come from the filth of that place. It's positively archaic. It used to all be holdings for prisoners down here."

"It still is," I say.

She smirks. "True, isn't it?" she says.

I don't understand why she's trying to make conversation. The king's children are isolated from society and have never set foot in the academy unless it was to make a political appearance with their father, but is she so lonely as to try to make friends with me?

"We haven't decided what to do with you yet," she says. "But . . ."

She hesitates. After a moment, she removes the bowl of grapes and kneels on the tray like it's a seat. She doesn't want to sully her clothes.

"Our father warned us about your family," she says. "Your brother is a jumper."

"There are plenty of families with jumpers," I say.

"Not families that know the way to the ground."

"There is no way to the ground," I say.

"Liar," she says. "There's a machine that can do it. My father is going to find it, you know. He's going to destroy it, because that's what the god of the sky would have him do. And he'll destroy your brother and everyone else involved with it, too, for treason."

"Then what do you need me for?" I say, not hiding my anger. "Why kill anyone if he's just going to destroy the machine?"

"So you admit it." She's smiling, her teeth perfect and white. "There really is a machine that could bring us to the ground safely."

"I didn't say that."

"There is. You've seen it. You know."

Her eyes brighten, but there's nothing maniacal or cruel in them. Worse, there's hope.

25

There's majesty in the ability to create. Look at an art-
ist's hands—sullied by colors. Powerful and strange.
— "Intangible Gods," Daphne Leander, Year Ten

Pen returns with complaints that the
prince was trying to spy on her while she used the water
room, but she's otherwise unscathed.

"If that isn't the silliest thing I've heard today," the princess says, helping me to my feet. "If it were a *boy* in the
water room, maybe he'd spy then."

"Leste!" he cries.

"You're more interested in my betrothed than I am,"
she says. "His cheekbones— Honestly." She takes the lantern from her brother and pushes me toward the door. For
the first time, I'm able to see the stairwell that brought me
here, but it's all I'm able to see on the way to and from
the water room, which isn't even a fitting name because it
has no running water and is little more than a hole in the
ground.

But I'm still thinking about the prince being attracted to his sister's betrothed. Could the decision makers have done something wrong? Is his own betrothed not appealing to him? Is he irrational? The prince isn't the first to be attracted to his own gender; although it isn't talked about, I remember my brother denouncing the serum and the surgery purported to treat this kind of attraction. Even before Alice's forced termination procedure, there were elements of medicine that he despised.

"Oh, your wrists are so red," the princess says as she's guiding me back to my prison. "The twine will do that, I suppose."

I say nothing. I can hear footfalls above me, and doors closing and opening. People going about their business, believing I'm dead because of tainted pharmaceuticals. Unaware of the king's sour practices, the corruption in his reign, and the absurdity of his children.

All of it leaves an ache in my chest. I consider running. The princess doesn't appear to be armed. But my hands are still tied, and I can't leave Pen besides.

My only hope is that Judas saw us being taken. And even if he doesn't care enough to pursue us himself, he'll tell Basil. Basil will come for me. The alternative would be living the rest of his life alone. I would try to save him if it were the other way around.

Though I'd be sour that he left me while I was sleeping, without so much as a note of explanation, which is what I did to him.

I wasn't thinking rationally when I left him. Looking back, it's all a haze of grief that overtook me. It made the craziest ideas seem possible. It made logic as far away as a beige patch of the ground.

The princess stops us walking. She holds the lantern up between us, and she looks at me with the eyes of all the princesses and queens in the history book. Eyes as old as Judas the Hero and Micah's boat of stars. She is ancient and profound, and she has Internment fascinated, copying her hair and her clothing in an attempt to understand.

She looks at me now the way the whole floating city looks at her—hoping for some sort of answer she'll never have.

"You can tell me," she whispers. "What does the machine look like? Smell like?"

"Smell?" I say.

"I want a full sensory experience," she says. "I imagine it smells like freshly printed paper and old coins."

It smells like mold, though old coins isn't inaccurate. But I don't tell her this.

"There is no machine," I say.

"Last night when you were talking to your friend, you said 'I wasn't even supposed to come out.' Why would you have said that if you hadn't been hiding in the machine?"

"I was being general," I say. "It wasn't safe for me to be outside, and clearly we can both see why."

She truly doesn't understand. She spends her life hidden away in this tower with her private instructors and her plum uniform and her braided crown. Her mother and father are alive. I hate her for that. I hate her in a way no princess in a tower can ever understand.

"There is no machine," I repeat. She can rot here.

The hope hasn't left her face. I don't know what it will take to kill it, but if I'm going to be trapped here, I'll have time to think up ways.

The door opens and the prince says, "What is taking so long?" He's still angry about his sister's jab.

I slump back to the ground beside Pen, hoping our captors hear the rumble in our stomachs. We don't touch the grapes.

If we refuse to eat, maybe it'll make them nervous and they'll consider letting us go so we don't starve to death. Though, given their oblivion, it isn't likely they'll notice.

The clock begins its set of ten chimes. "We should just kill the blond one," the prince says, perhaps thinking we won't hear him over the noise.

"Don't be a dolt," the princess says. "She might know something, too."

Pen leans closer to me. "If they're going to kill me," she whispers, "I wish they'd be quicker about it."

"Don't say that."

The prince makes a gesture to his sister like slicing a throat, and though Pen's tactic has been to appear unfazed, this is more than I can stand.

"There is a machine," I say, just as the tenth chime is finishing.

The duo looks at me, stunned.

"I've seen it, that's true. I've ridden in it. I've been to the ground and back."

The prince is the first to break his hopeful gaze. He narrows his eyes. "Impossible."

"More than once," I say. "Lots of us have gone."

"Half a dozen trips, at least," Pen says, playing along. "I can't believe it's gone on under your noses and you never suspected a thing. I'd have thought you'd be more clever than that."

"We're clever," the prince snaps.

"Very," the princess agrees. "I knew the whole while, didn't I, Az? I've said it plenty of times."

"You can't be the children of the king and be stupid, you know," the prince says.

"Clearly," Pen mutters through gritted teeth.

The prince and princess turn their backs to us in tandem, begin speaking quietly to each other, glancing back at us more than once.

"Where is it, then?" the princess finally asks. "The machine."

"That is the question," I say, looking right into her eyes. "Isn't it?"

"We don't disclose our secrets to kidnappers," Pen says.

The princess opens her mouth, but a voice echoes down the stairwell. "Celeste? Azure? You aren't playing down there, are you? You know what your mother said."

The prince looks to his sister, panicked. "Our instructor

can't know we're down here," he says. "She can't find them." He points at us.

"We'll go out the other way," she assures him. "We'll make like we were outside." She points to me as she's backing out of the room. "This isn't over, you. I'll have my answers if I have to crack your head open and take them out myself."

She's still pointing when she closes the door.

"She has a way with words," Pen says, now that we're alone. "A bit stupid, though. Does she not realize secrets aren't actual things sitting in our heads?"

But I'm not thinking about the princess now. I'm thinking about that voice that called down the stairwell.

"That was the specialist," I say. "The woman the prince called their instructor—that was Ms. Harlan."

"Are you sure?" Pen says. "You're probably dehydrated. Maybe you're imagining things."

"No," I say. "You don't forget the voice of the woman who poisoned you."

"Yesterday you were just a sweet schoolgirl," Pen says. "Now everyone wants you dead. I'm a little jealous of your intrigue."

"They want you dead, too," I remind her.

"You think?" She beams.

I see where the twine has made her skin raw, and despite her verve I know she's as miserable as I am, and as frightened. It's selfish of me, but I'm glad I'm not alone.

"Why did we tell them there's a machine?" she says.

"They won't kill us if they want our secrets. I was hoping to buy us some time."

After a pause, she says, "Morgan?"

"Yes?"

"What are we waiting for? We can't stay at the mercy of those two. They're insane."

"Basil will come for me," I say. "Maybe Judas, too. He was hiding when we were taken. He must have seen."

"No," she says. "We're on our own."

"He'll come," I say, forcing myself to believe it.

"He won't know where to find us. Morgan, look at me. Nobody is going to come. We are on our own."

I want to argue, but I know she's right. I think I've always known. Basil will try, and maybe Judas will try. But they won't know to find us in this strange dungeon and they won't be able to reach us. We have to free ourselves. "Then what do we do?"

"I say we knock them out," Pen says. "Push them, maybe. Or I could get behind one of them and use this twine to strangle them."

There are many ways this could go wrong, but is it any more dangerous than waiting? With dread, I accept that her plan makes more sense than mine.

"Nothing that violent," I say. "We can't just lunge blindly at them. We have to think it out. For starters, we have to make sure they don't have any syringes or blades on them."

"The prince might," she admits. "He seems the paranoid sort. Then again, the princess likes to be in control of situations. She probably still has your knife."

She sees my crestfallen expression and hooks her arms over my shoulders and brings her forehead to mine. "Let's make a promise," she says. "To be brave and go for it. We can plan it as best we can, and if it goes horribly wrong, we keep trying until we're free or they stab us. Maybe even after they stab us."

"If we can keep moving, we move," I say.

"And not leave each other behind," she says.

"I promise."

"I promise, too."

And in hushed voices we begin planning our mutiny.

It will have to be when they come to check on us next, likely tonight, we decide. We'll ambush them and try to buy a few seconds so we can lock them in while we make our escape.

The princess mentioned a back entrance so that their instructor wouldn't see them sneak outside. We'll look for that first, and if we can't find it, we'll hope the main floor of the clock tower is empty after dark. There may be patrolmen; we'll have to risk it. My brother and Judas made it seem as though many of the patrolmen are secretly opposing the king; it's too much to hope that we'll encounter some of them and they'll let us go.

Pen continues trying to saw through the twine that binds her wrists. But even when she finds a bit of protruding brick to work with, it does no good. "Definitely good stuff for strangling," she says. "I would say I could lure the prince over to me by flirting, but it doesn't seem that would work, does it? Given his preference."

"We can't kill them," I say.

"What's this from the girl who wanted to slit the king's throat?" she says.

"I wasn't thinking clearly then," I say.

"And now the dehydration and lack of sleep have enlightened you?"

"No," I say, and the firmness of my tone makes her stop sawing at the twine and look at me.

I hate the prince and princess—I hate the whole family more than I would have thought possible—but I don't want to do to them what they've done to me. "I don't want to be the reason anyone is dead, Pen, and I doubt you do, either."

She stares at me a moment longer before looking away, mouthing words I don't catch.

Then she says, "I make no promises," but I know it's her way of agreeing to my demand.

She goes back to working at the twine, trying to loosen the knots around my wrists now. But it's no use. Maybe the prince and princess have never had a hostage before, but they tie knots with precision, and the more we struggle, the tighter the restraints become. Pen finally gives up when I begin to bleed, and instead she helps me draw my knees to my chest, making me small enough to loop my arms under me until my hands are in my lap. For the first time I see the damage to my skin, swollen and red and oozing. Probably infected. Basil would be angry to see what they've done to me. Angry like when he found out about Ms. Harlan prodding into my head.

He's so careful with me, always.

When I return to him, he'll pull me into his arms. Sweep me up. I'll close my eyes.

I feel his chest against mine. Feel his breath on my neck. My skin swells with little bumps. And then the memory of him is gone. I said that I wouldn't kill them, but I know that I would. To return to him, I would.

By the seventh chime in the evening, Pen and I make the difficult decision to blow out the candle. We'll hide on opposite sides of the door and we'll use the darkness to ambush the prince and princess when they bring us a new candle.

Pen stands by the flickering light, staring into the flame before smiling at me. "One last look before it's lights-out," she says. "If this goes wrong, we'll never get a good look at each other again."

I narrow my eyes. "You always know what to say."

She winks.

I'm standing by the door, arms out to help guide her back to me in the blackness.

"You really are a beautiful girl," she tells me. "I never tell you that. I'm always fussing about your hair and things. But you are."

I feel the blush burning across my cheeks. "You too," I say.

She takes a deep breath, exhales, and we're in the dark.

We settle on opposite sides of the door, and I press my back to the wall. My heart is pounding and I feel myself shuddering with it. This isn't real darkness. This is unnatural, devoid of clean air and stars. The moon wouldn't be able to find us here.

We don't talk for the longest time, listening, waiting, knowing it could be hours before it's time to strike. The clock strikes eight. Then later, nine.

I hear a strange rustling sound, like stone grinding against stone. It startles me before I realize the sound is coming from Pen, not the stairwell. "What are you doing?" I whisper.

"Nothing."

"I thought I heard—"

"Shh!" she says.

There's a noise from the other side of the door. Whispers. A little laugh. Faint gold threads of light appear through the wooden door. I hear the locks being unlatched, and just as Pen and I planned, I scoot away from the door so that I'll still be in the shadows when the prince and princess step inside. The plan is to startle them and try to knock them down, then rush outside and lock them in. I've gone over and over it for what has surely been hours, hoping it will be as easy as it seems in my head.

The door creaks open, and Princess Celeste and Prince Azure cease their whispering when they realize we aren't on the floor where they left us. The prince holds the candle up, and he doesn't see that Pen is behind him. The princess does, though, and she draws a breath to speak, and I know it's time. I spring forward and hook my arms around her, pin her against me.

She struggles wildly, but the twine that binds my wrists is keeping her in place. "No." Her voice is desperate. "Please, no."

I'm not going to hurt her. I'm just about to tell her that, when I realize she isn't paying me any mind—the words are for Pen, whose eyes are dangerous in the candlelight. She's got something in her hands and she's raising it above the prince's head, and now I understand what that noise was. She discovered that a rather large stone had come loose in the wall.

"Don't!" Princess Celeste and I cry out at the same time.

We're silenced by the sound of the stone colliding with Prince Azure's skull.

He crumples, and the candle flies from his hand.

His sister explodes into a scream, and both of our bodies shake with it. Panicked, I let her go and she drops to his side. "Azure!" she's saying. "Az!"

In the next instant her lacy sleeves are red with his blood. He doesn't move. She lowers her ear to his chest, and her long, long hair wraps over her brother's still form like a shield. Her braided crown holds firm, as if to insist that she is something great, even on the floor, even like this.

The candle rolls along the stones, and just as Pen is reaching for it, it goes out, leaving us in darkness.

26

*Time was our very first king. We all live our lives to
the aggressive ticking of the clock. We don't question
that our lives are a grid of seconds; even our pulses
oblige. No succeeding king can hope to hold this kind
of power.*

— *"Intangible Gods," Daphne Leander, Year Ten*

Pen pushes me through the door. I can't see a
thing, and I rush to keep up with her. We pick a direction
that I think will take us toward the water room, and we run.

The princess is screaming and screaming. The stairwell
is alive with footsteps. We stop and spin around to see the
candlelight coming toward us.

We crouch behind a crumbling slab of wall, likely the
remains of an old prison cell, and force ourselves to quiet
our gasping. My lungs burn. My heart is racing. I'm furious. As Pen presses herself against me, I'm remembering
what she said.

I make no promises.

How could you?

From where we're perched, I can see the patrolmen rushing to the prince's aide. I think it's too late for him. The princess is sobbing that he needs a medic. Moments before she opened the door, she and her brother had been giggling.

One of the patrolmen leads her to the doorway and grabs her shoulders, trying to get something coherent out of her. "Who did this?" he asks several times before she seems to hear him.

Her arms are folded and she's staring at Prince Azure when she swallows and says, "Men. They—they stole us from our beds and dragged us down here."

"Men? What did they look like?"

"It doesn't matter; they've gone." She pushes his hands from her shoulders. "The heir to the throne is going to bleed to death if you don't help him. Do you want that to happen on your watch?"

Murmurs and footsteps. Some of the patrolmen rush upstairs; there are too many of them to count, and my stomach is sick when I realize that Pen planned it this way. A scream from Princess Celeste would summon every patrolman on duty. All we need to do is wait them out.

Medics hurry down from upstairs, carrying a cushioned board for the prince's body. And there's someone else, too. King Furlow himself, his thin white hair disheveled, his white robe open, revealing his doughy stomach. To see him in such a state is to see Internment for the soil. He is as ordinary as the rest of us. No greatness to him at all.

And I know Judas was right—I wouldn't have been able to kill him.

This is the man who had my parents murdered. But I take no satisfaction from the pain on his face when he sees his son, sees the blood all over his daughter's white clothes as she chews her lip and trembles.

"Papa," she croaks. "Make them help him."

"They are, love, they are."

Shadows move in the candlelight. Medics are carrying the prince up the stairs on the cushioned board. I can't tell whether he's breathing. All I see is that much of the cushion has gone red with blood, drops of it falling out of reach from the light.

Pen is trembling beside me. "Morgan?"

My wrists are burning from where the princess's struggle dug the twine into my wounds.

"Shh."

It seems the entire tower has gathered here. Except for the queen. There have been rumors that she has taken ill; looking back it does seem strange that she wasn't in any of the broadcasts.

Maybe the king poisoned her too, I think bitterly.

But he puts his arm around his daughter to console her, and it's an echo of my father comforting me when we stood over Lex's hospital bed, not knowing if he'd pull through.

King Furlow and Princess Celeste follow the medics up

the stairs. Patrolmen escort them on all sides. As they go, they take the candlelight with them.

The clock strikes ten, drowning out the sounds they make. But I can still hear Princess Celeste's sobs; I suspect I'll hear them for a very long time in my dreams.

Pen and I stay huddled in the dark after the last chime.

"We won't have long," I whisper when I'm sure it's safe. "Let's try to find a way out."

"We shouldn't take the stairs," Pen says. I can tell by her voice that she's fighting for calm. I don't know how long she was planning to attack the prince, but she's seen it played out and she's seen the damage she caused, and it's ugly.

I'm the first to stand and begin walking. She clings to my shirt hem.

"Morgan?" she whispers. "You understand that I had to, don't you?"

"Just hope he isn't dead," is all I say.

"She didn't tell on us. She could have. Why didn't she?"

"I don't know." My arms are out in front of me, and I'm feeling along the grimy bricks, hoping for an out. My eyes are trying to adjust to the darkness, but there's nothing.

And then, suddenly, there is. A glimmer of moonlight breaking through a wooden door.

I fumble for the doorknob, and it turns, but the door doesn't budge. Pen helps me undo the series of locks. It's taking so long, I feel we're in a dream where air has been replaced by sweetgold.

I pull the knob again, and the door opens with a creak that I'm sure will summon the patrolmen. But no, they don't come. They'll be busy with all that blood.

If Prince Azure is dead, will his father tell Internment it was Judas Hensley? Say it was another act of treason?

Moonlight, so familiar and beautiful when we make it outside that my chest aches at the sight of it. It's trapped in a shimmering triangle on the ground. We're standing before the plum court; it's made of glass, its lines and circles waiting for players to come and follow their rules. Pen and I run across the court, which is scuffed from the prince and princess's last game. We're trying to get momentum though our wrists are bound, and no one is there to stop us. Pen's plan is almost perfect. Almost.

I push through a row of shrubs, scratching my arms, legs, and face as I do. Pen winces at the sound of fabric tearing. When I look at her, I see the lace from her dress collar is now dangling in the shrub. She tries to free it, but it won't come loose, and she has to leave it behind.

The clock tower is located in a wooded area, not far from where Sections One and Two meet. I know exactly where we are. My apartment is to the left in Section One, Basil's to the right in Section Two. I allow myself a moment to stare at my building several paces away, partially hidden by its neighbors. Lights are still on in some of the apartments. It isn't too late for people to be awake, but the streets are empty. Probably from fear that murderers are running rampant. The patrolmen surrounding the clock tower are occupied, but there will be plenty more in the city, and it probably won't take long for word to spread that the prince has been attacked. We have to move quickly. We have to be invisible.

Down alleyways and through the woods, we move. It's only when we reach the charred flower shop that Pen asks, "Why are we here?"

"It's where the machine is kept," I say, doing nothing to hide the bitterness in my voice. If she hadn't hurt the prince, possibly killed him, here is where I would tell her to go home to her parents, to Thomas. But her ring catches a bit of starlight and I know she'll never see her betrothed again. After what she's done, she can never be safe in this city. She'd be declared irrational if she weren't dispatched for her crime. I have to take her with me, and hope the metal bird really will fly us to the ground.

She's quiet and contrite, because she knows it too.

I pry back the familiar board, granting a small passageway in through the window. Without full range of motion from my arms, I tumble forward, landing hard on my shoulder. The pain hardly registers. I catch Pen as she tumbles in on top of me.

Even after several days, the burnt smell lingers in this place, and memories of the day at the theater rush back to me. In my nightmares, I couldn't have imagined that the fire would destroy as much as it did. I couldn't have imagined this feeling I get now knowing I can never go back.

When I was little, my brother drew an image for me on the train ride home from the academy. It was a map of Internment. Only, instead of the real city, he'd drawn a castle for the clock tower. And the buildings were all different somehow. Mysterious. And right at the edge he drew a ladder that went down and disappeared into the clouds. It was the most spectacular thing I'd ever seen, and getting ready for my bath that night, I discovered that the map had fallen from a hole in my skirt pocket. I wanted to go out and look for it, but my mother told me the sweepers had already come. The paper would be collected with all the other forgotten-about things and it would be compressed and recycled into something new.

I looked for it the next day, anyway, to no avail. I couldn't believe such a wonderful thing could be destroyed so simply. I learned that it could. Anything could be destroyed.

"There's a machine in here?" Pen asks.

"Under here." I'm on my hands and knees now, struggling to crawl, until I find the door that will take us underground.

This poses a new problem. There are several locks on the other side of it, and even if I manage to break through them, I'll be faced with the pulleys and ropes of the lift; there's no way I'll be able to operate them while my wrists are bound.

"We have to find something to cut the twine," I say.

"I can't see anything," Pen says. "There must be scissors, though."

We begin fumbling through what's left of drawers and

cabinets. "Careful," I remind Pen. But I say this a moment too late, because there's a creaking sound as one of the cabinets gives way and crashes to the ground. Glass and metal fall around our feet.

"Sorry!" she says. "But there's probably a glass shard we can use now."

Carefully, I crouch among the debris looking for something sharp, and I hear Pen rustling about beside me for a few moments before she stops. "Listen," she says. "Did you hear that?"

I stop fumbling and then I hear it, too. There are faint whining and creaking noises coming from beneath the floorboards. Someone is using the lift.

Hurriedly I crawl for the door, scraping my knee as I do. I see light through cracks in the floorboards, and my heart is on my tongue.

The noise stops, and next I hear the pound of shoes on the metal ladder. A voice says, "Who's there?"

"Judas?" I say.

Latches being hastily unlocked. The door is pushed open, granting a square of candlelight to come through the floor. Judas sets the lantern on the ground before starting to hoist himself up. But Basil pushes past him—he's heard my voice and now he can't move fast enough—and in a beat I'm in his arms.

I want to hold on to him like he's holding me, but I can't, and so I bury my face in his neck and I press my lips there. I don't belong on Internment itself anymore, but I'll always belong with him.

"I see you've brought your friend." Judas's voice is dry.

Pen stares aside into the darkness. I know she's thinking about what she's done, about the boy soaked in blood in the clock tower.

"I had no choice," I say, reluctantly drawing back when Basil notices my bound wrists. He tries to free them, but stops when I cringe.

"We were coming for you," he says. "We tried last night, and there were too many patrolmen. We had to come up with a plan."

"We were going to start a fire this time," Judas says, sounding proud. "I figured it couldn't hurt our reputation. Everyone already thinks we started this one."

Violence is the only way to achieve freedom, it seems. I wouldn't have thought so before all of this. My escape plan was a more peaceful one, but I know now that it wouldn't have been successful.

Judas draws a knife from a makeshift sheath at his hip and saws through our restraints. It isn't as much of a relief as I'd hoped for. The pain is still there, tightening around the bones like bloody phantom ropes.

"So you're the fugitive," Pen says, grinning.

"Look at that," Judas says. "We've just met and already we have something in common."

During the rickety ride down in the lift, I press my body against Basil's. I pretend that we're in a shuttle on the way to the academy, not sinking down into a place where the stars won't find us.

Pen gasps when she sees a side of the metal bird emerging in the lantern light. "It's really here," she says.

"What people have been dying for," Judas says, easing up a fistful of rope.

"Is everyone angry with me?" I ask Basil.

"Yes, very," he says. "I can't imagine what you were thinking."

"I wanted to say good-bye to Pen, and to see the stars, and possibly murder the king."

Judas snickers.

Basil kisses my hair, which has gone lank and stringy from my time as a prisoner. I look at him and quietly say, "I wanted to go home."

He touches my nose, my lips. "I know."

I press my ear to his heart, and the steady force of it makes strange music with the creaky lift. Last time I rode it, I was afraid. Now I dread only the moment we stop.

"Lex will have my head," I say.

"He'll just be glad you're back," Basil says. "We all thought, when you were taken to the king in the clock tower—"

He doesn't finish the sentence.

"The king never knew we were there," Pen says. "It was his insane children."

"The princess asked about the machine that would take us to the ground," I say. "I misled her, but she knows. She was adamant."

"Wonder why," Judas says. "What's the princess want

with the ground? Her life here is charmed enough."

"I think she's just lonely," I say, looking at Basil. His eyes are dark and worried.

"Lonely and *insane*," Pen says. "They had us locked away from the sunlight for ages."

"How did you get away?" Judas says.

No one answers him. But it's no matter; we've stopped.

Pen is still in awe of the machine, though it's hardly visible in the dim. She feels along the metal slope of it, tries to peer at what's in the shadows. "What are those claws for, underneath?" she asks.

"You know how dirt warrens have claws for fingers?" Judas says. "That's so they can dig through the dirt faster than we can walk it. There are claws like that on all sides of this thing so it can do just that."

"To get us up to the surface so we can fly away?" Pen asks.

"To get us below the surface," Judas says. "We'll dig a tunnel and break out through the bottom and then sail down to the ground. Assuming we don't fall to our deaths, or that the force surrounding the edge doesn't throw us back."

"But how will we get back up?" Pen says.

"We won't."

She already knew that, of course, but the confirmation has her staring at her betrothal band. Somewhere above us, Thomas is worrying for her. He hasn't learned yet that he'll spend his dodder years alone. He won't ever stop searching for her, even if they tell him she's dead. But that search will be fruitless, and Pen knows it. When she thinks I'm not watching, her lips move.

"I'm sorry," is what they say.

27

When my betrothed asked me to marry him, the second time, I didn't answer right away. I held the possibilities on my tongue. Carried them with me for days. I thought about choices. I imagined myself leaving Internment on the wings of a great bird or perhaps down a very strong length of twine. I tried to imagine what the ground would be like, and I couldn't. I would try to see shapes, but all I would get is the bright light that cloaks the unknown when the human mind strives for a knowledge it can't possess. But even then, even without the ability to imagine, every time I conjured that bright haze, I could feel him standing beside me. No god has ever felt as tangible as flesh and bone. I can love only what I have experienced.

"Yes," I told him.

—*"Intangible Gods," Daphne Leander, Year Ten*

When my brother throws the glass, it hits the wall first, then shatters on a patch of floor that was clearly recycled from an old door.

"You could have been killed!" Lex says.

Alice sees me wince. "All right, enough of that now," she says, standing behind Lex and stroking his trembling arms. "Sit," she tells him, but he doesn't. His jaw is quivering. His eyes stare through me, and though my brother can't see me, he can hear me breathing, sense my weight shifting. He always knows where I stand.

I try to say I'm sorry, but the words catch in my throat. He so rarely shows emotion that it frightens me when he does.

"She isn't hurt," Alice tells him. She looks into my eyes. "And she won't leave again. Isn't that right?"

"Yes," I manage.

"Who knows who followed you here," Lex says, an octave shy of bellowing. "And you dragged Pen into this!" I've never seen him this angry. Usually he just tells me I'm foolish and then storms off. And if I'm mad enough, I storm off, too.

But I can't go back to how it was before.

I take a step forward and I put my hands on his shoulders. "Hey." My voice softens. "I said I'd always come back."

He's still for a moment, and then he drops into a chair and turns away from me. I'm clearly being shunned.

Alice steps around him and pulls me into a hug.

She's quick to forgive me. So little ever needs to be said between us. She put her arms around me when we stood vigil over Lex's hospital bed, and when I came to visit after her termination procedure, and anytime I needed comfort while my mother slept and my father worked.

"I'm sorry, Alice," I whisper. "I won't leave again."

There's nothing left to leave for. Everyone in my life is either in this bird or dead.

Judas has taken Pen on a tour of the metal bird, and while Professor Leander has his doubts about whether she's to be trusted, he revels in the opportunity to show off his invention.

Basil and I are alone at the kitchen table. He brushes his fingertips through a jar of clear salve and dabs at my wrists.

"She has to go back home," he says. "She still belongs in the city."

After a hesitation, I say, "She can't. She may have killed Prince Azure."

He stiffens. "What?"

"In order to get free, we'd planned an ambush, and she got her own idea and attacked him. I would have stopped her, but there wasn't time. I don't even think she realized what she'd done until she saw it all happening in front of her."

"Morgan—"

"It's bad. I know."

"Very bad. What if someone followed you?"

"They didn't. It was the perfect diversion. Every patrol-man in earshot came running when Princess Celeste started screaming," I say. "That was the scream of something that can't be undone, right there."

He frowns. "Poor Pen," he says.

"She isn't to be blamed entirely. It's because I went to say good-bye; that's when they caught her."

"It's because of the king," he says, smoothing a lump of salve over my wound. "Don't let yourself think anything else."

To give him peace of mind, I mutter, "Okay." But I know it isn't true. It can never be as simple as that. So much of this is my fault.

"And I don't care who is to blame," Basil says. "I'm here because I love you."

There's that word again. "Love." It's so easy for him to say. But it makes my stomach ache, my head fill with bramble flies.

He doesn't even wait to hear if I'll say it back this time. He rustles my hair and leaves to return the medical kit to the supply closet.

When he returns, he coaxes me to eat something. I suppose it's meant to be bread, but it's so stale that it hurts to swallow.

Basil uncorks a glass bottle of orange liquid. "Professor Leander concocted it," he says. "Supposedly it has a day's nutrients in case we run out of food. Take slow sips."

I try not to cringe, but it tastes like dirt and citrus fruits.

"Do you remember the story of Saffron?" I say.

"The uncorrupted?" he says. "From the history book?"

To be an uncorrupted is the highest honor in the history book. There are only six of them, and Saffron was the last. There's only one artist's rendering of her, and in it she's melancholy, with a gaunt face, dark hair and eyes, holding a blond-haired baby she was in charge of raising. Back when Internment still adhered to rankings, her parents sold her to a noble family as their servant.

Her life was fraught with hardship. The family she served was cruel. The husband had his way with her, and though it was never spoken, the wife knew and she sought revenge on Saffron by giving her impossible and dangerous tasks. Repairing wind-damaged shingles with a broken ladder. Retrieving children's toys from frail branches.

Saffron didn't even get to rest in her dodder years. She spent them caring for the family that owned her.

"I've never understood why Saffron gave the sky god her absolute faith," I say. "I thought she'd be angry with him."

"She was rewarded for her faith," Basil reminds me. When she died, before she could be committed to ashes, her body ascended to the sky god whole, so the story goes. "She's one of the few who can walk along the tributary. She can hear its souls whispering to her. She can wash her hair in it like it's a stream if she wants to. She gets to have a perfect afterlife."

"How could she be so good all of the time?" I stare at the orange liquid set before me. "What about this life? Couldn't she ever be angry that *this* life wasn't fair?"

Basil scoots his chair closer to mine, and he works a lock of hair behind my shoulder, smoothing it down over and over again. "Maybe Saffron wasn't angry," he says, "but I am."

"Me too." I try to laugh, but it sounds more like a

whimper. "No walking along the tributary for us. Guess we'll just be lumped into it like all the lowly others."

"It's never comforted me much," Basil says. "The tributary, I mean. I don't like the idea of blending in. I imagine a giant ribbon of people all sewn together and waving about on the wind."

This time, I do laugh. "I've always thought the same thing," I say, and as he sweeps his hand through my hair again, I grab his wrist to keep it still. I like the way his fingers feel against my temple. "Daphne said in her essay that the tributary frightened her, too," I say. "'Who decides what is saved and what is lost from our souls?'"

"We seem to have much in common with a girl who was killed for her ideas," he says.

I lean against his hand, granting myself a moment of melancholy.

His sad smile tells me he understands. I don't know how he always understands me when I haven't a clue myself.

"Take a few more sips if you can get them down," Basil says. "Then let's get you cleaned up so you can rest."

Water is in small supply on the metal bird, I come to realize. There are no running faucets; Professor Leander rigged a tap somewhere in the dirt and there's a device that filters it clean, but the pressure is very weak and he's particular about how much we take.

Pen and I sit in our undergarments, bathing ourselves with cloths we dip into the same shallow basin. We lather our hands with soapberries. Normally the berries would be pressed into a bar and are often scented, but raw berries will work in a pinch.

"I'll wash your hair if you wash mine," she says. "Try not to lather too hard. It frizzes the curls."

"You might have to get used to uncooperative hair," I say. "There's a lot of moisture underground." I don't mention what Judas said about the theory of water being absorbed from the clouds, rather than it being a gift from the sky god. I'm still angry with her, but not enough to make her question her beliefs.

I lean back on my elbows, dunking my hair into the basin while Pen cups water in her hands and massages my scalp.

For a while it's just the sound of the water, and then Pen says, "I didn't want him to die."

I focus on the ceiling, trying to determine what pieces of machinery it once was. Old gears from the clock tower melted down, maybe, or parts from an old train car.

"He probably isn't dead," she says. "Medical technology is so advanced nowadays, and the prince would be top priority."

She wrings water out of my hair. "Say something."

"How long were you planning it without me?" I ask.

"I noticed the loose stone when Prince Creepy was leading me to the water room. Later when you fell asleep, I got up and made sure I could work it free. I knew you'd never go for it, so I didn't tell you. Look. I didn't want to really hurt him, but it was the only way out, and they *had* been threatening to kill us all along."

"They weren't going to kill us," I say. "You heard the princess. She didn't tell on us. There's some reason she wanted me to lead her to this machine."

"She shouldn't be so greedy," Pen says. "If I were living her life, I'd count my blessings, not ask for more of them."

She's right about this much. I'll never understand the prince and princess's reasons for kidnapping us, and I'll never know if they were being greedy, or lonely, or just bored.

But despite my anger, I find myself talking to the god in the sky. It's the first time I've done so in a long time.

I ask that Prince Azure will live.

28

*I have wondered if Internment is an afterlife. I have
entertained the idea that we are a glorious dream . . .*
—"Intangible Gods," Daphne Leander, Year Ten

I'm exhausted, but I can't sleep. Every time I
close my eyes, I see the quartet flutterling I bought for
Pen. A hand pulls the cord, and it flies around and around
behind my eyelids. It won't be still.

I open my eyes. Basil is pressed against me on the tiny
mattress and is watching me. I wouldn't let him blow out
the candle in our lantern; the darkness would feel too
much like my prison in the clock tower. "Can't relax?"
he says.

"It wasn't midnight yet when I came back underground," I say. "I didn't get to hear the clock tower strike
twelve. I just wish I could have heard the chimes once
more." I reposition myself, finding it difficult to find a soft
spot amid these blankets. "Basil? Do you think they have
clock towers on the ground?"

"I read somewhere that the idea for the clock tower came from the ground," he says. "A lot of the city's designs did. Maybe things won't be very different from Internment. Just much more room."

"If we don't crash and die," I remind him.

"Yes, that too."

I try to imagine what the ground will be like. All I see is another version of Internment.

"We probably won't make it," I say. "Our top engineers have been trying to get to the ground for centuries, and they've all failed. You know that, right? That we'll probably all be killed?"

"I don't know any such thing," he says.

"Basil, really."

"Call me irrational if you like," he says. "But I believe we'll make it, and I've no doubt the girl I'm betrothed to would believe it too."

"When I put aside all of the ugly thoughts, it feels poetic," I admit. "We're inside this sleeping machine, just waiting to see where it takes us when it wakes."

"There's the Morgan I know."

The Morgan he knew is dead. I don't know who's lying beside him now.

He seems to know what I'm thinking. "Don't bury your sense of wonder," he says. "It's a rare thing, and one of the things I adore most about you."

"Amy thinks they'll be fascinated by us on the ground," I say. "She thinks they'll throw us a party."

I look up at the hanging lantern, trying to imagine that

this metal bird can be as much a home to me as my apartment was. The Morgan Stockhour that lived in that apartment would envy me. Maybe it's silly of me to envy her now.

"Close your eyes," Basil says. "Try to sleep."

I close my eyes, and this time I see ashes being thrown upon the wind.

The bed lurches beneath me, and I awaken with a gasp.

"It's okay," Basil says before I've opened my eyes. The urgency in his voice is hardly reassuring.

The lantern swings over our bed, and Basil reaches up to steady it. "Professor Leander is testing the claws. That's all."

"We're moving?" I say. "Actually moving?"

The shadows of his grin dance in the candlelight when there's another jolt. This is the happiest he has looked in days. "We're moving."

The door to our bunk room whips open, and there's Pen, her hair somehow pristine though the look in her eyes is a bit deranged. "My lantern nearly fell off its hook," she says excitedly. "It's like Internment is shaking on the wind."

"Not Internment. Just the bird," Judas says, coming up beside her. "Professor Leander was up all night fiddling with the gears. He says there's no time left. Thanks in part to the two of you, and that little stunt with the prince."

Pen gives me a flat stare. "You told?"

"I only told Basil!"

"Voices carry," Judas says. "And you've put us all even more at risk, you know."

Pen crosses her arms, indignant. And I know she isn't angry with me for telling Basil; she's angry with herself. "It's sacrilege, what that professor is doing," she says. "If we were meant to be on the ground, we'd be able to fly like birds."

"Not much religion in hitting the prince with a rock," Judas fires back.

She opens her mouth, but I interrupt. "I don't hear an engine."

"We have to generate our own electricity down here," Judas says. "Get the gears turning, and with luck they'll take over for us once we take to the sky. Right now it's all brute strength."

"Can I help?" Basil asks.

"How are you with heavy lifting?" Judas asks.

"He's incredible," I say. Basil would be too modest to let on how strong he is.

"It's true," Pen agrees. "Makes Thomas look like a weakling. Not that that would take much." She folds her arms and scoffs, the way she would if Thomas had just claimed her cheek for a kiss.

But of course, no kiss comes, and her expression slowly falls.

"Come on, then, if you think you'd be useful," Judas tells Basil.

We all follow Judas down the narrow hallway. Without the clock tower or daylight, I have no concept of time. I don't know if I can get used to the sun's absence. It makes me feel a bit like I'm trapped in a box; sometimes I struggle to breathe. I am a creature of the sky. I've always known that, but I didn't fully appreciate it until I was forced to live in the dirt.

I think of what my mother said that one afternoon about dreaming of living among the roots of a giant tree. That may have been her way of trying to tell me about this place; but she stopped herself, because she thought ignorance would keep me safe.

I become distantly aware of my own grief, and I realize how easily I'm able to force it away. It will come back, to be sure, but for now I'm in control, and when Judas leads me to a ladder, I climb up after him.

"Didn't you have a dream like this?" Pen says, climbing the rungs beneath me.

"Yes, but we were side by side," I say.

"Still. How eerie."

Judas grabs my hand and helps me onto the upper level. Then he stoops down to help Pen, but she ignores him, preferring to stumble on all fours before coming upright. "Did you know our Morgan is something of a clairvoyant?" she says.

Judas is looking at me when he says, "She's something."

How unusual for me to smile at such an innocuous thing. Basil climbs up beside me, bringing me back to my senses. I stoop to gather the lantern Judas set on the floor.

We find Professor Leander in the control room, sitting before a wall of windows, each different in size and shape.

He must have been hoarding pieces for decades in order for this bird to exist as it does.

There's an alcove off to one side, surrounded entirely by dirt-darkened windows, containing levers that seem to move on their own without needing any human force.

"Do those control the claws?" Basil asks.

"Sure do," Judas says.

Amy is hanging over her grandfather's chair, pointing to the levers and asking questions, but she spins around when she hears our approach. "I knew you'd be back," she says cheerily. "The others said you were dead."

"Nobody said that," Judas says.

"You did."

He scratches the back of his neck. I decide to forgive him. If he thought I was dead after my capture, it was with good reason. All his friends who have crossed the king are either in this bird or dead. I heard Alice and Lex murmuring that if the other jumpers haven't found their way to the bird by now, it's time to leave them behind.

"We're quite alive," Pen says. "What can we do to help?" Her voice is bright, though she exudes weariness. Well after midnight, I heard her enter Basil's and my bunk room. I guess her loneliness made sleeping on a cushion on our floor more appealing than the couch in the common room.

"There is a gear that's giving me trouble," Professor Leander says. "Sticking. There's some grease in a yellow can."

"I'll go," I say. "Where is it, exactly?"

"I'll show you," Amy says. As she brushes past me, she grabs my hand, and the gesture is so nonchalant that I wonder if she's aware of it. It makes me feel honored. Trusted.

Behind us, Professor Leander has already begun assigning tasks to the others.

"You must tell me all about the clock tower," Amy whispers when we get to the ladder. "I'm infinitely jealous that you met the princess."

I blink. "Are you an admirer?" Princess Celeste is a popular role model for the girls of this city, but Amy doesn't seem the sort to buy into that, especially with the king's role in Daphne's death.

"I just wonder what it's like to be her, is all." Her eyes are wide. "My sister told me that the princess shoots deer for fun and nobody is bold enough to stop her."

"She collects antlers and mounts them to her wall," I say, beginning to climb down.

"Ghastly," Amy says. I can hear her grin. She reminds me a bit of Pen when we were younger—fascinated with the macabre, excited at any small scrap of adventure to be found. I wonder if Daphne was the same way. I'm sorry we never spoke, though surely we passed each other nearly every day at the academy. She wasn't among the faces to judge and shun me after Lex's incident. With a sister that had done the same thing, maybe she even sympathized. I have a feeling we could have been friends.

The bird lurches to the left with a chorus of metal whines. Amy loses her grip and topples backward. We're close enough to the bottom now that I can catch her as I set one foot on the floor. Miraculously, I don't drop the lantern. But she's dead weight when she hits me. The bird goes still, and I realize that she's quaking in my arms. Her eyes are all white, lashes aflutter, limbs and torso shuddering as though some creature is trying to burst out of her.

Alarmed, I lay her on the floorboards.

"Judas," I cry. My voice is shrill. "Judas!"

In a blur, he's leapt to the bottom of the ladder and is crouching at her side.

"She just— I caught her when she fell, and . . ."

"It's okay," Judas says. "It wasn't anything you did. Stand back."

He looks up to where Pen and Basil are perched at the top of the ladder. "Tell the professor to stop tinkering with the bird. She's going to need stillness until she comes out of it." His voice is calm, but his eyes are sharp with worry.

"I'll get Lex," I say. "He can help."

"No," he says. "It'll run its course."

This is how the edge ruined her. Her arms thrash. Her ankles pound at the floor. A low, hiccupping cry comes out of her.

I just want it to stop. I'd do anything to make it stop.

I think of the yellow pill her betrothed forced down her throat after we found the murdered university student. "Doesn't she have a pharmacy bag?" I say. "Something."

"Doubt she brought it here," he says. "A lot of good those things will do, anyway."

"This—this happens often?" I say.

"Now and again."

Mercifully, she goes still. For a moment I wonder if she's dead, but then I hear her moan. Judas sighs with relief. "We should get her to bed."

"Maybe Morgan and I should clean her up first," Pen says. I don't realize she's even descended the ladder until she's beside me. She nods to the stain that's formed on the skirt of Amy's uniform.

Judas looks away, cheeks flushed. "I'll go find something else for her to wear."

"A bucket of water and some cloths would be ideal, too," Pen says. "And don't let anyone come in here until we're done. The poor girl's having a bad enough day as it is without becoming a scene."

I stroke Amy's forehead, which is flushed and warm. She leans into my touch, helpless and utterly at my mercy. I'm ashamed of myself for having envied her, for thinking she was able to brave the edge without consequence.

"Oh, stop looking so serious," Pen says. "Really, I've cleaned my share of messes, and I've seen some worse things, let me tell you."

She's trying to make me feel better, and I'm grateful. It makes the task more bearable.

By the time we've finished dabbing Amy with warm soapy cloths and gotten her into an oversize shirt, she's beginning to stir. She mumbles something about the smell of burning hair.

"There are no fires," I assure her.

She opens her eyes, as vacant as a doll's, and stares at me. "You're not her," she says. Then she's gone again.

"You stay with her," Pen says, gathering the wadded uniform. "I'll go wash these."

I'm not sure what else to do, so I hold Amy's head in my lap and run my fingers through her hair. I can't be certain where this delirium has taken her, but maybe she can sense that someone is caring for her, the way that I could after I'd been poisoned.

"Soon," I tell her, "after you've awoken, this bird will fly us away. The people of the ground will throw us a party bigger than Internment itself. Everyone will love us. It's going to be wonderful."

A strange thing, words. Once they're said, it's hard to imagine they're untrue.

The bird is moving unsteadily through the dirt. Judas argued with the professor that Amy needed to recover, and the professor told him that his grandchildren weren't made of glass, and anyway we didn't have the time to waste. He added, "Coddling the living sister won't bring back the dead sister," which I thought was especially harsh.

Now Judas and I are standing in the doorway to Amy's bunk room. It's been more than an hour since her episode, and Judas looks as exhausted as if he'd been the one experiencing it.

"Poor kid," he says. "All she's got now is me."

"What about her parents?" I ask.

He shakes his head. "They would have had her and Daphne both declared irrational if they'd known about the bird. They wanted perfect daughters and nothing to do with scandal."

It's happened before that parents have had their children declared irrational. The sentence can usually be dropped after the child has agreed to give up the rebellious behavior, such as falling in love with someone else's betrothed or admitting attraction to the same sex. I've heard of it happening, but I still have trouble believing it's done.

"I can't imagine my parents ever declaring me irrational," I say. "Even after Lex jumped, they would never have done that to either of us."

"Lucky you, then," Judas says.

He sees the hurt in my eyes and adds, "I'm sorry. That was stupid of me."

Now, after more than an hour of still sleep, Amy's limbs begin to move under the blanket. When she opens her eyes, they're glassy and gray.

"Hey," Judas says, back to her side in an instant. "Hey, you. Welcome back."

She rolls her head to the side, realizes that I'm watching her, and groans with embarrassment.

"The turbulence got you," Judas says. "We said it might. Remember that?"

His soothing tone is for her, though he seems to be more in need of comforting than she does. She's the only thing like family he has left.

"I was listening for Daphne," she says. Her voice is hoarse. "Listening for her ghost. But they cut her throat. They took her voice away."

Her eyes fill with tears, and Judas is quick to dab at them with his sleeve. "No they haven't," he says. "I hear her all the time."

"You do?" she says.

"Of course I do, silly girl. She's in this bird. She's holding all of the bolts in place and she's begging for us to sail across the sky."

Amy squeezes her eyes shut, closing herself away from us living things.

"Those are only echoes," she says. "People die, and everything they've ever said just echoes around and around. There's nothing new. Only the same nonsense from their lives."

I fear she's right.

29

. . . or a not-so-glorious dream . . .

—"Intangible Gods," Daphne Leander, Year Ten

I pace about the bird for a long while, pressing my hands to the wall when it lurches. I've seen what the edge did to my brother, and I've just seen what it did to a little girl. Whatever it is that keeps us here, whether it's a god or a ghost or something atmospheric, it doesn't discriminate. What will it do to a metal bird that tries to leave? Will the bolts come loose? Will the floors splinter while the walls crumple in on us?

"How certain are you that we won't die?" I ask.

Professor Leander is inspecting the window at his control panel; there's nothing to see but dirt on the other side. "Remarkable stuff, this sort of glass. Nearly unbreakable. Several decades ago, long before our times, they tried to build a dome around this city. Thought it would discourage the jumpers. And this beautiful glass was made to withstand the wind pressure. To test it, pieces were flung from the edge, and they shot back into the city, unscratched."

I heard about this, not in my history book, but from my father when I asked why more wasn't being done to deter jumpers.

"But despite all the clever engineering of the dome and this glass, the sun's glare through it would have caused us to burst into flame."

"How did you come across it?" I ask. "The glass."

"It was buried by my great-grandfather, one of the dome's engineers. He willed the map of the burial site to my father, and my father to me. Now, after generations, it's finally time to put it to use. So I can't assure you, child, that we won't die, but I can assure you that this bird has been building for longer than you or I have been alive. The time has come and there's to be no backing down."

This does little to reassure me. I feel that familiar wave of claustrophobia coming up in my stomach, and I force it down.

"When?" I ask.

"Maybe this evening," he says. "Or tomorrow. We've already moved several hundred paces from the flower shop. I expect that soon we'll have reached the swallows."

My heart is in my ears. "The swallows?" I say. "Why would we want to be there?"

"The pressure of the sinking dirt will be enough force to get us to the bottom of the city. We'll be thrust into the sky. Think of it as a birth."

"What if we're crushed?" I gasp. "What if we cause a

gap in the bottom of the city and all the dirt leaks out to the sky, and—"

The professor is chuckling. "What if we stay here?" he says. I assume he's being rhetorical, but he spins his chair around to face me and waits for an answer.

"We'd run out of food," I say, feeling as scrutinized as when I'm caught daydreaming during one of Instructor Newlan's lessons. "And now that we've moved, we would have difficulty tapping another water supply."

"And without food and water, we would . . ." He holds his arm out toward me, a line on a page waiting for a sentence.

"Die," I say.

"We would die," he agrees, turning back to his controls. "That is a fact. So we can face a certain death, or I can try to make this girl fly."

Well, it's hard to argue with that.

"How is my granddaughter?" he asks. "I haven't had time to check in on her. I hear she had a fit."

"She's resting," I say. "But she's better. She was talking for a bit earlier."

He nods. "My granddaughters are always strong," he says, and then he begins muttering to his controls. I take that as my cue to leave.

The lantern casts a dim glow on the metal hallway; there are windows in the ceiling, but they're dark because of the earth on the other side of them. This tiny upper platform has been deemed the Nucleus: bird's head, Judas told me. I like it here. The voices of the others are small and tinny, and it seems like a great place to think, if only my thoughts didn't all turn a dark corner right now.

I find Pen and Basil in the kitchen, huddled over a rumpled piece of paper.

Basil looks up, forehead creasing when he sees my troubled face. "Amy's not doing any better?"

"It isn't that," I say, shaking my head. I don't want to tell him about my fear of being crushed. "Never mind. It's been a long day. What are you doing?"

"Mapmaking," Pen says. "We're trying to guess where the bird is now. If we're going around the lake and not under it, of course, then we've probably passed under our apartments by now."

She's working with a pen stone that's been crudely sharpened, and her hands are ashy. Normally the pen stone would be cut and rolled into a wooden pencil, but down here she's had to make due with raw materials. It's easy enough to find pen stone in the dirt. The old piece of paper, she must have found lying around.

Basil pulls out a chair for me and I sit between them. Even though it's a rough sketch, Pen has a talented hand. The lines are clean and carefully scaled, and the shaded squares of buildings are evenly spaced apart. For the lake, she even doodled some trout with *X*s for eyes.

"So we started here," she says, tracing her finger around the square labeled *flower shop*. "And if we've been moving toward the swallows, that's west, which puts us about here, or maybe not quite that far yet." She points to the academy. The map doesn't say anything for the students inside it, learning in our absence.

"You knew about the swallows?" I say.

"I asked what his plan was," she answers. "I like to know where I am and where I'm going at all times."

"Does anyone else know you've been working on this?" I say. "It would be a big help to the professor, I'm sure."

She smiles at the page. "You think?"

"It's quite good," Basil agrees.

She wrinkles her nose. "I just wish I had some proper colors," she says. "Do you think they have decent coloring materials on the ground? They must, right?"

"Of course," I say. "The people who run the scopes have reported that the buildings down there are all sorts of colors. They must like to decorate the way that we do."

Pen seems satisfied with this. She blows on the tip of her pen stone and draws the princess falling from the clock tower.

Tentatively, I peer into my brother's bunk room.

Alice has gone to the helm to try to help with the efforts, and Lex is sitting alone on the mattress, his fingers tracing the raised letters on a roll of paper from his transcriber.

His lips stop moving when he hears me.

"Are you through being angry with me?" I ask.

"Are you through making foolish decisions that could get you killed?" he says.

"We're in a metal bird that's set to be hurtling toward the ground soon." There's a laugh in my voice. "What could be more foolish than that?"

He makes a small tear in the page to mark his place, and then he rolls the paper and sets it down.

"I'm sorry if I scared you when I snuck off, Lex, truly."

He grunts, but the raised corner of his mouth is more of a smile than he gives me on good days.

"I've brought you something," I say. I sit next to him and begin tying the scrap of white cloth around his wrist. "I'm wearing one, too," I say as I finish the knot.

He runs his fingers over the frayed edges of the fabric. "For Mom and Dad, then," he says.

Traditionally, family members and exceptionally close friends would cut a strip of fabric from the deceased's clothing and wear it in remembrance. "I know we're supposed to make these after the ashes have been thrown to the tributary," I say, "but we aren't going to have that."

"What did you use?" Lex asks.

"The shirtsleeve from my uniform." Another piece of my life I'm grieving.

Lex is still for a while, and I begin to wonder if I've done the wrong thing in tying the fabric around his wrist. Maybe I've forced my grief on him, and he doesn't want to share it with me. He does seem adamant about moving on.

But then he puts his arm around my shoulders and squeezes me close.

Neither of us have words for this loss. We expected to say good-bye to our parents the way our world dictates, years from now when we were prepared. But our world turned out not to be what was promised to us. There will be no ashes thrown to the tributary. There will be no festival of stars with our paper desires burning in the sky.

Our parents are gone now. Our home, where we teased each other and squabbled as we grew, is out of reach. It is only Lex and me, escaping the city that wants us dead.

I stare at the fabric that's around my wrist. "I never properly thanked you for saving me after I was poisoned."

"No thanks necessary," he says. "Just repay me by staying alive, if it isn't too much to ask."

I'm about to tell him that he has a deal, but I don't get the chance. The bird jolts sharply in one direction, then the other, and I careen into the wall with Lex still holding on to my shoulder. The lantern is swinging dangerously overhead. The next jolt extinguishes it.

I do my best to stay close to the wall. "What's happening?" I say.

"Could be anything," Lex says. He doesn't sound at all worried, and I'm not sure whether he truly believes we'll be all right, or he's just content to die here if the alternative would be capture by the king.

"Morgan!" Basil is shouting for me.

"Stay wherever you are," I call back. "It isn't safe."

Beyond the doorway of the bunk room, there's nothing but darkness and the sound of gears whining and hissing. All of the lanterns have blown out. Small metal plinking sounds make me fear the worst: that the bolts are coming undone and we're being crushed.

I prop my leg against the adjacent wall for traction, grateful these bunk rooms are so tiny. Why, with all of the planning that went into this bird, did no one fashion something for us to hold on to?

Mercifully, the bird eventually goes still.

Lex stirs in the darkness. "Are you hurt?" he asks.

"No," I say. "But the lanterns blew out."

"Don't light them yet," Lex says. "It might not be safe. We're still moving."

He's right. I can feel a pull. "We're still spinning a bit, aren't we?" I say. "And sinking."

"We must be in the swallows," Lex says. "The bird hasn't been crushed by the weight of the churning dirt yet."

"If you're trying to make me feel better, I'd much prefer you stop," I say.

When the calm has gone on a while longer, I relight the lantern. I hear murmurs down the hall.

"Basil?" I call. "Pen? Alice?"

A dim glow forms in the bunk room across the hall. Alice.

A sphere of light flickers up the stairwell as Basil and Pen find us. "I should go see if the professor needs help with the gears," Basil says.

"Be careful," I say, raising my cheek to accept his kiss as he passes me.

I turn my head in time to see Alice's worried expression before she smiles at me.

Pen's hands are shaking as she smoothes her map against the wall and studies it. "I suppose I was wrong," she says. Her voice is tight. "We've reached the swallows sooner than I thought."

"It's almost over," Amy says. I raise the lantern to better see her. Despite the weariness left over from her ordeal, her face is alight. "We'll be in the sky in moments."

"Nobody knows how deep the swallows run," Pen says. "It might just give us a boost before we hit more solid ground. It might still be a while."

"It won't," Amy says.

"You don't know that. No one knows that."

I note the hysteria in her voice. "Pen?"

She chews on her trembling knuckle. There are tears in her eyes.

"Everyone alive?" Judas calls from the bird's head.

"Barely," Pen says.

"Come on up if you all want to see something you'll never forget," he says.

For as long as we may have left to live, anyway.

Everyone on the bird gathers at the helm with the professor: my brother and Alice, Pen, Basil, Judas, Amy, and me.

Pen is still shaking, though it's nearly imperceptible, and with all the excitement no one else seems to notice. She has always had the cool head, and to see her coming undone makes me somewhat nauseous.

Through the window at the helm, I can see the dirt churning furiously. There's a story I read years ago; in it, a castle stood beside something called a waterfall. I wasn't quite able to picture it then, but now I can see that the water must have been like this—restless.

"What is this 'something' we'll never forget?" I ask, holding up my lantern.

"We've reached the bottom of the swallows," the professor says, not turning away from his controls. He rubs at his chin, and I can hear the scrape of his white stubble. "We've hit some solid ground. I suspect we're a hundred or so paces from the sky."

I don't quite believe the words, and yet something within me must, because my palms are sweaty and there's a chill at the back of my neck. Whether we're to soar across the sky or sink through it like a rock, it's only a matter of moments. I'm working my way through varying degrees of panic, and I want to yell for us to stop. I want to undo this journey and return home, even if it's to an empty apartment. But I know that is only the fear and the grief talking.

"No." Pen has gone white beside me. "I don't want to go," she says.

"There's no turning back now," the professor says.

I try to touch her shoulder, but she pushes away, takes a step for the doorway. Even her curls are trembling. "Let me out of this thing. I don't care what they do to me. I'll go to trial for what I did to the prince. I could live the rest of my life as an irrational, I don't care, so long as I can stay in the sky."

I set down the lantern and reach for her again, and this time I make fists around her hands. "Pen, listen—"

"I can't leave. And my mother, I—"

I bring my forehead close to hers. "Pen, if we got out of this thing here, it wouldn't be possible to dig our way back up to the surface. We would be buried in an instant."

I meant to console her, but my words cause me to feel trapped. No matter; Pen has always been my strength and this is my time to return the favor. "Here," I say, and dab at her runny nose with my sleeve.

"Thomas," she says miserably. "He won't even know what's happened to me."

There's nothing I can say to make this better. I'm not surprised that she's letting it show how much she cares for him, after a lifetime of hiding it; there's something about imminent death that makes all the threads weave into a picture like one of my mother's samplers.

"But we must be brave, remember?" I say.

She nods, watching her tears fall onto her betrothal band.

The next violent jolt has Basil at my side. He surprises me by putting an arm around Pen as well as me. He's never been very familiar with her, but now we have our fear in common. We are all part of this floating city we'll never see again. This city I love so much that I fear I'll cease to exist once I'm off it.

I steady the lantern between my feet to keep it from sliding. We stay huddled together as the bird struggles to burrow the rest of the way to the sky. We count the seconds until our little world is lost to us for good.

"Have any visions about this?" Judas asks Amy over the incessant noise of the levers and the bird struggling its way through the last of the dirt.

"A dream," Amy says. "And you don't want to know."

"Don't take stock in that," I whisper to Pen, whose sobs

have lost their sound. I do wish she'd be calm. I can't bear to see her in such pain. I would hijack the helm and claw this bird up to the surface to take her home if I could.

"It would be unwise to remain standing," the professor says. Obligingly, we huddle on the floor.

A pace away, Alice is holding Lex's hands. He's saying something into her ear while she stares worriedly at the windows. Poor Alice, still wearing a pretty dress, though its underarms and chest are darkened with sweat. Bone and bead earrings still hang from her ears. Dragged into this. All she wanted was a life with my brother. To go out sometimes. To have a child. To grow flowers in the apartment without Lex blindly clomping into them. To grow old in dodder housing, having lived a complete life. Instead she's being forced out of her home.

Now isn't the time to be angry with my brother, but I suppose the anger I feel for him never goes away. I cover it with love and with patience, but it doesn't undo what he's taken from all of us.

I'm angry with my parents, too. For not telling me. For dying.

"Breathe," Basil says, and I realize I've begun to hyperventilate.

"Tell me again what you said earlier," he says. "About the sleeping machine."

"Sleeping?" Pen whispers.

"I said that we're all inside this sleeping machine, and we're waiting to see where it takes us when it wakes."

"Good," Basil says. "You believed it, then. All you have

to do is hold on to that belief a little longer. And then we'll be in the sky."

"There aren't maps of the sky," Pen says. "We're flying right off the page." She looks as though she'll be sick. But if she's going to say anything more, she doesn't get her chance. The bird tilts to one side and we all go sliding toward the wall. The lanterns go wild from the spill, and all but one are extinguished.

I bite down on a mouthful of my shirt and scream into it. The professor's cursing does nothing to console.

"Keep that damned thing lit," he tells Judas, who holds the dying lantern. "It's all we've got."

But he's wrong about that. In an instant all of the windows fill up with brightness.

30

Free will isn't quite the same as freedom.
— "Intangible Gods," Daphne Leander, Year Ten

I see no blue sky, and no clouds. The brightness churns in a way not unlike the swallows.

There's a terrible grating sound, which I come to realize is the side of the bird scraping against the bottom of the city. The howling can only be the wind.

The turbulence undoes a piece of metal in the ceiling, and it comes crashing to the floor with the spattering of bolts. Lex calls out for me.

"I'm okay," I say. I try to crawl toward him, but Basil tightens his hold on me.

"Keep your head down," he tells me.

But that's impossible with the temptations these windows hold; I keep trying to make out shapes in the brightness.

"Is the bird strong enough to make it?" Judas asks, clinging to the professor's chair, which is bolted in place.

"This design is superior to the earlier models," the professor says.

"Earlier models?" I say. "You mean—you mean this isn't the first time this has been attempted?"

"Of course not! There have been half a dozen tries," the professor says, shouting to be heard over the wind. "People have been attempting this for generations."

I don't want to ask what came of those attempts. The answer is obvious anyway. The birds were destroyed, probably sent hurtling through the sky if they weren't ripped apart by this wind. This is the wind that throws jumpers back. Escape is impossible from the surface; why should it be any more feasible from the bottom?

Then the tumultuous bird calms. And I see what no other resident of Internment has ever seen: the bottom of the city.

It's jagged. From the outside I can now see a dome of wind that encapsulates the city, forcing clouds around and over and under it.

The bird trembles, and through the windows of the helm I can see the wings burst open, and we break into a smooth glide.

The professor punches down on a large brass button and there's a sharp chemical smell. Judas told me the professor had been brewing his own fuel to keep us in the air. There was no promise it would work. We could be crashing to the ground right now, but we aren't. The weight leaves my chest.

I'm too stunned to move. Beside me, Pen's sobs have

ceased. There is nothing but the howl of air and the creaking of the gears and the popping of the metal.

"What's happening now?" Lex says, unaffected by the
view. This snaps Alice out of her trance and she grabs his
hands, brings them to her face.

We are sinking into the sky. Our tiny city is getting
smaller. Something within me is sinking, too.

I wrap my arms around Basil because for the first time
since all of this began, he looks truly pained. His parents
and his brother are out of reach now. He could blame me,
if he wants. I would understand. But no such words come
from him now. He's choosing me; no regrets.

"It's just like the maps have come alive," Pen says,
streaks of tears still on her face.

Amy is the first among us who's brave enough to stand.
Basil is next, taking my hand and guiding me up from my
shaky knees.

The head of the bird is a sphere of windows. Light
comes in from above and all around.

Judas still clings to the lantern, and the look in his eyes
is further away than Internment as it gets smaller behind
us. He watches our city get left behind. A city that turned
its back on him, took away the girl he loved.

Pen slowly rises, holding on to my shirt hem like this is
her first step.

All my skin is covered in tiny bumps, and my blood
has gone cold. The whirling clouds conceal Internment
almost entirely. I can see the city for a moment at a time,
but mostly it's a white sphere. From the ground I suppose

it wouldn't seem much like a city at all. All they would see is the dirt that holds our city together. Maybe the people of the ground haven't attempted to reach us because they don't think such a place could be inhabited.

We've all gone silent. The levers groan to a stop, no longer causing the claws to move as though digging through the dirt.

Judas is first to snap out of our collective trance. He crouches in front of Amy and says, "Are you feeling all right?"

"Yes," she says.

"Really?"

There's a little laugh to her voice. "I promise. Just enjoy the view."

But a crash somewhere on the lower levels interrupts us. We look at one another, everyone in the bird accounted for.

"Oh, the bloody—" the professor says. "Don't tell me another chunk of the ceiling has come off."

The noise repeats itself, a loud thump like someone kicking a wall. A voice cries out for help, and at first I'm sure I've imagined it, but Judas reacts, moving toward the ladder.

"Everyone stay here," he says, but I follow him anyway, with Pen, Basil, and Amy at my heels.

"Don't," Alice calls out, but she doesn't come after me. She won't leave Lex.

We descend the ladder, and the daylight no longer reaches us. Judas uses the flame of his lantern to light another that used to hang from the ceiling.

The kicking noise persists, and a scream, not of fear but seemingly of frustration.

Pen and I look at each other.

"That sounds like—"

I shake my head. "It can't be."

Judas tugs at the heavy door of a storage closet where spare clothes are kept. And, of all things, Princess Celeste is perched on the floor, having been prepared to kick at the door again.

As if that weren't strange enough, someone is slumped behind her in the darkness. I feel relieved to think that the prince survived Pen's attack, but when Judas holds up the lantern, I see that the ruffled blond hair and sleeping face don't belong to Prince Azure.

"Thomas," Pen gasps.

He doesn't move, and Pen balls her hands into fists. "What have you done to him, you bloody lunatic?" she cries. I hook my arm around her waist to keep her from lunging.

"Yes, right," the princess says. "I thought that might be your reaction." She reaches into the collar of her dress and extracts something that's wrapped in a cloth. Even before she has unwrapped it, I know it's the knife I was carrying when she and her brother kidnapped me. She pulls Thomas's limp body under her arm and holds the knife to his jugular. I can see the blue vein in his throat dangerously close to that blade. The bird is already so rocky, she might kill him even if she means only to bluff.

Preemptively, I clasp my hand over Pen's mouth. She screams in protest, but Thomas can't afford any chances.

The princess clearly hates Pen after what she did, and Pen is already so distraught from the journey that she could say something she'll immediately regret.

"I thought you might try to kick me out, even after we took to the sky," the princess says. Her eyes are on Pen. "I planned to use the boy as leverage, but I believe I could return the favor and kill someone *you* love."

Pen bites my hand, hard, but I don't let go.

"What is it you want from us?" Judas says.

"Shouldn't it be obvious?" the princess says. "I want you to take me to the ground."

"Well, good news, then, because we couldn't let you out even if we wanted to," Judas says. "Opening a door right now would get us all killed at this altitude."

I pity her. She's known for her poise, and here she is, undone. Her braided crown is frayed. Her eyes are desperate and vicious. She's the most popular girl on Internment, but she'll find little kindness among the lot of us. She looks at me. "Is that true?"

Is it? I have no idea. "Yes," I say. "Of course. Everyone knows that."

Princess Celeste has a steady hand on that knife, but the unpredictability of flight makes me nervous.

Pen stops squirming and she has her eyes on her betrothed. His chest rises and drops. His breaths disturb the lace of the princess's collar just so.

"You," the princess says. "Patrolman's daughter." She pats the small bit of space beside her on the closet floor. "Let's have a chat, shall we?"

I let go of Pen. "Don't be stupid," I whisper, and kiss her cheek. She's growling.

"Bring the lantern," the princess says. "It gets dark in here."

As soon as I'm beside her, she reaches forward and pulls the closet door shut.

She releases Thomas, letting him spill backward into a pile of once neatly folded clothes. I notice that she keeps hold of the knife.

"Don't blame him for what Pen and I did," I say. "He didn't know anything about all of this."

"Didn't he?" she says. "He knew where to find you. I followed him all the way to the flower shop."

I don't know how Thomas knew to go to the flower shop, unless he'd somehow seen me leaving it with Judas, or had been nearby when Pen and I had been kidnapped.

"I wasn't planning to hurt him," she says. "I just needed some kind of backup plan in case you tried to toss me out. And he *did* seem to already be heading this way."

"How did you sneak into the bird without anyone catching you?" I say.

"I had to hide in the dark for a long time. But then, before you started moving, everyone stepped out into the dirt to"—she clears her throat—"use the water room behind this thing. I presume there isn't one on board." She smirks, clearly impressed with herself. "Anyway, the door was left open. My brother and I have been sneaking out of the tower since we were toddlers, practically."

"I suppose you can't be the child of the king without

being brilliant," I say, trying to keep the conversation going. It seems to keep her from doing anything rash.

"No, my brother is stupid quite most of the time," she says, not without fondness.

"'Is'?" I ask. Not "was."

She looks at the darkness beyond the lantern, crestfallen. "He's breathing, if that's what you're asking."

"Will he live?" I ask.

"Never mind that," she says, and attempts to pat down her frizzed hair. "He isn't here, and we are, aren't we? And I need your help. Call me daft, but I like you. You were at least honest with me about this thing existing."

I wonder if she remembers that she kidnapped me, and that her father is the reason Lex and I no longer have our parents. They should be on this bird, not her.

I swallow my anger. For Thomas. For Pen. For sanity's sake.

"As you can understand, I don't feel very safe here," the princess says. "Especially with that Hensley boy. If he'd murder his betrothed, I can imagine what he'd do to me."

Judas did not murder Daphne. I'm so tired of hearing the accusation that I could scream. But it isn't the worst thing for Princess Celeste to fear him.

"And you want me to protect you," I say.

"I don't require your protection," she says. "I require your sensibility. When your beastly friend raised that stone to my brother, you tried to stop her. You saw that it was a bad idea. You don't act irrationally even if you're angry, do you?"

It was my irrational need to leave the bird that got me kidnapped in the first place, but I don't say that. "I have been called a diplomat."

She sighs. "Being the king's daughter doesn't mean much now that we're no longer on Internment," she says. "But I will kill this boy if anyone tries to harm me. He'll wake up soon, but that won't stop me. And don't let anyone get ideas about leaving me on the ground, either. I'm to return safely to the sky, or, believe me, my father will make you wish you hadn't returned. I've left him a note explaining where I've gone."

She doesn't know that this is a one-way trip. Not even the king will be able to retrieve her. It would give me too much pleasure to tell her. But this would be unwise; she's scared, scorned, likely hasn't slept, and she's holding a knife. And the fact that she snuck onto this bird tells me that she must have a compelling reason. Something worth risking as much as she has, leaving her home and surrounding herself with people who might cause her harm.

"I know Pen, and she won't care how sensible I am. Not if I'm defending a girl holding her betrothed hostage. You have to let Thomas go. If you do that, I'm confident I can keep her from strangling you."

"And the Hensley boy?"

"I'd just avoid him if I were you," I say. "He's not a fan of your family's."

The princess stares at me for a few seconds. "And you?" she says.

"I'm not a fan of your family's, either," I say. "All you

341

know about me, for sure, is that when Pen attacked your brother, I tried to stop her. It may not be a lot to go by, but there it is."

She considers this.

Then, without saying anything, she grabs Thomas under the shoulders and hoists the dead weight of him into my lap.

It is a peace offering. She nods.

I kick at the door, and I hear the sound of listening ears backing away. "You can let us out now," I say.

Pen dabs at Thomas's face with a wet cloth. She presses it to either side of his neck, under his chin.

It's just the three of us in the bunk room. The others are trying to make themselves useful in the Nucleus. Judas is keeping watch over Princess Celeste away from the others; with all the grace of her lineage, she allowed herself to be searched. She allowed me to remove my knife from her hand, and the tranquilizer darts from her belt and from the rims of her stockings, while Judas and Basil awkwardly averted their eyes.

"He seems unharmed," I offer now by way of comfort.

Pen undoes the top buttons of his shirt, and she peels back the collar until she can see the bruise on the side of his neck. "It's one of her stupid tranquilizers. He can probably hear everything we're saying right now," Pen says. "Thomas, you idiot." She kisses his parted lips. "Why did you follow me?"

I can't rid the smile from my face before she notices.

"What?"

"It's just that I've never seen you act so fond of him before," I say.

"Of course not," she says. "He's repulsive." She brushes away some drool at the corner of his mouth with her thumb. "But he belongs to me."

They're still betrothed. Willingly, it would seem. Maybe the ground won't change us at all.

I stand.

"Where are you going?" Pen says.

"To find Basil."

I hurry down the hall, up the ladder, and nearly bump into Basil in the doorway to the Nucleus. He's carrying the pieces that fell from the ceiling as we broke free of the city. "Careful," he says. "You could cut yourself."

I stand on the tips of my toes and bring my face close to his. "No I won't," I say. "Because you're here. You wouldn't let anything happen to me."

I kiss him. The back of his neck is warm when I touch it.

He stoops to set the debris on the floor, and then he's touching the sides of my face, his hands as soft as air. His eyes have changed, gone hazy the way they do when our bodies are close. I like that I'm the only one that does this to him; I'm the only one who gets to see him this way. "Never," he murmurs.

He gathers me up and I'm weightless before he sets me on the railing that overlooks the next level. He's the only thing keeping me from falling back, out of the reach of daylight. I'm not afraid of falling. I don't fear the sky beyond

343

the train tracks like I did before. I can go anywhere just so long as it's with him.

He has one arm around my back, while his other hand bunches my skirt up to my hips.

Say it, that voice is telling me again. *Say that you love him.* But what I say is, "I've never seen you like this."

All I want to do is kiss him under these windows that are full of sky.

His mouth tastes the same as it did that afternoon when he told me he would follow me to the edge. We're both still wearing our uniforms, which have been laundered and made to smell of soapberries, but there's a familiarity to them.

"I don't care if it's in the sky or on the ground," he says against my neck. "I want to spend the rest of my life with you."

"Even without the decision makers?" I say, drawing back.

"Especially then," he says. "It wouldn't have mattered whether or not we were paired up. It's always been you, Morgan."

I push forward so that my nose and forehead are against his, and I'm smiling so wide it hurts. "You'd choose an irrational like me?" I say. "Without being forced."

He kisses me. "Yes."

"A girl who's terrible with math—"

"Yes."

"A shameless daydreamer—"

"Yes."

344

"Who's brought you nothing but trouble?"

"Yes." He holds my chin in his hand. "Yes. Daydream all you like."

Over us, the sky goes dark. At first I wonder how evening could have come so quickly, but then I realize it's the clouds that have gotten dark, not the sky. Though they don't make a sound, it's as though they're growling at us.

Basil notices it too. I hop down from the railing and we both stare up at this strange new sky.

31

We are taught that curiosity is a thing to be feared.
But our first trains came from curious minds. As did
medicine, and clocks, and first kisses.

—"Intangible Gods," Daphne Leander, Year Ten

Get your fingers off my windows, kid," the
professor says. Amy doesn't even hear him. She's too busy
gaping at the flecks of white that are whirling around us.

"What is this?" she gasps.

"I think they're ice shavings," I say. "Lex, you told me
about this happening when clouds release water and it freezes."

He raises his head toward the windows as though he'll
be able to look. I immediately regret what I've said; it's got
to be killing him that he can't see any of what's happening.

"It shouldn't hurt us," he says. "Not unless it's coming
down fast."

"They're like lightbugs," Amy says. "Daphne and I
used to catch them in jars."

"Where are you going?" Basil says when I let go of his hand.

"Pen has to see this," I say.

"Take the lantern, then," he says.

It's hard to believe the rest of the bird is dark while this fantastic thing is happening in the Nucleus.

When I find Pen in Amy's bunk room, she's speaking to Thomas in a low voice. His eyes are open, but murky. "Don't worry," Pen tells him, raising her voice when she hears me approach. "You're free of that crazy princess now. We'll kill her later, no matter if Morgan thinks she can stop us."

"I'm on your side, you know," I say.

"I still haven't forgiven you for not letting me punch her."

Thomas draws a sharp breath and then hoarsely says, "Not a good idea."

"See?" I say. "He agrees with me."

"No he doesn't," Pen says. "He's been speaking non-sense for the last several minutes."

"I only told you I love you," Thomas says.

"Shush. How did you end up in the hands of that lunatic princess anyway?"

Weakly, he raises his arm, reaches into his shirt pocket, and retrieves a scrap of lace. Pen looks at her dress and realizes it's the piece that's missing from her collar. "She told me that she had you prisoner," he says. "She said she would kill you if I didn't follow her."

"We should just leave her somewhere to fend for herself

when we land," Pen says. "I hope the people on the ground are savages with an appetite for blondes." She looks over her shoulder at me. "Did you want something?"

"Remember that frozen dust I told you about?" I say. "We're flying in it."

She turns her attention back to Thomas. Her fingers are trembling when she smoothes his blanket. Delirious though he may be, he notices and grabs her hand.

"Pen? Don't you want to see it?" I say.

"No," she says softly.

"But it's unlike anything—"

She closes the door on me.

I know that it isn't these icy white swirls that have Pen so scared. It's the idea of leaving Internment and surviving it. It's the idea that our god doesn't care whether or not we return, and that the history book may be wrong.

Amy says the ice shavings are like lightbugs, but they remind me of the funerals I've attended. Of the dusted bodies released onto the wind. In the dusting process, all the bad of a person's soul is burned away, so that only the goodness will carry on to the afterlife. It's a cleansing.

"It's like we're flying through the tributary," I say, leaning back against Basil's chest.

"They're flurries," Lex says, annoyed. "Don't turn something scientific into a cathartic experience."

"Be nice," Alice tells him.

I don't offer a response. Lex is entitled to his bitterness for having to miss this sight. I wouldn't know how anyone could describe it in a way he'd appreciate.

"I think I've found a landing spot," the professor says. "Where's Judas? Need him to help me with the wheels." There are so many pieces to this bird, and they serve so many different purposes, that it makes my head spin. Once it's on the ground in broad daylight, I want to inspect it. I hope they have image recorders on the ground so that I can take images.

"He's watching the princess," Amy says, adding a flourish to the word "princess." "She can't be left alone, apparently."

"I'll get him," Basil says, before I can volunteer.

"I'll go with you," I say.

"Me too!" Amy chirps.

Judas is keeping the princess in one of the bunk rooms. We find him standing in the doorway with his arms crossed, as the princess re-braids her hair.

"We're landing," I tell Judas. "The professor needs you. Something about wheels?"

The princess stands, her face alight. "Landing?" she gasps. "As in, on the ground?"

"Watch her," Judas says as he leaves the bunk room. "She'll try to seduce you."

"We'll try to resist," I say.

Princess Celeste wrings her hands. "So we're near the ground, then?" she asks. She blinks several times when she notices Amy staring at her. "Hello," she says. She cheerily shows a row of white teeth, and her eyes squint pleasantly when she smiles, the way she smiles in every image and at every ceremony her father hosts. She would have no way of knowing that this girl before her is the famous murdered girl's sister. Maybe she doesn't even know her father's role in Daphne's death.

"I heard you collect deer antlers," Amy says.

"Not only the antlers," Princess Celeste says. "The whole heads sometimes, if my father lets me. Most of the body gets sent to the food and bone factories, to make jewelry like the necklace you're wearing there."

Amy touches the bone-carved star hanging from her neck. I've never noticed it before.

"Living things make the greatest art," the princess says.

"Dead things, you mean," Amy says, hoisting the star up in her palm. "This is dead."

"Once living, then," the princess says.

From somewhere on the bird, Judas calls, "Brace yourselves!" And it's not a moment too soon, because a jolt has us all going sideways. Basil grabs on to my waist, and I grab Amy, fearing she'll go into another of her fits. The princess backs herself into a corner and presses her hands on either wall. I could swear she looks excited.

The turbulence persists for another minute or so, and there's an instant of reprieve before the floor shakes beneath us, like we've crashed into the ground and now we're skidding.

"Pen!" I call. "Are you guys okay?"

"Lovely!"

This is it. The moment when we reach the ground, or die trying. My nerves are jumbled and I'm starting to feel nauseous. I've already endured more in one day than the whole of Internment's population would deem possible. Generations of rebels have plotted for this. Several have died in failed attempts. It's foolish of me to think that I'd be among the ones to finally achieve it.

But fantastic things are possible. I've learned that.

When the bird goes still at last, Amy stumbles into the hallway, drops to her knees, and gags like she's going to be sick.

I kneel beside her.

"My body hates this endeavor," she says, coughing.

"At least it wasn't another fit," I say. "You won't miss any of the fun."

She smiles wearily at me.

The bird hitches, and Amy claws at the floor and closes her eyes.

I think she's whispering to the god in the sky.

32

This was to be an essay on the history of my city. But how can I tell the story of a city in the clouds without questioning what's above the clouds, and what's beneath them? All my life I have felt caught between two worlds. Here's what I know for sure: Internment is only a piece of what's out there. I know all its sections by heart, and I've memorized the times at which the train will speed by my bedroom window. It isn't enough. I want to know more.

—"Intangible Gods," Daphne Leander, Year Ten

Pen and Thomas are the only ones missing from the Nucleus.

We all stand at the windows, trying to reconcile what's before us. A ground covered with white dust. White dust that falls from the clouds. Beyond that, more water than I've ever seen in one place. It's nothing like our modest lakes. The waves are like roars. The water stretches on toward the sky, making a hazy, unreachable seam.

Basil stands behind me with an arm across my collarbone, as though to protect me from danger lurking in this gray-and-white place. Pen asked if they had color on the ground, and I assured her they did, but suddenly I'm not so sure. There's no blue even in the sky.

I wonder if we're dead. I feel as though we have been cast beyond the reaches of the living, and we're to remain forever here, neither alive nor dead. For all the daydreaming I've done about the ground, I suddenly cannot imagine that life exists beyond my floating city.

The professor shuts the engine. The metal pops and groans.

The princess is the first to speak. "This is it?"

"Of course not," Judas says. "We're only facing the water, that's all."

"See you later, then," she says, turning for the door. "You can all stand around gaping at this monstrosity of a lake if you'd like, but I'm on a mission."

Her footsteps clomping down the metal platform stir us all into motion. Everyone follows her for the door, except the professor, who stays behind to be sure the engine cools properly. Not that I see what it would matter; I doubt this thing has the strength or the means to return us to the sky, and even if it does, we're all fugitives. We aren't returning.

We parade down the hallways and the spiral staircase, through the kitchen and down the ladder that will take us to the door. Judas shoulders his way to the front. "Sorry, Princess," he says. "Usually I'd say 'Ladies first,' but this could be dangerous."

The princess folds her arms. "So chivalrous."

I'm worried about Pen, but I know that it will do no good to call for her. She can't be rushed. All her life she has believed in our history books, and we've just fallen into a world where perhaps none of what we've been taught will matter.

I grab Basil's hand and peer down the ladder as Judas undoes the series of locks.

"Wait," I say. "What if the air is different? What if it's diseased, or those ice flurries are dangerous?"

Judas smirks at me. Then, having undone the last lock, he pushes the door open.

The cold is immediate, assaulting my skin. My hair flies away from my face. We have chilly days on Internment this time of year, but they're nothing at all like this. Cold like this could kill a person.

Over the sound of the wind, I hear the laugh on Basil's breath. He squeezes his arm around my shoulders. "Would you look at that," he says.

I stare at the white ground, accumulating more whiteness from the sky, until I see a strip of red fluttering about on a post. The only thing in sight. It must be some sort of flag.

Judas sets one foot outside the bird, preparing to climb his way down the side, and a voice calls out, "Halt!"

The voice is so loud that it echoes in all the metal walls. *The god of the sky,* I think, my heart on my tongue. He has followed us here. He's come to decide our fates.

Judas is too stunned to step back into the bird or to go forward.

There's a mechanical quality to the word. Not a god. A machine that's being shouted into. And the word is heavily affected. No one on Internment speaks quite that way.

Amy grabs Judas by the collar and tugs, which brings him to his senses, and he climbs back inside.

Vehicles appear on the horizon, smaller and more colorful versions of Internment's emergency vehicles. A peculiar mist trails behind them. Their lights are like pairs of eyes, and the flurries glimmer in their rays.

None of us move. Uncertain.

I like to think we're brave.

Lex starts to say something, but Alice holds his arm and tells him to be quiet. "Where's Morgan?" he says. I find his hand, and he squeezes hard. Whatever's to happen to us, we'll be together. I want him to know that, but I can't speak. How can I? What words would be enough for this?

There are more vehicles than I can count, surrounding us on all sides. And then in that affected way, a voice says, "We won't hurt you. Exit slowly. When you get to the ground, put your hands up where we can see them."

When we get to the ground.

A hand touches my back, and when I turn around, I see Pen and Thomas behind me, clinging to each other. I don't know how long they've been here. For her, I muster the words, "It'll be all right."

She doesn't seem convinced.

Judas climbs the ladder on the outside of the bird first, Amy behind him, then Alice so that she can help Lex.

The princess is left to stand in the doorway, shivering.

She looks at me, and a wicked grin begins to form. "Don't look so glum," she says. "This is going to be an adventure."

Her hair is full of icy wind and daylight. She is every princess, every queen, in the history book. In this instant, I don't see a bratty princess, but rather I see greatness in her.

She doesn't bother with the ladder. She turns to face the strange world beyond the door, and she jumps.

Morgan, Pen, and Basil may have escaped Internment, but their adventures are just beginning once they reach the ground. Turn the page for a sneak peek at the second installment in the Internment Chronicles.

burning

kingdoms

Lauren DeStefano
New York Times bestselling author of the Chemical Garden Trilogy

When the world was formed, the people soon followed. It has been a balancing act of life and death from that day on. It is not the place of any man to question it.

— *The Text of All Things*, Chapter 1

Snow. That's the word the people of the ground have for this wonder.

"Goddamn snow," our driver mumbles for the second time, as mechanical arms sweep the dusting from the window.

It's like a stab to the heart hearing a god referred to so unkindly. I wonder which god he means. I'd think the god of the ground would be less forgiving than the one in the sky. Vengeful. It would make sense, the god of the ground having interned us to the sky for being too selfish.

But I don't ask. I haven't spoken a word since I told Pen that it would be all right.

All the whiteness is blinding, and despite the blustery

cold, the inside of this vehicle is so hot that beads of sweat are forming at the back of my neck. There's a metallic taste to this air.

I have a thought that my parents will be worried, before I remember that they're gone. Not at home. They're colors in the tributary now, a place that can't be seen by the living.

I squeeze Basil's hand. And on the other side of me, Princess Celeste has her hands to the glass as she stares through the window. A city has begun to materialize through the snow. It's all boxy shadows at first, and then ribbons of color shoot through the sky, squares of light wink from the buildings.

My brother is in one of the surrounding vehicles. When we left the metal bird that brought us down from Internment, the men in heavy black coats split us up as they saw fit. They pushed us into the seats. They said they'd take us somewhere warm and safe. They don't seem to realize that we were banished from this place, hundreds of years ago.

The driver raises his eyes to us in the mirror. "It was swell luck that you came down before the blizzard."

I don't know what that means. "Blizzard" is a new word, and it bounces on my tongue, begging to be said.

Basil is looking up into the sky as though to chart a way back home, but the whiteness that falls from the clouds is his only answer. Now would be an apt time for him to regret following me here—regret our betrothal. Maybe the decision makers were wrong to bond us to each other for the rest of our lives; we've always cared for each other, but he's logical while I'm a dreamer. He's patient while I'm careless. And now he'll never see his parents or his little brother again because of me.

I want to say his name so that he'll look at me, but I'm afraid of what speaking might do to this odd balance between the driver and the three of us.

Our driver's coat appears to be some kind of uniform. He's a patrolman perhaps—or whatever they have on the ground. Maybe they don't keep order down here at all.

Princess Celeste elbows me. And now that she has my attention, she nods to her window. Outside, a large machine is set some distance from the buildings. It's like a giant metal bug, its legs suspended in the air. Each leg is painted a different color, and at the tips are what appear to be clouds.

I can't tell if the princess is attempting to smile. Her eyes still have their sparkle, but she is, for once, subdued.

Our vehicle rolls to a stop. I look out the window on Basil's side and I see the other vehicles stopping alongside us. I want to run out and join my brother and Alice, and Pen, who was fighting tears the last time I saw her.

But I don't move. Basil puts his other hand on my arm as though to protect me.

The driver steps out into the snow, and the cold air cuts right through my skin before he closes the door again.

The princess speaks first. "This is it? There isn't a soul in sight out there. This is what we've been banished from?"

Doors open in the other vehicles. I see Alice first. A man is trying to escort her toward the building where we've parked, but she dodges him and reaches into the car to help Lex.

The sight of my brother, pale as the snow, causes me to abandon reason. I open the door.

"Wait," Basil says.

"I have to let him know I'm okay," I say.

Basil understands. He climbs out first and keeps hold of my hand. "Lex," I call.

My brother's head immediately rises from its weary drooping. "Morgan?" His voice is panicked and relieved. "Sister?"

"I'm here," I say. "I'm right here." The words are heavy on my tongue. This cold is freezing me to the bone. I try to reach for my brother, but one of the uniformed men is steering Basil and me toward that building. Even before the door has opened, I can smell the strange and unfamiliar foods cooking inside.

I bite my lip and take one last look over my shoulder before I'm guided inside. I can see Lex and Alice, and behind them, just a flicker of Pen's blond curls for an instant, a flash, a thought I can't catch.

I hold on to Basil's hand as though my life depends on it. It might.

They bring us to a row of metal chairs, and we're each given tea.

It looks strange in its cup. Weak. They probably have different herbs on the ground. A different ecosystem, too.

I don't drink the tea. I don't trust it. But I still appreciate its warmth against my palms. Though we've come in from the snow, we're all shivering. What a sight we must be for these uniformed men: people who fell from the sky in a metal bird, sitting in a row, not a word uttered among the lot of us.

The professor is the only one of us who's missing. I heard one of the uniformed men say that he refuses to leave the aircraft.

"Aircraft" is a new word also.

A different uniformed man is sitting behind a desk, staring at us. He glances between us and an open ledger on his desk. "None of you are going to talk, are you?" he says.

Silence.

"They always stick me with the weird ones," he mumbles, more to his ledger than to us. "Last week, the caped vigilante, and this week, the party on an aircraft made of windows and doors."

I suppose he's referring to the metal bird. I got a fleeting glimpse of it as we were hustled away, for the first time seeing it in the daylight. This man's description isn't far from the truth.

"Is this them?" a man cries as the doors burst open. I flinch, and Basil grabs hold of my arm.

This man wears a long black coat that is dusted with snow, and yet his hair is pristinely combed and dry. He looks at us with the excitement of a child. "You are the ones who fell from the sky, yes?"

"They don't talk," the uniformed man says. "Don't think they understand a word we're saying."

"We can understand you just fine, thank you," the princess says. "It's just that no one has offered us an introduction." She daintily sets her cup on the ground, stands, and extends her hand to the man in the coat. She means for him to kiss her knuckles, but he shakes her hand instead, so roughly that her body jolts. But if the princess is surprised, she doesn't show it, retaining the poise that has made her an icon for all the young girls of Internment.

"My apologies, then," the man in the coat says. "I'm Jack Piper, the one and only adviser to King Ingram IV."

Delight flashes in the princess's eyes.

"I'm Celeste," she says. "The one and only daughter to King Lican Furlow." She pauses. "The first."

Jack Piper laughs, and I can't tell whether he finds her delusional or charming.

"You will have to tell me all about your father and his kingdom," Jack Piper says. "But for now, I've arranged proper accommodations for all of you."

The princess looks to me, her shoulders hunched with excitement.

She's completely mad. She knows it, too. It's her madness that made her the only one among us brave enough to speak. She means to remain a princess, no matter whose kingdom she may have fallen into.

We are whisked back into the vehicles. "Cars," I hear someone call them. They're all black with spare wheels fastened near the front doors. They emit dark clouds through pipes, and the seats rattle as we move. I try to find comparisons to the train cars back home, but there is no comparison. We have nothing like this. This is a different world.

"They won't hurt us," the princess says into my ear. "It wouldn't be civilized."

"I don't know how you can be so certain," I say.

"It's standard diplomacy," she says. "Papa says I have a real talent for it. He thinks I might even become a decision maker once I'm old enough. I'll have to find something to do with my time once my brother is king."

Decision making is one of the few professions that can't be chosen. Decision makers are scouted and trained privately. They hold our society in their palms, deciding which queue applicants will have boys, which will have girls, and who should be betrothed to whom. And that's only a small part of what they do. It's as powerful a position as one could have. Next to being royalty, that is.

I shudder to think of Princess Celeste as a decision maker. We became acquainted after she and her brother shot Pen and me with tranquilizers and imprisoned us in the basement of the clock tower.

Not that any of that matters now.

The car stops before a building barely visible in the whiteness of the storm. I can see that it's the color of sand and has curved edges, and it's larger than any of the buildings on Internment. Again, we're hustled from the cars and through the front doors.

Everything inside is red and gold.

Behind me, Alice is murmuring things into Lex's ear. He can't see any of this; I wonder if he senses the differences between the ground and home at all, aside from the ridiculous cold.

"Welcome, welcome to my humble home," Jack Piper says. He sheds his coat, and one of the drivers is standing at the ready to collect it.

Pen and I exchange incredulous expressions. Home? This place is easily larger than our entire apartment building.

"Children," Jack calls.

With the rumble of footsteps overhead, they emerge at the top of the steps, pushing and shoving one another and then, upon realizing their audience, straightening their clothes, smoothing their hair, and marching down the steps single file.

They assemble before us in order of height, all of them with Jack Piper's light brown hair. The smallest is in ringlet ponytails, and the tallest is long and lean, with round lenses around his eyes. They appear to be magnifying glasses, though I can't imagine why they're on his face.

"This is my son," Jack Piper says, gesturing to the boy with the lenses. "Jack Junior, though we all call him Nimble. Like the nursery rhyme. I don't suppose you know how it goes. And this is Gertrude." The second tallest lowers her eyes shyly. "And that's Riles." The third tallest, a boy, smirks at us. "And Marjorie. And that's Annette."

The littlest girl curtsies with all the petite grace of a dancer in a jewelry box. "A pleasure to meet you," she says.

"Is it true you came from the floating island?" one of the children says.

"Riles, manners!" snaps another.

The boy with the lenses regards us wryly. "Welcome," he says, "to the capital city of Havalais."

I don't understand that name he's just said. *Have-a-lace.* He gestures theatrically to the letters etched into the wall behind him:

HAVALAIS: HOME OF THE FLOATING ISLAND

Pulse It

Did you love this book?

Want to get access to
the hottest books for free?

Log on to simonandschuster.com/pulseit
to find out how to join,

get access to cool sweepstakes,

and hear about your favorite authors!

Become part of Pulse IT and tell us what you think!

Margaret K.
McElderry Books   SIMON & SCHUSTER BFYR   SIMON
                                                        PULSE

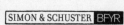

From #1 *New York Times* bestselling author

KRESLEY COLE

LET THE CARDS FALL WHERE THEY MAY. . . .

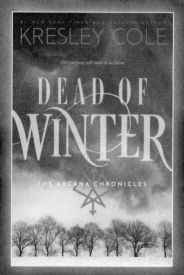

thearcanachronicles.com

PRINT AND EBOOK EDITIONS AVAILABLE

SIMON & SCHUSTER BFYR

TEEN.SimonandSchuster.com

THE NUTCRACKER IS ALL GROWN UP.

"DEFINITELY NOT YOUR GRANDMOTHER'S NUTCRACKER TALE."
—Marissa Meyer, *New York Times* bestselling author of *CINDER*

CLAIRE LEGRAND
WINTERSPELL

A TALE OF MAGIC, LOVE, AND INTRIGUE.

PRINT AND EBOOK EDITIONS AVAILABLE

From SIMON & SCHUSTER BFYR

TEEN.SimonandSchuster.com

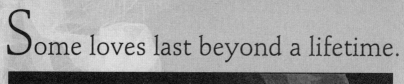

Some loves last beyond a lifetime.

"A beautiful, haunting read."
—Tahereh Mafi, *New York Times* bestselling author of *Shatter Me*

Sublime

Christina Lauren
New York Times Bestselling Author

From *New York Times* bestselling author **Christina Lauren**

PRINT AND EBOOK EDITIONS AVAILABLE • From **SIMON & SCHUSTER** BFYR • TEEN.SimonandSchuster.com